FIGHTING FOR WHAT'S HIS

A WARRIOR FIGHT CLUB NOVEL

LAURA KAYE

READ HARD WITH LAURA KAYE

Warrior Fight Club Series
FIGHTING FOR EVERYTHING
FIGHTING FOR WHAT'S HIS
WORTH FIGHTING FOR
FIGHTING THE FIRE - September 2019

Blasphemy Series
HARD TO SERVE
BOUND TO SUBMIT
MASTERING HER SENSES
EYES ON YOU
THEIRS TO TAKE
ON HIS KNEES

Raven Riders Series
HARD AS STEEL
RIDE HARD
RIDE ROUGH
RIDE WILD
RIDE DIRTY

RIDE DEEP

Hard Ink Series
HARD AS IT GETS
HARD AS YOU CAN
HARD TO HOLD ON TO
HARD TO COME BY
HARD TO BE GOOD
HARD TO LET GO
HARD AS STEEL
HARD EVER AFTER
HARD TO SERVE

Hearts in Darkness Duet
HEARTS IN DARKNESS
LOVE IN THE LIGHT

Heroes Series
HER FORBIDDEN HERO
ONE NIGHT WITH A HERO

THE WARRIOR FIGHT CLUB SERIES

*This fight club has one rule:
you must be a veteran...*

FIGHTING FOR EVERYTHING
FIGHTING FOR WHAT'S HIS
WORTH FIGHTING FOR
FIGHTING THE FIRE - September 2019

To Christi Barth
For always being with me until the very end
Oh, Christi!
(she'll understand why...)

CHAPTER ONE

SHAYNA CURTIS STARED at the locked door, debated for about ten seconds, then decided to pick the lock.

Rain pounded down on her as she fished the kit from the worn hobo-style bag on her shoulder. Having an overprotective big brother who'd decided his little sister needed survival-skills lessons before his first deployment came in handy sometimes, as much good-natured eye rolling as she'd done at the time.

Now, to break in before one of her new neighbors called the police. Being arrested for breaking and entering probably wouldn't be the smartest way to kick off her fresh start here in DC or to make the best first impression on her new roommate. Though, since said roomie was late to meet her and not answering his phone, she thought that earned her a pass.

She inserted the tension wrench, raked the pins, and twisted the wrench until the lock gave way.

"Annnd I'm in," Shayna said to herself, mentally fist pumping as she opened the door and stepped in out of the rain. "Thanks, bro." No doubt Ryan would get a kick out of knowing she'd picked her way into his best friend's townhouse. Hopefully the best friend would find it humorous, too.

She dumped her purse on the hall table and then dashed back out into the downpour to grab her laptop, toiletries, and one bag of her clothes. The rest would have to wait until the rain let up, though she wasn't happy to leave her camera equipment in the car.

Back inside, she dumped her things and turned on the lights, illuminating a space that was surprisingly modern compared to the old red-brick rowhouse's exterior.

Gray hard woods stretched throughout the first floor, connecting the open living room dominated by a cushy, stone-colored sectional sofa with a gleaming white kitchen. A large sliding door with transom windows above at the back of the space looked out on a fenced-in brick-paved patio with a hammock that had her name written *all* over. The property backed up to a narrow road and a tree-lined field beyond.

She turned away from the view and trailed her fingers over the smooth surface of the silver quartz breakfast bar. The kitchen was spotless—not a dish in the sink or a crumb to be found. Her gaze scanned over the living room. *Everything* was neat as a pin with nary a pillow askew.

That was going to make things interesting, wasn't it?

Perhaps the coolest—or freakiest?—feature was the floating staircase that connected the first and second floors. The stair treads were stone rectangles that protruded from the wall but weren't otherwise connected, and the hand rail was nothing more than a sheet of plate glass, which added to the illusion of being suspended in thin air.

"This thing is a trip," she said to herself as she made her way upstairs, each newly explored part of the townhouse offering only the barest clues about the man who'd be her roommate for the next two months.

Billy Parrish. One of her brother's best friends and a former Army Ranger who now worked as a private detective.

If the interior reflected the guy, she'd guess he was either the kind of anal military man who'd been able to bounce quarters off his rack. Or he was never here. God, she hoped it was the latter.

The gray hard woods continued up here, where four door-ways extended off the hallway—two closed, two open. She went to the open ones first and found a basic but spotless bathroom and a large bedroom she suspected might be the guest room since, in addition to a queen-sized bed, it had a large curved desk and two sets of bookshelves that probably comprised Billy's home office.

And *finally* Shay found something that looked lived in.

The desk wasn't messy—certainly not by her standards—but there were tidy stacks of books, file folders, and legal pads. Two cups filled with pens and paper clips. The bulletin board above the desk represented the most personal thing she'd seen yet, covered as it was in neat rows of pinned phone numbers, photographs, and papers of various sorts.

She leaned over the desk to get a better look at a picture of two guys in camo sitting in beat-up beach chairs, beers in hand. Her brother grinned back at her. And so did Billy.

She'd first met him eight years ago when Ryan had brought him home for Christmas over one of the Rangers' typically short stateside rotations. She'd been a high school senior, busy with the school newspaper, the winter dance committee, and the nail-biting excitement of college acceptance decisions, while Billy had been a tall, broad-shouldered, belly-laughing *god*.

Despite the fact that she only saw him occasionally, she'd crushed hard each and every time she had the chance.

Not that he'd looked at her. First, because he was six years older than her and, as such, way out of her league. And second, because her brothers would've killed him. Killed him *dead*.

Well, there was just one brother who might possibly interfere in her love life now. If she had a love life, which she decidedly didn't. Though, it was funny how she no longer hated the thought of her brothers' overprotectiveness the way she once had now that she'd lost one of them.

On a sigh, she shook the thought away.

Fresh starts and all that.

Right.

Which brought her back to Billy. She wondered what Ryan had told him about what'd happened. Her gut squeezed, because she shouldn't wonder. Not if Ry blamed her the way she blamed herself.

"I really hope it's not going to be weird living here with you," she said, staring at Billy's picture for one more moment. It'd been more than three years since Shayna had last seen him, so there was a better-than-average chance of weirdness.

First, because it'd been so long and, really, she barely knew him. Second, because once upon a time she'd crushed on him so bad. And third, because there was no way that a single, thirty-three-year-old man could be thrilled about her invading his space for two months. For free.

When Ryan had raised the idea of staying with Billy, she'd offered to pay, of course. After working an unpaid internship for the last year, she didn't have a lot of savings, though her second part-time job had allowed her to set some money aside for the relocation. But the guys had insisted she put that toward the deposit she'd need on an apartment in the city.

She just hoped that Billy was really okay with that. Otherwise...awkward. And awkward sucked so bad.

A chill rushed down her spine as the air conditioning kicked on.

Shayna hugged herself, her hands pressing damp fabric to her skin. After driving all day from upstate New York and getting caught in the cold September rain, a hot shower sounded like heaven. She peered down the quiet hallway. Waffled on how bad of an idea it might be to shower in someone's home after having broken in. Checked her phone, still finding no texts from Billy.

And then she uttered a "fuck it" as she dashed downstairs to retrieve her things. This was her home, too. At least for a while.

She dropped her belongings on the bed, yanked out her toiletry bag, and closed herself into the hall bathroom.

Shay made quick work of getting undressed. In the shower, the hot water raining down on her nearly made her moan. Seven hours of driving had left her achy and stiff, and the needling heat relaxed her muscles and chased away the chill.

But it didn't ease the guilt she felt in her heart of hearts.

No, nothing could do that.

———

THIS DAY FUCKING SUCKED.

That was the tenor of Billy Parrish's thoughts as he fought through Friday night rush hour traffic on the way to his rowhouse in Upper Northwest DC. The leads on his case had gone stone cold. His charging cord wasn't working and his phone had died an hour ago. And he was late.

He fucking hated being late.

Especially when it involved a favor for one of his brothers. Didn't matter that Billy wasn't enthusiastic about this particular favor. He'd known Ryan Curtis for more than a decade—since West Point, had fought and bled by his side, and owed the guy for having saved his life. So when Ryan had asked, Billy had said yes. Simple as.

Not that he thought having Ryan's kid sister in his house for the next two months was going to be simple. Not when her very presence and his obligation to look out for her was going to be one helluva cockblock.

Finally, he turned into the alley that ran behind his rowhouse on Farragut Place and pulled into the parking spot behind his house. He killed the engine and, for just a few moments, sat still and listened to the rain hammer on the roof of his Explorer.

Christ, he was tired.

Problem was, he slept like shit unless he did one of three things—fuck, fight, or choke down one of the year-old Percocets his doc had prescribed back when things were bad. Or, at least, worse than they were now. Billy tried like hell to avoid taking the pain pills, especially after he'd had a bad experience with them, but that required the fucking or the fighting.

Neither got rid of the phantom pain. Hell, both often made it worse. But they managed to quiet all the shit in his head, and that was what he needed more than anything else.

He blew out a breath and forced his ass out into the rain, and it was with his first steps in the direction of his house that he noticed. The lights were on inside.

Prickles ran over his scalp and his blood turned to ice. Because he hadn't left them on. On the fucking day that Ryan's sister was arriving, some asshole had broken in?

Unfuckingbelievable.

He raced to the basement door and let himself in as quietly as he could. He traded his dead cell phone for the gun in the holster at the small of his back. And then he went in search of the scumbag whose day was about to get even worse than his.

Billy eased up the steps to the door that opened into the kitchen. He winced at the creak of the hinges, cleared the corner, and then stepped into the light. One, two, three heartbeats, and he swung around the corner to find that the first floor appeared empty. Still, he cleared the entire space methodically.

Thump.

Billy's eyes drifted to the ceiling above him. *Gotcha.*

He kept his footfalls light as he ascended the stairs, stopping to check the second-floor hallway before climbing all the way to the top. His bedroom door remained closed, but light poured out of his office and from under the bathroom door.

He frowned in confusion.

Gun at the ready, he made for the bathroom, his free hand reaching for the knob.

The door swung open on its own.

"Freeze!" he bit out.

Four things happened pretty much at the same time.

The woman screamed, jumped backward into the door, slamming it against the wall behind her, and dropped a pile of clothing to the floor.

And then the towel she wore around her chest came unknotted and swung open, baring every inch of her.

"*Jesus fucknugget, Billy!*" the woman screeched, her hand going to her heaving chest just above her breasts. Her bare breasts. Full with pink nipples that tipped upward. She had a heart-shaped watercolor tattoo on her right hip. And her hair was red everywhere...

Oh. Oh hell.

In a heartbeat, Billy whirled away and lowered his gun, his mind racing as he reholstered the weapon. "Shayna? How the hell..."

Small brushes of fabric against fabric sounded out from behind him, as if she was resecuring the towel. Over her body. Which he'd just seen naked. "You were late. So..."

"So...?" He went to turn back and reconsidered, bewilderment morphing into regret of the *holy shit I just pulled a gun on Ryan's sister* variety. "You, uh, decent?"

"As decent as I get," she said with a kind of hysterical humor in her voice. Her footsteps retreated toward his office—her room, now.

And that little bit of humor had his regret morphing yet again into somewhere north of pissed off. Billy turned just as she disappeared inside the bedroom. He stalked after her. "How the hell did you get in here? I thought you were a burglar and nearly shot your ass."

Picking clothing from the exploded disaster that he assumed had once been a packed suitcase, she gave a rueful chuckle. "Number one, my ass was the only part of me you didn't nearly shoot. And, B, would a burglar seriously take the time to close the door while they were using a stolen bathroom? And three, my brother's a Ranger."

A Ranger who'd taught his little sister to pick a lock, because of course he did. Billy nailed her with a glare as the rest of what she'd said sank in. "You said number one, B, and three."

Her laughter, even a little nervous as it was, was like the sun cresting the horizon—it brightened the whole fucking room. "*That's* what you want to talk about right now?" she asked, peering at him with those blue-green eyes as she pulled a pair of black underwear from the jumble. A blush still colored her cheeks and chest. And the waves of her wet red hair set off the pale creaminess of her skin, as had the reds and oranges of the watercolor heart.

None-the-fuck-of-which he should be noticing or thinking about. Billy crossed his arms. "You're not funny."

"I'm a little funny," she said, coming to stand right at his side. She knocked her arm into his. "But I *am* sorry for scaring you. Also, hi. Nice to see you again."

He inhaled a deep breath meant to calm, but it was a mistake. A big one. Because he got a lungful of peaches and a sweetness that was all Shayna.

Shayna, who was Ryan's *kid* sister. Except...nope. Not one

goddamn thing about the woman standing next to him belonged to a kid. And he would know since he'd seen nearly the whole beautiful package.

"Hi," he said. "Welcome to D.C. Sorry I nearly shot you."

She grinned, and it was crooked, with one side of her mouth drawing up higher than the other. "No harm, no foul," she said, and then she held up the ball of clothing in her arms. "I'm going to go get decent*er*."

Between the smile and the sarcasm, *now* he was thinking about her mouth... "You do that, Goldilocks."

Her brows cranked down, and then she chuckled. "Ha ha. Except I didn't try out your bed, just your shower."

And. Now. He. Was. Thinking. About. Her. In. His. Bed. "Don't you have some clothes to put on or something?" Which was *not* something he typically said to a woman. But Shayna Curtis wasn't any woman.

She was one of his best friends' sisters. A best friend who'd asked him to watch out for her. And therefore she was ten kinds of off-limits.

"Yup," she said, nearly running back to the bathroom.

Billy just stood there and dropped his head forward. He was so fucked.

CHAPTER TWO

SHAYNA WASN'T sure whether to bang her head on a wall or burst out laughing. Both reactions seemed appropriate to having dropped her towel in front of Billy Fucking Parrish. *Of course,* that would happen to her on her first day living with the guy, who'd quite possibly moved faster than any human being ever when he'd turned around and given her his broad back.

Good going, Shay.

She chuckled to herself as she dropped the towel—on purpose this time, folded it, and hung it on the bar behind the door. It only took her a minute to slide on a pair of leggings and a long, lightweight sweater, and then there was nothing to do but brazen it out and face the guy like she didn't care that he knew her pubes were a few shades darker than the hair on her head.

To the extent that she'd ever imagined anything happening with Billy—and she had to admit she'd fantasized about it a few times—it had never begun with anything so ridiculous and humiliating as what'd just happened. For crap's sake.

"You like pizza?" Billy called from just outside the door.

On a deep breath, she opened it to find him standing in the

hall again. His dark blond hair a sexy finger-raked mess as if he'd been tugging at it. The square of his jaw set in a tight line. Serious brown eyes trained on hers. No gun in sight, this time. Which made her say, "Before we talk pizza, can we just agree that Ryan should never know about what happened the last time I opened this door?"

He nailed her with a droll stare. "Please, God. I'd like to live."

She snickered as she flicked off the light switch. "Good. And I love pizza."

"Come on down, then." With a sideways tilt of his head, he beckoned her to follow. Which gave her the opportunity to really take him in. While she'd dressed, he'd removed the brown bomber-style jacket he'd had on, revealing just how much freaking justice he did to a pair of blue jeans. Because lordy did he fill them out nicely. His white T-shirt was plain but highlighted the breadth of his shoulders and the bulk of his biceps. It was only once they got downstairs that she noticed his feet were bare.

His look was at once nothing special and crazy hot because *this* was how he looked when he was just chilling at home and not even putting in an effort to make panties drop. Yet, drop they still metaphorically did. She bit back a smile.

He went to the double ovens and set them to preheating, and then gathered flour, sugar, salt, a bottle of olive oil, and some dry yeast from the cabinets. Next, he collected mixing bowls and measuring spoons. He laid everything out in neat, precise rows. Shay stared as he moved about, obviously comfortable in the kitchen. "I thought you were going to order out."

He shrugged with one big shoulder. "Mine's better, Goldilocks."

Shayna rolled her eyes even as the confidence in his tone drew a smile from her. "All righty, then." She rested her elbows on the counter and watched him start on the dough. "If I'm Goldilocks, who are you?"

Billy smirked. "Papa Bear. Obviously."

"Oh, obviously," she said mockingly, earning a wink from him. It was either mock or stammer in an embarrassment she didn't quite understand. At least she hadn't blushed, which given how fair she was, happened often enough. "Can I help?"

His dark-eyed gaze lifted to hers, and he gave a single nod. "Suit yourself. Grab the cans of tomato sauce and paste from the pantry." He nodded his head toward the cabinet. "And then the spices are next to the stove. We need the dried oregano and onion powder. I'll mince the garlic and chop the basil while the yeast stands."

"I'll have you know that you're putting my pride in being able to make a mean bagel pizza to shame right now," Shay said as she collected everything.

"A decade of missed meals and MREs makes a man crave something real, something homemade."

She nodded, a little niggle taking up root in her belly. Because Ryan was still out there. Still going places and doing things that he could never tell her about. Still sacrificing his comfort and his time. Still putting himself in harm's way. No homemade meals in sight.

"Ryan lives and breathes it, Shay. He loves what he's doing. Don't you worry about him," Billy said in low voice. He tossed an observing glance her way, then got busy starting the sauce.

Shayna blinked. How had he known? She didn't ask, though, because Billy had insight into her brother's life that Ryan himself would never give her. Would he share it with her? "Did he say that?"

"He didn't have to."

"Was that what it was like for you?" she asked.

A muscle ticked in the side of that angled jaw, and the knife with which he chopped the basil *thunked-thunked* harder against the cutting board. For a moment she thought he wasn't going to answer.

And then he did. "It was."

Was. As he'd moved about, she'd seen a small stretch of scarring that ran up his neck and under his shirt. Her gaze trailed over the tee again, and she wondered just how extensive his scars were from the burns he'd suffered in an explosion a few years ago. An explosion that he and Ryan had survived but that a lot of the other Rangers in their squad hadn't. That was all she knew, and it'd taken her a lot of coaxing to get Ryan to share that much with her.

Silence rang loud in the room, clearly communicating that it wasn't something about which he wanted to talk. She regretted asking and searched her mind for something to lighten the mood, watching as he combined the sauce ingredients in a blender.

"Have you always been good at cooking?"

A single shake of his head. "My mom came to stay with me for a few months. After I was discharged."

So much for changing the topic, because she heard what he didn't say. That his mom *had* come to help him as he recovered...for a few months. Just how bad had his injuries been? "If you cook this good, she must be amazing."

It was his first genuine smile since their unfortunate reunion upstairs, and man, was it a stunner. "She is," he said. "Could whip up a fantastic meal and whip me into shape with one hand tied behind her back."

The affection in his voice was utterly charming. "That's impressive," Shay said with a chuckle.

He smirked. "It really is because I was a fucking handful when I was growing up."

Shayna grinned. "Oh, so you're not a handful anymore?"

He gave her the strangest look, and then burst into a speechless guffaw.

Heat absolutely flooded Shay's face. *Oh. My. God.* Did she *seriously* just ask him if he was a handful? "That's...that's not what I meant!"

Grinning like a shithead, he turned the blender on high. One hand on his hip and the other on the blender, he yelled, "What? I can't hear you!"

"You are a total ballbag, Billy Parrish!" she said, crossing her arms and glaring at him. Even though she knew she totally deserved whatever shit he gave her, because she'd walked right into that. Mostly she didn't *really* mind, since it seemed to have chased away the tension that her earlier question had caused.

And playful Billy was a thing to behold.

He hit the *stop* button on the blender. "What did you call me?" he asked, amusement still plain in his voice.

"A ballbag." She gave him a challenging look.

He snickered. "How am *I* the scrotum? You're the one—"

"Yeah, yeah," she said, feigning indignance. "Obviously you answered the question about whether you've grown up. In the *negative*."

"You can't lob a man a softball and not expect him to swing for the fence. Or at least want to..." His mood seemed much lighter as he finished the dough, divided it into two balls, and spread it out on two pizza pans. Then he made quick work of cleaning up after himself, leaving his workspace nearly spotless. Meanwhile, part of the reason Shayna disliked cooking was because she made such a mess. "Now for the fun part. What do you want on it?"

"Surprise me," she said. "I like almost everything."

"Mmm, an adventurous girl, I see," he said, gathering the mozzarella, pepperoni, and a few vegetables from the fridge.

Shayna couldn't resist giving him a hard time, just to try to make him laugh again. "Woman."

"What?"

"I'm twenty-six, after all. An adventurous *woman*," she said, arching a single, teasing brow.

But laughter was decidedly not his reaction. His gaze flashed suddenly and tantalizingly hot, and he gave her body a slow once-over before his eyes met hers again. Shayna felt his perusal as if it had been a physical caress. Heat bloomed over her. Was he seeing her as she was, standing there in leggings and a sweater? Or was he seeing her as she'd been earlier, completely naked, flushed from her shower, and pressed up against a door?

Because it sure as heck didn't seem like he saw her as the girl whose teenage infatuation had often left her hanging on his every word. And she wasn't at all sure what to do with the possibility that her unattainable teenage crush...might find her attractive in return.

Or maybe she was reading too much into the whole thing.

He cleared his throat and returned to stand beside her. "Duly noted," he said, an odd tone to his words that she didn't know him well enough to understand. Minutes stretched out as he chopped and diced the toppings.

In the wake of their exchange, her heart kicked up inside her chest, even as Billy busied his hands—and eyes—with sprinkling the mozzarella evenly over the pies. He wasn't looking at her any longer, but she had the strangest sense of certainty that he was utterly aware of her where she stood beside him.

"These look really great, Billy," she said, watching his big hands work. "You didn't have to go to all this trouble, but I think I'm going to be really glad you did."

He kept his eyes on the pizzas as he finished preparing them and finally slid them into the ovens. "Anything for Ryan's kid sister," he said, his tone much more reserved.

Oh. So *that* was how he saw her. All righty, then. What she'd thought she saw in his expression had been wishful thinking, after all.

Which was fine. Probably even for the best. Because Shay's fresh start definitely didn't include renewing her silly crush on her brother's best friend.

THE BEST THING about it being Saturday was Warrior Fight Club.

Which meant that Billy could attempt to fight out all the shit in his head and the restless energy in his body that had kept him awake all night.

Awake picturing Shayna's beautiful body. Awake with her voice in his ear saying that she was an adventurous *woman*.

Which was about a million times better than the other images and sounds that had been keeping him awake lately. On the same call where Ryan had asked for the favor for Shayna, he'd also informed him that one of their buddies hadn't survived the injuries he'd received on an op a few weeks ago. And that knowledge seemed to have revived Billy's old nightmares.

So, yeah, imagining Shay was far preferable, even if she'd been a constant torment in his head, keeping him hard enough that he'd been tempted to take himself in hand. But no fucking way was he jacking off to the thought of her just a few hours after she'd moved into his house.

And that left fighting as the best way to chill his damn self out.

Even better? He was meeting a few of the guys beforehand to work out. With any luck, by this evening, he'd be drained—

and therefore a significantly less horny and moody moth-erfucker.

One could hope.

He pulled his ass out of bed and grimaced at the stiffness of the right side of his body. Some of which was muscular, and some of which was his ruined skin.

In the bathroom, he pulled off the shirt he'd slept in and gave himself a once-over in the mirror.

"Shit," he murmured. All that tossing and turning had opened up the ulceration on the top of his shoulder. Given how extensive his scarring was, he supposed he was lucky that he only had one place where the skin remained so fragile.

He frowned at his reflection. He *was* lucky. That, he couldn't deny.

Of the eight men on his Ranger squad, five had died in the fucking trap that had been set. There'd been no reason to ques-tion the well-vetted intelligence they'd received about a large munitions stash hidden in the basement of a house in the middle of a densely inhabited part of Baghdad. No reason at all.

Until the explosives detonated, revealing that the whole thing had been a set-up and they'd been played.

Why did I survive that shit when so many others didn't?

He'd asked himself that so many times over the past three years...

Needing to shake off the fog of sleeplessness, guilt, and regret, Billy took a quick shower, and then he treated the crack in his scar tissue with antibiotic cream. He debated bandaging it, but it wasn't bleeding, and he really didn't want to call atten-tion to it. Next up came moisturizing the nearly forty per cent of his body that had suffered second- and third-degree burns, the most serious of which had been down his right side—the side that had been closest to one of the devices his squad hadn't seen until it was too late.

A lot of his scarring had matured and mellowed enough now that it wasn't super obvious, but the skin on his right shoulder, ribs, and back, that covering a lot of his right arm, and going down the outside of his right thigh, remained shiny and melted-looking and was where, if he was going to have skin irritation or scar breakdown problems, they occurred.

At first, he'd been too sore, too demoralized, and too stiff to do something as simple as rub cream on himself, but for most of the last three years, this had been part of his daily morning routine. Like brushing his teeth or hair. Just what he had to do if he wanted to have nearly full function of his right arm and shoulder.

But the tear in his skin meant he was either going to have to wear a tank that wouldn't further irritate his shoulder, or wear the compression shirt he used to have to wear all the time. Four hours of working out argued in favor of the tank. He dressed in his gear despite the fact that he wasn't meeting the guys until mid-afternoon, then headed downstairs to put on some coffee.

Except, he'd only made it to the top of the steps before he smelled the warm, rich scent of French roast on the air.

Sure enough, he found Shayna downstairs perched on one of the stools at the breakfast bar. Her shoulder-length red waves hid her face as she stared down at an iPad on the counter, and he cleared his throat hoping not to scare her for the second time in less than twenty-four hours.

"Oh, hey," she said, her gaze cutting to him.

"Hey. You made coffee."

She nodded. "Coffee is life. I hope you don't mind."

He wiped up a little spilled sugar and poured himself a cup. "I woke up to ready-to-drink hot coffee and you think I'm gonna mind?"

She gave him a smile, and it struck him again—as it had while they'd made and eaten dinner—that she was so damn pretty. Even sitting there in an old T-shirt and a pair of men's boxers, without makeup, and with those curls going every which way. She'd always been a cute kid, though the infrequency of his visits to the Curtis house, the regularity of their deployments out of country, and the age difference between them had kept him from really getting to know her as anything other than Ryan's little sister.

Which was exactly how he should keep thinking of her. Even though, she was right, she wasn't a girl anymore.

"Just don't want to overstep. I'm sure my invading your home for two months is inconvenient enough."

He mentally winced, because he'd thought that very thing about her. But he certainly didn't want her to feel like she was a burden. "My house is your house, Shayna. Make yourself at home any way you want."

"Thanks," she said, her gaze landing on the cut on his shoulder and skating away again. "You headed to the gym?"

"Later," he said, throwing some bread into the toaster and wondering if Ryan had told her anything about how he'd sustained his injuries. Billy hoped he hadn't, because there were only so many times someone could say *Billy was lucky to survive!* without it sounding like *How did Billy survive when the others didn't?* And for Billy it was a really fucking short trip from that question to the guilt-drenched worry that others deserved to have survived more than him. Like Laurens, who was married, or Coffman, who had kids.

On a sigh, Billy held up the loaf. "Want some?"

"Not much of a breakfast eater," she said, shaking her head.

Quiet fell between them as he buttered his toast and sat beside her at the bar. "Work?" He nodded at her iPad.

"Yeah. Just reviewing the emails about my orientation for the new job."

"When do you start?"

"I have a week of orientation starting on Monday, and then I'll get assigned to an editorial team and learn more about my actual schedule."

The excitement was plain in her voice, and it made Billy think about how long it'd been since he'd last felt that excited for something new in his life. He was damn grateful that he'd been able to parlay his experience as a Ranger into private investigating, because he knew for a fact that a lot of post-service Rangers struggled. First, because it was fucking hard to go from life-or-death to a nine-to-five. And second, because while the spec ops guys were among the most elite soldiers in the military, they didn't have the kinds of readily transferrable skills as someone whose occupational specialty had been in communications or IT or engineering or medicine.

Not to mention that sitting around doing nothing was *not* good for Billy. This he knew for sure. But being a P.I. wasn't his passion. And he wasn't even sure what was. Not anymore.

"What will you be doing?" he asked, forcing himself out of his head.

Her smile showed off more of that excitement. "I'll be working for the *Washington Gazette* as a photographer, doing a mix of on-the-streets assignments and photo editing."

"That sounds impressive," Billy said. Even as the back of his brain added, *And potentially dangerous...*

She shrugged, but the gesture wasn't convincing in its nonchalance. "I'll probably be assigned to pretty fluffy stories at first."

"Even if that's true, people could use more feel-good stories in the news these days," he said, taking a bite of his toast and washing it down with a sip of coffee. She'd made it perfectly.

"That's true," she said.

"Did you go to school for photography?" he asked, wondering what had led her down this path. His curiosity in the whys behind people's behavior was part of what made him enjoy private investigation. Even though what he learned was sometimes painful for his clients.

"Yeah. I studied journalism and visual arts because I wasn't sure what direction I wanted to go in with photography at first. But it didn't take me long working in the museum field to realize I wanted to do something with greater immediate relevance. And then interning with a newspaper confirmed what my gut was telling me. I wanted to capture history in the making." She sipped at her coffee as a soft pink filtered into her cheeks, like maybe she thought he'd find what she said to be stupid.

He didn't. Not at all. In fact, that sentiment portrayed her as being pretty damn similar to her brother. Both of the Curtis siblings wanted to make a difference in the world.

And Billy knew first-hand how important journalists of all kinds were from having worked with them on the front lines. It could be a pain in the ass to have a journalist embedded with your platoon, but it took a lot of fucking courage to carry nothing more than a pen, voice recorder, or camera into a war zone.

His gut squeezed around the toast and coffee he'd eaten. Because the thought had him imagining *Shayna* as one of those war correspondents, and...no. It made no goddamn sense to imagine such a thing. Or to let it impact him so badly.

"I think that sounds great," he managed, pushing off the stool and feeling all kinds of off-balance.

He cleaned up his mess and put everything away where it belonged. The only thing out of place in the whole room was the cup Shayna was using and the chair upon which she sat. A lot of years in the Army, with its constant and often surprise inspections, had made him into a neat freak. And then losing control of his life three years before had turned up the knob on that particular character trait. By a lot. He *needed* things where they belonged or it drove him fucking nuts.

He eyeballed her empty mug, and then gave into the urge. "Done with that?"

"Oh, uh, yeah," she said.

Billy made quick work of rinsing and tucking it away in the dish washer.

Shayna pushed off her stool and grabbed her iPad. "I need to bring in the rest of my things from the car," she said. "I know your guest room is also your office, so do you want to show me where to put stuff so it won't be in your way?"

"I can bring it in for you. Where's your car?"

"You don't have to do that," she said, her gaze flickering to his shoulder again.

He frowned and shoved down a tendril of anger. Did she think he couldn't do it? "Nope, but I'm offering." And, truth be told, he wouldn't mind the break from being in her presence, because something about Shayna Curtis sent his thoughts—and his body—in directions he shouldn't and didn't want to go.

"Well, okay. Then I'm about five cars down the block. The silver CRV with New York tags. I'll grab my keys." She made quick work of retrieving her keyring from upstairs, then held it out to him. "Thanks. I'll need to use my own vehicle for work from time to time, so everything needs to come in."

"Got it," he said, coming closer to grab the keys.

Those blue-green eyes peered up at him, questioning, appreciating, maybe even admiring. And it was all suddenly more than he could handle. "Can I help?"

"I'll handle it," he said, partly speaking to himself, which was why the words came out more harshly than he intended. Damnit. How long was it until fight club again?

"Okay." She stepped back from him as if she knew he was a pressure cooker about to explode.

Damn it all to hell, she wasn't fucking wrong. Not that it was her fault. It wasn't. And it meant he needed to get his shit together.

Billy forced a smile. "Let's get you settled in so you're all ready for your new gig."

CHAPTER THREE

By the time Billy got across town to the Full Contact MMA Training Center, he was nearly desperate to release some of the pent-up frustration and restlessness that had been barreling through his body all damn day.

Walking through the front door of the gym was a little like coming home. The familiarity of the modern reception area, with its cases of trophies and ribbons filling one whole wall. The scents of air conditioning and cleaner and sweat and determination. The symphony of sounds—equipment clanging, weights dropping, feet beating out a rhythm on treadmills, boxing gloves hitting their targets.

Just the promise of release was enough to fire a shot of relief through his veins.

And he had Warrior Fight Club, which met at Full Contact every Saturday, to thank for every bit of it.

He'd belonged to the WFC for almost two years, and it had done more than anything else he'd tried to screw his head on right. Talk therapy was fine. It was whatever. He didn't hate it but it just put him further into his own feels. And that was generally the last place he wanted to be.

Whereas his fists took him way the hell out of his head—while also proving to himself that, despite his injuries and his pain and the loss of his military career, he could still take care of himself and, when necessary, others, too.

He wasn't surprised to find that he was the first one there. He'd left way earlier than he needed to, but he'd had to get away from Shayna.

He'd brought her belongings in from her car just like he said he would, and when he'd expressed surprise at how many cameras she owned, she'd shown him each one and explained its advantages and uses. She'd been cute and almost contagiously enthusiastic while she'd done so. But she'd created such a disaster in his office—he really needed to stop thinking of it that way, didn't he?—that he'd just gotten the hell out of there rather than risk waving his freak flag at her.

It was all for the best, because now he had time to pound out a few miles on the treadmill before anyone else arrived. He was on his fourth mile when a deep voice pulled him from his thoughts.

"How's it going, Billy?"

He turned to find a big mountain of a man grinning at him as he dropped his bag of gear to the floor. Moses Griffin, who was also a Ranger, though they hadn't been in the same battalion.

"Hey, Mo. It's going."

Mo palmed a dark hand over his bald head, the movement emphasizing the bulk of the man's biceps. "That good, huh? Did your company arrive yet?" He got onto the treadmill next to Billy's, feet straddling the belt.

"Roger that," Billy said. Mo had been there the day Ryan had called in his favor, and he and a few others had heard Billy vent about it. But now that he'd met Shayna, he felt a little bad about having done so. "It'll be fine, though. She's cool."

She's beautiful. And interesting. And uses hilariously random curse words.

Mo's eyebrows went up and he slanted him a glance as he adjusted the settings on the machine's LED screen. "Glad to hear it," he said, his tone flat.

Which wasn't really like Mo, who seemed to have two settings: happy and gregarious, or sarcastic as fuck. He was just one of those guys who came at life with humor and optimism, and who looked at every stranger as a friend waiting to be made. Billy had always admired that about him. But today, something seemed off.

"You okay, big guy?" Billy asked as Mo started running.

"Yeah, I'm fucking fine," he said, not really sounding fine at all. Billy arched a brow, and it made Mo laugh. "Okay, so I'm not. Got rejected from a job I applied for and I'm in a mood over it."

"Shit, I'm sorry, Mo. Is it that time again?"

"My contract's up in about six weeks. I have some other irons in the fire, but this one looked sweet." He shrugged. "Something will come along."

He tacked on that platitude almost like he was keeping Billy from being the one to say it.

The two of them had something in common when it came to their post-service jobs—they'd both chosen things that gave them flexibility and kept their routines from being all about the same-old, same-old. After years of living right on the edge of life or death in high-adrenaline, high-stakes operations, monotony was enough to drive men like them insane.

So Billy had chosen private investigation, where he could control which cases he took or didn't. And Mo had been doing government contract work since he'd retired five years ago. His current position with the Department of Defense had been his longest, at a year.

"You still feeling the contractor route?"

"Maybe. I don't know. I'd like to do something that feels like it makes a damn difference. You know?"

"Hell, yeah. I get that." Billy's favorite cases involved tracking down missing persons, because he felt like what he learned *mattered*. But as good as he was at investigating—and he was—he'd more fallen into it then felt called to do it.

At first, he hadn't cared about that distinction. But lately, it was on his mind more and more. Especially since Ryan had shared the news of the death of another of their friends.

Why did I survive the trap when so many others didn't?

Before they could say anymore, Noah Cortez came into the gym, bag of gear hanging on one muscular shoulder, big grin on his face. "Am I late to this party, or what?" he said, dropping his bag next to Mo's.

Billy hit five miles and jumped his feet onto the rails as he powered down the machine. "Right on time," he said, clasping Noah's hand when he extended it.

And, Jesus, what a difference a couple of months had made in the former Marine's life. An IED had given him a traumatic brain injury that'd damaged his left ear and eye, and when Billy had first met Noah right here at Full Contact about four months ago, the guy had been a gaunt shell battling some serious depression. Now, he'd put on a good thirty pounds of muscle. The dark circles were mostly gone from under his eyes. And he walked taller, like a weight had been lifted off his shoulders.

"How's your girl?" Mo asked, moving to the younger man's good side.

The expression on Noah's face hit Billy uncomfortably in the chest because he'd never once felt the fundamentally happy way Noah looked. He'd seen Noah and Kristina together, and it was crystal clear that they were a match of the happily-ever-after kind. Billy was happy that so many things had turned around for the younger man—Noah had fought for it and deserved it. But it was still a sucker punch to realize you might never find that for yourself.

"She's too fucking good for me, but otherwise she's great. Busy now that the new school year's underway," Noah said, pride plain in his voice.

And for some reason, that had Billy thinking about Shayna. About the excitement in her voice as she'd talked about her new job and wanting to do something meaningful. About the enthusiasm she'd demonstrated as she'd shown him her equipment.

To be that young and fresh again, your whole life stretching out in front of you full of potential and possibility. As jaded and world-weary as he was, even though he was only six years older than her, he could barely imagine it.

"When are we gonna get to hang out with her again?" Mo asked. "It's been too long. You gotta come up for air every once in a while."

"Oh, right. Halloween," Noah said, not taking the bait even as Billy snickered.

Mo frowned. "That's over a month away, son."

Noah chuckled. "No shit, but Kristina gave me marching orders to invite you all when I saw you tonight. We're going to throw a Halloween party at my parents' house. So you officially all have plans or Kristina will track you down. Feel free to bring dates." He looked at each of them expectantly.

"How about roommates?" Billy asked as he wiped down his treadmill.

Noah's gaze suddenly felt too observant. "Your buddy's sister? Absolutely. How's that going?"

"She arrived yesterday, but she seems cool." He took a long pull from his water bottle to avoid any looks they might be giving him.

"She's cramping his style," Mo said, smirking.

"No," he said, almost reflexively. "She's just...keeping me on my toes."

Mo arched one dark eyebrow. "Is she now?" He waggled his eyebrows at Noah, who laughed.

"Not like that, assholes," he said, wiping the sweat from his face. Even though she was fucking attractive. There was no denying that.

Noah scratched at his chin. "There's a story there."

"There's definitely a story there," Mo said.

Billy rolled his eyes. "Fine. She broke into my house when she got there yesterday because I was late and it was fucking pouring. And I thought she was an intruder so I pulled my gun on her."

He wasn't sharing the bit about the towel. That was all his.

His dickhead friends burst out laughing. Mo laughed so hard, he had to jump his feet onto the rails.

"How did she break in?" Noah asked, clutching his stomach.

Billy scowled. "She picked the lock."

Noah's brows went up. "Resourceful."

Mo nodded and grinned. "Ranger brother teach her that?"

"Yeah. I should've known, too."

"Did she flip out about you pulling the gun?" Noah asked.

"No," Billy said, realizing just how fucking cool her reaction had been. "She teased me about it and made me agree that we shouldn't tell her brother."

Mo and Noah traded impressed looks. "I like this girl and I haven't even met her," Mo said. "When are we rectifying that?"

"Any time," Billy said. "She's new to D.C. so she'd probably appreciate making some friends."

Just then, Coach Mack, Hawk, and Colby arrived, and Billy

was glad for the interruption. Because he felt like talking about Shayna was making him think about her in ways he really shouldn't.

He greeted each of the new men in turn. John "Mack" McPherson was in his forties and had started WFC about a decade before. Leo Hawkins and Colby Richmond were two of Coach Mack's original members, and they often helped instruct and supervise training within the club. And, of course, all three of them were veterans, because that was the only requirement for membership.

Which was a big part of the reason that WFC meant so much to Billy. The worst part of losing his career hadn't been his injury, as bad as that had been, it'd been the loss of his community, the place where he belonged.

WFC had given that back to him. These guys had been where he'd been. They knew what it was to be out there serving. And they understood the struggles you faced coming home—even if you were physically whole—like no one else.

Finally, all the chit chat was out of the way, and they got down to business. First, with an ass-kicking workout of free weights, and then with class and matches.

And Billy was so keyed up that he won every round.

She lived next to a cemetery.

Shayna discovered this when she took a walk around the neighborhood to see what was nearby. She'd found a few convenience stores, a pharmacy, a couple of schools, and a fantastic-looking Indian restaurant.

And a sprawling cemetery, part of which was the final resting place of famous writers, diplomats, and politicians, and part of which was the Soldiers' Home National Cemetery, the country's first national cemetery, founded even before the more famous Arlington.

It had been created to bury the thousands of dead soldiers from nearby Civil War battles. And at the edge of the cemetery was the cottage where President Lincoln had spent the hot summers of his presidency, watching as more and more graves filled the surrounding fields outside his front door.

It was a cemetery.

And, camera in hand, Shayna had stumbled into it, lured by the beautiful gardens, unusual little chapels, and haunting statuary.

For the span of several long minutes, she found it hard to take a breath.

Because the last time she'd gone to a cemetery, it had been for her brother's funeral. Dylan. The middle Curtis sibling. Who'd died helping Shayna.

She'd never gone to visit him again.

Shayna couldn't feel him there. And the empty hollowness felt like an accusation. *It's your fault he's not here. It should've been you.*

The tightness in her chest made her a little dizzy, and she realized that she was gulping for breath. Bracing her hands on her knees made it a little easier to breathe, but also caused the camera she wore strapped around her neck to swing down.

Shayna grasped at it like it was a lifeline.

It was, of a sort.

Because putting the viewfinder to her eye narrowed her field of vision down to what was immediately in front of her. To what was *manageable.*

From behind the camera, she could control what she saw, and with what clarity, and at what distance.

It was part of what made her fall in love with cameras in the first place. That and the fact that when you held a camera, people looked at the lens, not at the photographer. You could observe exactly as you wished without being observed in return.

At least, that's the way it felt sometimes. And years of looking at the world through a viewfinder had trained her to find the light and the dark and the detail and the emotion of life.

Right now, she felt grief for Dylan and fear that her family blamed her the way she blamed herself.

And in those emotions, what stood out to her on this beautiful day were all the shadows cast by the sun. The gingerbread cutouts cast intricate shapes upon the siding of Lincoln's cottage. The circular spokes of a Civil War cannon's wheel upon the grass. The way her own shadow laid on the ground next to that of an angel's statue, as if they were both nothing more than a formless play of light.

Shayna finally allowed herself to wander into the heart of the cemetery, where rows of little white grave markers made interesting patterns of lines and diagonals depending on just how you looked at them. And she grabbed those images as well. The strange geometry of it. As if the grave diggers had attempted to impose some order on death.

When there was nothing orderly about it. Because it couldn't possibly make sense that an otherwise healthy twenty-seven-year-old man should get killed by a drunk driver. Two months before his wedding. Because his stupid sister had asked him for help.

Yet that was exactly what'd happened to Dylan.

Suddenly, Shayna was bone tired. From the drive yesterday. From sleeping in a strange bed. From the long walk she'd taken in the heat today. From the way that grief could sneak up on you years later, as if reminding you to never get too comfortable in your own skin.

She wanted to go home. But the cemetery was a maze of paths, and from behind the view finder, she hadn't been paying the closest attention. She followed the sound of traffic, hoping to get to the road, but found herself blocked by a tall, ornate iron gate. Locked.

Which was when she realized that her cheeks were wet. She batted the tears away and headed back in the direction from which she came, where she took a different path hoping it would lead her out.

"Are you okay, miss?" came a deep, rolling voice. An older black man sat on a bench, a brown and white dog laying against one foot, and a cane leaning against the opposite knee.

"Yes, thank you. I just got turned around."

"Easy to do in here, unless you come all the time like me and Ziggy." Upon hearing his name, the dog's tail pounded out a rhythm on the sidewalk.

"Now I know," she said, mentally pulling herself together. "I was taking pictures and wasn't paying attention."

The man tilted his head. "Well, I imagine you were paying attention to different things."

Shayna blinked. "Yeah, I guess I was. Would you...mind some company?"

His smile offered the kind of warmth that made her think of seeing an old friend after a long time apart. The kind of friend who was so close that neither time nor distance could impact your friendship. You just picked up right where you left off every time.

"I like nothing better than company. Isn't that right, Zig?"

Shayna's butt had no more hit the bench then Ziggy sprang into a sitting position against her calf, so close that his paw was on her foot. She laughed. "Well, hello to you, too."

"Now, now, Ziggy," the man said.

She guessed that the dog was a terrier/pit bull mix. And as

it looked up at her, its mouth fell open and its tongue fell out, making it look like the dog was goofily smiling up at her. "It's okay," she said as she patted his big block head. "I like dogs."

"Well, I'm just warning you that once you start you can't ever stop."

Grinning, Shayna nodded. "I suppose that's fair." She looked up at the man. "I'm Shayna, by the way."

"Pleased to meet you, Shayna. I'm Reuben."

She held out her hand, and they shook. "Nice to meet you, Reuben," she said, laughing as Ziggy put a paw on her knee as if protesting the pause in her petting.

"Told ya so," Reuben said, chuckling.

God, Shayna felt so much better being around the friendly man. No longer lost or alone. Which she knew was an exaggeration of the situation. But clearly she felt that way on some psychic level, too.

Which was why she was here. In D.C. After messing up so badly, she desperately wanted a shot at a fresh start. She really hoped such a thing was possible. And that she deserved it.

"You new around here then, Shayna?"

She nodded. "Just moved in with a friend on Farragut Place."

"No kidding? We're on Farragut, too. A new friend and a new neighbor, then. What do you think of that, Ziggy?"

The dog pushed his head into her hand, making her chuckle again.

"He's a very good judge of character," Reuben said. "I'd say he likes you."

"Well, the feeling's mutual," she said, scratching his ear.

Reuben looked out over the cemetery, where the shadows were beginning to stretch out across the grass. "I suppose we best be getting back. Would you like to walk along with us?"

"I'd like that," Shayna said, being sure to match her stride and pace to Reuben's. He walked sure, but slow, and with a slight limp on the side where he used his cane. Off leash, Ziggy trotted right between them, never leaving his owner's side.

On the way back to their street, she told him about her new job, and he told her about his daughter and grandkids who lived outside the city in Maryland. His wife had passed away five years before, so it was just him and his dog in the row house where they'd raised their family.

"Well, this is me and Zig," he said, pointing to a row house with an old lawn chair on the front porch.

Shayna nodded and pointed down the block. "We're the fourth one from the end."

"Good to know. If you need anything, just come on down and knock."

"I will," she said, bending down to pet a wagging Ziggy. "I hope you'll do the same." She rose and felt so grateful to the man for being there for her, whether he realized she'd needed that or not. "Maybe you can come over for dinner some time, Reuben."

"I know I can't refuse an invitation to dinner. You just tell me the time and date," he said with a wave. "And have a good night, now."

"You, too," she said, continuing down the sidewalk. At home, she opened the door—and nearly walked directly into Billy. "Whoa, sorry." She braced her hands on his chest in surprise.

He grasped her by the biceps to steady her. "Hey, there you are."

She blinked up into dark eyes unsettled with worry. "I'm sorry. Did you need me?"

Billy peered down at her for a long moment. "Uh, no. I

mean, I guess I was just curious where you'd gone because your car was here but you weren't."

"I was learning my way around," she said, aware that he was still touching her. She wasn't complaining. Up close, Billy Parrish smelled like soap and man and sin and she was in no rush to give it up. "And I made a new friend."

He arched a brow. "Did you now?"

"Reuben? Do you know him?"

Expression suddenly guarded, he shook his head.

"Old man, walks with a cane. Has a brown and white dog named Ziggy. His house is in the middle of the block."

His expression softened, which was when the question occurred to her—was he jealous that she might've met someone? No. Couldn't be. Probably just protective. That made way more sense.

He gave her arms a light squeeze and stepped back. "If you met one of our neighbors, then you officially know one more than me."

He said *our*. It was a little thing that probably meant nothing, but she still found it sweet. Not that she was going to mention it. "Really? But you've lived here a while."

"I know the immediate neighbors enough to recognize them and to give them a wave if we happen to be outside at the same time, but otherwise I'm usually either working, sleeping, or at the gym." He shrugged as he went in the direction of the kitchen.

Shayna shut the door and followed. "Well, I'll have to introduce you to Reuben because he's very sweet and he helped me today." The words were out of her mouth before she'd even thought about what she was saying—or admitting.

Billy frowned. "What did you need help with?"

"Oh." She waved a dismissive hand. "I just got turned around and he pointed me in the right direction."

His frown deepened. "You know you could've texted or called me, right? You need anything—anything at all—you can come to me, day or night."

The words were infused with a sincere intensity that spiked her pulse. "Yeah, okay, Billy. Thank you. And I will. I promise."

CHAPTER FOUR

SHAYNA WAS GOING ten kinds of crazy. It was nearly eleven o'clock in the morning, and she hadn't heard a peep out of Billy. And she really needed to ask him a question.

She needed desk space, but she didn't want to move things around on his desk without asking. They might only have lived together for two days, but she'd had plenty of occasions already to notice him straightening up after her or putting things away. And he was nearly fastidious in cleaning up after himself. So she was certain that he would not love her pushing his things to the side to make room for her laptop, photo printer, and supplies.

She'd debated long and hard on the idea of knocking on his bedroom door. But that felt too intrusive in case he just wanted to sleep late.

Instead, she sent him a text. *Hey, you feeling okay?*

When she didn't get a reply, she wrote a note, slipped it under his door, and left the house to solve this problem another way.

When in doubt, there was always Target. And luckily there was one not too far away.

And because Target was the land of things-you-didn't-even-know-you-needed, she not only bought a desk and chair, but she also loaded up on some desk organizers, office supplies, two new lip glosses, a super cute pajama set, and groceries for the week, because it wasn't like she could expect Chef Billy to cook for her every night.

The nickname made her chuckle, even though he *was* a really good cook. But she wanted to do her share, so she also bought a few replacements of his things that she'd been eating.

About mid-way through the magical, mystical land of *Tarzhay*, her phone dinged an incoming message from Billy. Finally!

Yeah, sorry I didn't see this sooner.

No worries, she replied. *Need anything from the mecca that is Target?*

He didn't answer for long enough that she thought he wasn't going to, but then he did.

Large non-stick bandages and medical tape. Only if it's not a PITA

Shayna frowned at the request, and immediately thought of the cut he'd had on his shoulder yesterday. Though, it didn't precisely look like a cut. More like an irritation had rubbed his scarred skin raw.

Yup I'm on it

She finished getting the things on her list and his, checked out, and headed home. Unable to find a parking spot on their block, she double parked on the street out front, grabbed as many bags as her arms and fingers could possibly hold—because she was too stubborn to want to make more trips—and waddled in through the front door looking like a pack mule.

Billy stood at the kitchen counter, head tilted back, drinking a glass of water. Shirtless.

Shayna did a double take that nearly had her dropping everything on the floor.

Her eyes couldn't decide where to focus first. On the obviously hard muscles of his shoulders and pecs? On the actual ridges of muscles on his abdomen? On the way his gym shorts hung low enough on his hips that they hinted at the muscled indentations that she'd find beneath? If she ever looked. Which she totally would, except she didn't have an invitation to go down under...

He arched a brow. She was so busted.

"Um, hey," she managed, brazening it out even as her face filled with heat. "Sleepyhead."

"Slept worth shit until it was time to get up, of course. Then all I wanted to do was go back to sleep." He watched as she awkwardly settled all the bags on the counter, then extricated her wrists from the looped handles. "Need help?"

"Um," she said again, because this close, she noticed two other things.

First, that he was a little sweaty, and the sheen of it over all those muscles was sexy as hell. It made her want to shower with him. Or lick him. Or both, but maybe not in that order.

And second, she saw for the first time just how extensive his scarring was. Save for the area around the cut on his shoulder—which looked bigger today—most of the scarring wasn't a markedly different color, but it was smoother and shinier in some places and raised in others, compared to the skin that hadn't been burned. And it covered the whole right side of his ribs and part of his back, from the waist of his shorts to his arm pit.

"I kinda do need help...in the form of muscles...which you seem to have a lot of."

Now her face was on absolute *fire*, but she didn't care,

because she wanted him to know that her staring was about those hot-as-fuck muscles, not the scars.

"Is that right?" he said, eyebrow arched.

Shayna rolled her eyes. "Do you need confirmation of this fact?"

He shook his head. "Nope. Doesn't suck hearing that a pretty girl noticed, though."

Pretty girl! That internal squee was her first—ridiculous—reaction. Clearly, his muscles made her a little stupid.

"Woman," she said, arching a brow of her own.

A slow smile crept up his handsome face. "Okay, *woman.* What is it you need muscle for?"

She led him outside to her car, then popped the hatch. "Meet my new desk and chair," she said, pointing to the boxes that filled the back. Of course the desk needed to be assembled.

He frowned. "You could've used mine."

Shayna shrugged. "I didn't want to assume. Besides, I'm messy and you're not, so I didn't want my stuff to drive you crazy."

He peered down at her like he was trying to figure her out, and something about the look made her belly go on a loop-the-loop. "I appreciate that, but I still would've made room for you."

Before she could think of how to respond, he tugged the heavy box out of her trunk. His biceps bulged under the strain of the desk's weight.

She managed the box containing her new chair and followed Billy back inside.

As they dropped the furniture in her bedroom, he said, "Gimme your keys. I'm going to give you my parking spot out back while you're here. That way you don't have to circle looking for a space or end up having to walk a couple blocks at night."

"That's really sweet, Billy, but I don't want to put you out

—" Her gaze latched onto his shoulder, where a thin stream of blood oozed down his back from his cut.

He turned, saw where she was looking, and frowned. "I'm *fine*, Shayna."

Could he not feel the blood? "No, it's not that, Billy. You're bleeding."

His head whipped to the side, and he strained to see over his shoulder, but couldn't. He went into her bathroom and hit the lights. "Aw, shit."

"I got the bandages you asked for. I'll grab them," she said.

Without looking at her, he nodded once. She heard the frustrated breath he released as she left the room. It only took her a moment of sorting through the bag to find what she was looking for—and to stumble upon the ice cream which she threw in the freezer.

When she came back up, he was waiting at the top of the steps. "I got it from here, thanks."

"I can help—"

"I've *got* it," he said again, not quite meeting her gaze.

"You helped me, so why can't I help—"

"*Shayna.*"

"*Billy.*" She understood how guys like Billy and her brother thought. She'd been around enough of them to know they *hated* needing help. But that didn't mean they didn't actually need it. "You won't be able to reach. Let me help."

He let out a harsh breath, then turned away. "Fine." He disappeared into his bedroom at the back of the hallway.

Shayna followed. His room was all dark blues and browns, with a big queen-sized bed dominating the space. And it was as neat as the rest of the house, with not even an errant sock on the floor. She followed the rectangle of light spilling from the master bathroom and found him gathering supplies from the medicine cabinet.

For a moment, she just stood in the doorway, because she could feel the anger rolling off of him. "I'm sorry that carrying my stupid desk made your shoulder worse."

He slanted her a look, and it was clear that he was attempting to beat back his temper. "It didn't, so don't worry."

"I'm kinda predisposed to think things are my fault, so it can't be helped."

He frowned, and this time all the frustration bled from his expression. "Why do you say that?"

Because my idiocy and stubbornness killed my brother.

That was what she thought, but what she said was, "I don't know. Old habit."

Billy shook his head. "Well, this isn't your fault, Shayna. And I'd be willing to bet that whatever else you're worrying about isn't either." He closed the toilet lid and sat heavily, and Shayna was glad that he looked away, because his words had unleashed a sting at the backs of her eyes. "I hate that I need help with this, not that you're the one helping."

There went her belly again. "Just pretend I'm Ryan," she said in a quiet voice.

He smirked up at her. "Why would I do that?"

"Because you probably wouldn't care if a buddy was patching you up, right?"

He shrugged with one big shoulder. "Anyone ever told you that you can be too damn perceptive?"

"I'm a photographer, after all. It's literally my job to see things."

"Mine, too," he said, tossing another glance over his shoulder, this one appreciative.

Their gazes collided. Held. Made Shayna's heart beat harder.

"So, do I need to do anything special or just clean, bandage, tape?"

"Put antibiotic cream on before you bandage. And be sure to pat rather than wipe. Because of the movement of the joint, this spot is the one area that has struggled to heal. Otherwise, that's it."

She washed her hands and ran warm water over a wash cloth, then did as he said. "Let me know if I hurt you."

"You won't," he said. "I can't feel much where it's scarred. My nerves are mostly shot back there."

No wonder he hadn't realized it was bleeding. Shayna debated whether humor would help or hurt the situation, then went for it. "Well, in case you have one nerve left, I don't want to get on it."

One beat passed, then another. Billy chuckled, and the sound did funny things to her chest. "Appreciate that, smart ass."

She put a playful sauciness in her voice as she said, "You noticing my ass, Billy Parrish?"

He didn't answer, even though she could almost *hear* his mental debate as to how to respond, which made her laugh as she tended to him.

"This is pretty much the same thing I had to do when I got the tattoo on my shoulder," she said, smoothing antibiotic cream over the open skin. She grimaced as she did so, not because she found it unpleasant, but because she worried about hurting him despite his reassurances.

"How many tattoos do you have?" he asked in a low voice.

The question reminded her that he'd seen one of them, and heat filtered into her cheeks as she positioned the bandage. "Four. The one on my hip, and three on my back and shoulders. Once you have one, it's kinda addicting."

"Is that right?"

"Mmhmm," she murmured, concentrating on the tape. "I

think the bottom piece of tape might need to wrap under your arm a little to hold it in place. Is that okay?"

"Whatever you say, Goldilocks."

"That'll be Dr. Goldilocks to you, ya git." She smoothed the tape down. His muscles were every bit as hard as they looked. Gah.

He chuckled again. "What's with the colorful name-calling?"

She grinned. "I grew up with brothers. Am I offending your sensitive ears, Ranger Parrish?"

"Hell, no," he said. "I'm a fan."

"Good. There," she said, surveying her work. Satisfaction warmed her belly, because she'd gotten to help him. And he'd called her pretty. And said he was a fan of the crazy crap that came out of her mouth. "All done."

He rose and peered in the mirror. "Perfect, Shayna," he said, their gazes meeting in the glass.

And she could've sworn he said, "Perfect Shayna," *without* any hesitation between the words. Especially when he looked at her like he was doing right now.

As if she had on far too many clothes. And Jesus did she suddenly agree.

"Any time you need patched up, consider me your girl," she managed, still meeting the heat in those brown eyes.

Brown eyes whose reflection looked her up and down. "Don't you mean *woman*? Consider you my woman? You know, when I need patched up."

Shayna released a shaky breath. "Yeah. Exactly."

He gave a slow nod, then turned to look at her directly, bringing them toe to toe. "Then, consider me your man when you need muscle. Now, how about I go move your car and help you build a desk?"

With Shay's assistance, Billy built the desk and the chair, helped her reorganize his guest room so everything fit, and disposed of all the cardboard packaging. Then he'd put her behemoth photo printer in place and watched as she began to impose a Shayna level of order on all her things.

Which was to say, it wasn't very fucking orderly.

Of course, that drove Billy nuts. But he ignored it for the most part because he was enjoying spending time with her. She was funny and made him laugh and she was just...really easy to be with.

Having her around this weekend had made him realize just how much he was usually alone. And that it was actually nice to have some company around his place.

It wasn't going too far to say that he'd had more fun with her setting up her room than he'd ever had in this house since he'd moved in. Doing a whole lot of nothing special. And that was all due to Shayna.

That was all to say nothing of the million little ways she'd communicated consideration for him beyond patching up his fugly skin.

Her whole thought process around the desk situation told him—without judgment—that she respected that he was more concerned with neatness and order than the average bear. And when they made lunch together, he realized that she'd replaced some of the food and drinks she'd used since she'd arrived. He hadn't expected or needed that, but he'd appreciated it. Even the fact that she'd fought with him about helping with his shoulder spoke of someone who cared, even if admitting his weakness in needing help frustrated him, too.

They sat at the breakfast bar talking long after their sandwiches and salads were gone.

"So what kinds of investigations do you do as a P.I.?" she asked, turning on her stool toward him, just a little.

"Background checks are the bread-and-butter of my work, which is probably true for a lot of P.I.s. But I do a lot of surveillance work as well. Infidelity, workers' comp, some collection of evidence for litigation. And when I think I might have what it takes to be helpful, I take on missing persons cases."

Shay really listened when he talked. Like she was taking in everything he had to say. Ryan had been that way. You always knew you had his full attention, and it made you feel like you could always count on him having your back.

The comparison between the siblings was oddly comforting. Probably because Billy missed being out in the field with his brothers like a sonofabitch.

"Which is your favorite kind of investigation to do?" she asked.

He didn't have to think that hard about it. "Missing persons cases are the most meaningful thing I do these days."

She tilted her head, her expression thoughtful. "Do people come to you instead of the police, or after the police have given up?"

"Usually after the police have given up. Or in a situation where the authorities aren't responsive."

"Wow. That sounds like a lot of responsibility, Billy. Being someone's last hope."

"It is. But it's also good feeling like what I do matters." A knot lodged unexpectedly in his throat. Because in the Army, he used to live and breathe that feeling. And now he was sometimes fucking desperate for it.

Shay nodded. "Can I ask you something that might be kinda personal?"

Billy scratched his chin. "Uh, go for it."

She gave a little smile, but it melted away again. "How hard is it to go from being a Ranger to being a civilian?"

There was that perceptiveness again. He met those sea-blue eyes and gave her the truth, not just because her curiosity was sincere, but because some day she'd have a brother going through the shit of transition, too. Though, hopefully not until Ryan put in his twenty and was good and ready to retire.

"It's like...it's like going from a world where everything's in technicolor to one where everything's black and white."

Shayna's lips parted like maybe he surprised her. But he suddenly *needed* her to understand. He turned toward her, their knees touching under the counter.

"It's like, one day you're dodging bullets and jumping out of helicopters into deserts alive with hidden threats and you're taking really bad fucking people off the streets, and the next day, you're standing in a grocery store aisle with seventy-five types of cereal wondering if anyone knows how goddamn ridiculous it is that there are so many choices of one thing. And you're going to dinners and parties and people are talking about what some celebrity said or wore or what happened on the last episode of a TV show and all you can think about is that somewhere someone might be dying because you don't have their back. Which probably sounds arrogant as shit, but it's how you feel. How *I* feel. Sometimes."

And hell if that wasn't more than he'd admitted to anyone in a long-ass time.

Shayna's expression was a beautiful mask of emotion—more of that surprise, but maybe sympathy and sadness, too. And fuck, he really hoped none of what she felt was pity. Because even though he was capable of throwing himself a goddamn stellar pity party on occasion, he hated it from anyone else.

"So, uh, yeah. That was probably more than what you wanted, but, uh, that's one soldier's take." He finally took a drink to cut off the string of awkward nonsense coming out of his mouth.

She swallowed, and it was a thick sound, as if she were a little choked up. And then he saw the glassiness in her eyes.

"I'm sorry it's hard sometimes. And it must be harder because people who haven't been through it can't imagine it. Not really. We think soldiers come home from war and must be so happy about it never realizing..."

"That's the thing," he said, hardly believing how much he was laying bare—or how easy he was finding doing so. With her. "I *was* happy at first. I don't think you have any way of guessing at all the ways in which being in the real world starts to seem surreal. It's why so many people get out of the military and end up doing similar kinds of jobs as a civilian."

His friend Noah was only the most recent example of that very phenomenon. Guy worked as an ordinance disposal tech in the Marines, which meant he spent his time around things that exploded or threatened to do so, and now he worked for TSA as a bomb appraisal officer.

Some of that was skills and qualifications. But some of that was an urgent fucking need to return to the work you'd done before, *because* it'd felt meaningful, and *despite* the fact that said work might've been responsible for injuring your body or fucking with your head.

"Like with you doing investigations," she said.

He rubbed a hand over his face, needing that momentary break from laying himself so bare to her—and from how much Shayna fucking got him.

"Yeah. Exactly," he finally said. "I was actually drawn to private security, but my recovery was kind of a long, slow process and I feared my responsiveness wouldn't be what a crisis situation might require." Which had been a helluva thing to come to terms with.

"You're a good egg, Billy Parrish," she said, her expression suddenly shy.

And fuck if he didn't feel a little heat crawl up his face. "I think I preferred when you called me a ballbag."

She laughed, a full-belly laugh that eked a smile out of him in return. "Fine, knobhead."

And now he was laughing, too. How was it that this woman had taken him from some really damn intimate shit he'd barely been willing to tell his therapist to humor in the course of a few minutes? He didn't know, but he appreciated it. A lot.

"Much better," he said, nodding.

He could barely believe they'd been sitting at the breakfast bar talking for nearly two hours. Or that he'd enjoyed it so much when it'd involved digging into some of the shit he usually kept boxed up tight. But he had.

The LED clock on the microwave caught his eye. "Damn, is it three o'clock already?"

"Yeah. I'm sorry. I've taken up your whole day." She grabbed his plate and bowl and threw him a smile. "Here, I'll clean up. I hereby release you from furniture building and moving."

He grasped her arm. "Don't apologize. I liked getting to hang out with you. It's been a while. I just need a few hours to do research on a case that's been a pain in my ass."

Her expression went so soft and sweet. "I get it. Really. Go ahead. Do what you have to do. I'm just gonna chill out anyway."

"You sure?" he asked, pushing off the stool.

"Yes, knobhead, I'm sure."

He flipped her off and made for the stairs, grinning to himself as she burst into laughter again, and then he threw her a wink as he went up.

On a grumble, Billy settled into the recliner in the corner of his bedroom with his laptop and the file on his current stalled case and made himself work. He managed to focus for about two hours when his eyes started to cross from scrolling through databases and spreadsheets in search of alleged hidden assets in a civil investigation he was doing—and not finding any evidence of them.

Why had he taken this case? When background checks and surveillance cases were so much more straightforward? And while hardly ever straight forward, at least missing persons cases were rewarding. This shit was just a pain in his ass.

On a sigh, Billy closed his laptop and rose—and caught a flash of color from the corner of his eye.

He looked out the window next to his chair to find Shayna lying in the hammock on his patio. Wearing a navy blue bikini, though partially covered by a towel, as if she'd gotten chilly and pulled it over herself like a blanket. She was asleep.

And *fucking A*, she was pretty.

He stood there a long moment, staring down at her, thinking how cool she was and how much he'd enjoyed this day—despite the bullshit fragility of his skin and the fact that they'd kinda argued. She was as stubborn as he was...and he liked that about her.

So many times today, she'd reminded him of her brother in ways both good and bad. Like Ryan, she was stubborn and strong-willed and straight forward and caring to a fault.

All of that was also bad, though, because he knew that the last thing Ryan would want for his sister was a broken-down, washed-out Ranger who was, at best, coasting listlessly through life while rocking some major survivors' guilt and more than a little self-loathing for his part in failing his brothers.

He allowed himself one more glance at all her pretty curves. And then he reminded himself for the dozenth time: *She's Ryan's sister. She's Ryan's sister. She's Ryan's sister.*

Ryan's sister, who was easy to talk to and made him laugh and got him to open up in ways he rarely ever did...

Still, *Ryan's. Fucking. Sister.*

With that reality check in mind, for the next hour, Billy ignored the fact that Shay was lying in a bikini outside his window. Or tried to.

Fact was that ignoring just the idea of her presence was utterly fucking impossible.

Maybe it was the lure of the bikini. *Probably* it was just the bikini.

Jesus, he was acting like a teenage boy and not a man who had a whole list of numbers he could call of women who'd previously scratched his itch—and were willing to do it again.

As soon as his body had been able, he'd found sex to be one of the things that most helped him forget all that he'd lost. That most worked out the restless angst and agitation often roiling through his blood. He always made it clear that he wasn't in it for a relationship, and with most of his partners, that'd been more than fine. They weren't looking for that either—at least not with him. So, yeah, Billy had options that didn't involve perving on his best friend's sister who he was supposed to be looking out for as she got settled in DC.

So much for working...

He closed his laptop and tossed it on his bed. Got up. Stretched, but not so far that he pulled at the tape of his dressing. The dressing Shayna had put on for him.

At first, he hadn't been able to feel her touch, but then she'd smoothed her fingers under his arm and around to his pec.

And he'd fucking felt it.

Just like he'd felt how she'd looked at him when she'd come home from shopping. He'd had to resist the urge to cover up his ruined skin, but when her eyes had conveyed such interest, such *hunger*, he'd fought that urge right back into its box.

Shayna Curtis hadn't looked at him like he was a ruined man. And she hadn't touched him like it either.

Which was why he couldn't resist looking out the window again. She still lay sleeping, her hands curled around the towel on her chest. A few pieces of paper had blown off of the hammock to the brick paving of the patio. Shayna's red curls got caught in the breeze and blew around her forehead.

In the distance, thunder sounded out in a long, low rumble.

Billy frowned, then went downstairs. At the back door, he debated right up until he saw the first droplets of rain hit the glass in front of him.

And then he had the strangest fucking thought: he had to protect what was his.

As in, take care of Ryan's sister, like he'd said he would. That was what he'd meant. That was *all* he meant.

Fatter drops hit the window pane, not giving him the time to gut check any of the shit that'd just run through his mind.

Outside, he went right to her. A hand on her arm, he gave a light shake. "Shay, wake up."

A smile played around her lips. "Billy..." The word came out as little more than a breath, but he still heard it. More than that, things inside him *felt* it.

"Shayna," he said a little louder, trying not to look at the line of her collar bones or the scattering of freckles just above the fabric of her bikini top or the nearly bare curve of her hip that remained uncovered by the towel.

Her eyelids popped open, and those eyes the color of the Caribbean Sea looked up at him so soft and sleepy. And then awareness slid into them as she pushed up onto her elbows. "What's the matter?"

Everything, his gut answered. Then his gaze scanned over her face. *Or maybe nothing at all.*

He shook his head at himself *and* in answer to her question. "It's about to storm."

"Oh," she said, her gaze going up to the sky just as a fat rain drop nailed her between the eyes. "Aaah! I see that now." She chuckled as she wiped at her face and twisted her legs off the edge. "You know, you strung this hammock up like it's for the Jolly Green Giant. I had to make an acrobatic maneuver to get into it."

Her feet dangled nowhere near the ground, though that was hard to focus on when he got his first eyeful of just how much of her skin that bikini bared. Christ. "I think I'd like to have seen that," he managed.

"Can you make yourself useful and hold the hammock still so I can hop down?" she asked, amused frustration in her voice.

He swallowed hard as he bent to retrieve the scattered paper. No, not paper. Photographs. "Nope. I'm here for the dismount maneuver," he said, as the photographs—*arresting* photographs—captured his attention. They were a mix of color and black and white. Of a cemetery...

She gave an aggrieved sigh. "Come on, douchecanoe, it's starting to rain for real. Help me down so I don't splat all over the place."

The images in his hand were melancholy and haunting, and set off a weird feeling in his chest even as her words penetrated the way they'd captivated him.

With a half-hearted chuckle, he came toward her. "Douchecanoe, huh?"

"Uh huh," she said, smirking up at him, so playful and pretty.

He came close enough that his knees touched hers. Without giving himself a chance to rethink the wisdom of his actions, he put an arm around her back. "Fine. Grab on to me," he said, the words coming out low and rough.

"I don't want to hurt your sh—"

"*Grab on to me.*"

She did. Her hands clasped around the back of his neck, coming nowhere near the wound on his shoulder that he knew concerned her. And then he pulled her against his chest until all her soft curves were pressed tight against all his hard edges.

Their gazes collided.

Her breath caught and she glanced at his mouth. Just the slightest little glance.

Billy was instantly and demandingly hard. And so fucking hungry for just one taste.

Shayna's eyes flashed back to meet his. "Thank you," she said in a breathy, needful voice that ratcheted up the lust suddenly heating his blood. From that look and the feeling of her body against him and their whole day together.

"It's nothing," he said, putting her down.

But she didn't let go. "It means a lot to me."

"What does?" His body wanted more of her pressed to more of him again. Wanted it bad. He clenched his teeth against the need clawing through him.

"Everything you're doing for me." Her voice still had that breathiness that grabbed him by the balls.

"It's no problem, Shay," he gritted out. It didn't matter how bad he wanted more from this moment. He couldn't let himself have it. But he also wasn't pushing her away, was he?

Her gaze dropped to his mouth again.

"*Shayna.*"

Pink filtered into the fair skin of her cheeks and she dropped her arms. "I guess we should go inside."

"Uh huh."

She gave him one last look, then made for the door.

Which was the first time Billy saw the ink she'd mentioned she wore on her back.

From underneath her hair, he could just make out the symbol of an aperture on the back of her neck. The black was stark against her skin. But what caught his attention even more was the bigger piece she wore on the whole back of her right shoulder. A tattoo of several Polaroid photographs surrounded by watercolor flowers. Inside the Polaroid frames were images of a sun setting over mountains, the fuzzy seeds of a dandelion blowing away, and a little girl in a dress reaching for a red heart-shaped balloon as it floated skyward.

Wrapping the towel around herself, she disappeared inside, and he blinked out of his stupor and followed her.

As he closed the door, she said, "Oh, I'll take those." Shay gestured to where he still held her photographs.

"You took these?" he asked, happy for something else to focus on. Besides her gorgeous body and intriguing ink.

She nodded, but there was something about her demeanor that was suddenly off. Almost shy. Shayna accepted the pictures into her hand.

"They're fucking good," he said. "Beautiful and disturbing at the same time."

She peered up at him, a guardedness in her eyes. "Disturbing how?"

Billy frowned. He hadn't meant to offend her. "Just, I mean, they feel...sad." Or maybe that was his own bullshit coming through.

"Well, they are of a cemetery." Her tone was neutral though her gaze was questioning.

"But look at this one. It isn't obviously in a cemetery." He helped her shuffle through until he found the two shadows on the ground, one of a statue, he guessed. The photo was a black and white and powerful in its simplicity. "Is that you?" He pointed at the other shadow, and Shayna nodded. "Looking at this makes me feel a sadness. Because it looks like your shadow is about to turn into the angel's shadow for a hug." He shrugged, feeling like an idiot. "I mean, I'm no fucking art critic. I'm just saying how it feels to me."

She nodded. "That's fair. Thanks for saying they're good."

He shrugged, feeling like they just had a conversation that he only half understood. But clearly, he'd fucked something up. And it sat like a rock in his gut. "Hungry? I could make something."

"Oh, no. That's okay. Thanks though." She thumbed over her shoulder, and he could tell he was losing her even before she said the words. "I'm just gonna go change and get ready for the week."

Billy nodded and watched her go. And found himself battling about a dozen different urges.

To follow her. To ask what he'd said to bring her down. To pull her back into his arms. To ask where the third tattoo was—because she'd said she had three, but he only saw two, and the only other part of her back that was covered was her backside...

Not a single one of those were urges he should give into.

And food was *not* what he wanted.

Which meant he had to get the hell out of there before he caused trouble of the can't-take-it-back kind.

CHAPTER FIVE

SEAN *and I are heading to Ben's for chili dogs. You in?*

Mo's text had lit up Billy's phone about three minutes after Shayna went upstairs, and Billy had been only too happy to agree. Being in the presence of his friends would keep him from doing anything stupid.

Mo and Sean were already in line when Billy got there. It only took a few minutes until they were ordering some half smokes, dogs, and fries. While they waited for their food, they found a booth in the back corner.

"How the hell are you, Riddick? I feel like it's been forever," Billy said to the Navy vet. They'd met through Warrior Fight Club almost two years ago.

"Same old," Sean said with a grin. "Finding 'em hot, leaving 'em wet. Just like always."

"Fucking firefighters," Billy said on a laugh. Sean had worked as a firefighter in the Navy and did the same as a civilian. *Overworked*, if you asked most of his friends, because the guy covered every co-worker's missed shift and took on every bit of overtime he could.

Mo gave a deep chuckle. "Son, I think them fires done cooked your noodle."

Sean smirked. "Don't you worry about my noodle, Moses. The ladies don't complain. Trust me."

Holding up his hands, Mo shook his head and looked to Billy. "How's the new roommate?"

"You got a new roommate?" Sean asked, taking a sip of his beer.

Billy rolled his eyes. "She's not a roommate. She's a house guest. A temporary one."

Sean's dark eyes went almost comically wide. "Wait, your roommate is a woman?"

"An adventurous woman..."

Billy gritted his teeth against the memory of Shay's teasing voice in his ear and Sean's interest. Because the guy could be as relentless as a dog with a bone when he saw the chance to get under someone's skin. Most of the time it was funny and good-natured, unless he happened upon an actual exposed nerve. Which, *goddamnit*, Shayna was tonight for some reason.

"Thanks a fucking lot, Mo. She's *not* my roommate. She's new to DC and needed a place to stay until she can find her own apartment."

Wearing a shit-eating grin on his face, Mo slid out of the booth, hand to his ear. "Is that them calling our number? I'll get it."

"She single?" Sean asked.

Billy glared. He felt himself do it. He didn't mean to do it; it was just instinctual. And he knew the second he did it that he'd done something akin to waving a red flag at a bull. "Don't even think about it, Riddick."

Interest slid into the other man's eyes—interest in busting Billy's balls, that was. "So she *is* single. You warning me off because you're interested then?"

Jesus. Fucking. Christ.

"No, I'm warning you off because all you want is another fire station groupie to stretch your nozzle."

"Dude, you stretch the pipe, not the nozzle." Sean smirked again—it was pretty much his face's primary setting.

"What the hell conversation am I walking in on?" Mo said, placing two heavily laden trays of food on the table.

"Just trying to teach Parrish to talk like a firefighter," Sean said, grabbing for his half smoke and fries.

Billy took a big bite of his chili dog, glad that the food made it impossible to continue the conversation.

Though he should've known that wouldn't stop Sean, who dunked two French fries into the ketchup before pointing them at him. "Since when did you want a roommate, anyway?"

"I didn't *want* a roommate. Buddy asked me to help out his sister for a few weeks and I agreed. Simple as."

"How old is she?" Sean asked.

Billy gave him a look. "Twenty-six. And if you'd stop taking shifts during club meetings, you'd know all this shit already."

Sean shrugged. "The job's the job." They ate in silence for a few precious seconds, and then he said. "What's her name?"

"Jesus fucknugget!" Billy bit out.

"Jesus...fucknugget?" Sean blinked and looked at Mo, who was about three seconds away from busting a gut.

"That's a new one," Mo said, chuckling around a bite of his half smoke.

Which, of course, was when Billy realized he'd used the ridiculous curse that Shayna had thrown at him that very first night. When he'd seen her naked.

"Whatever," Billy said, somehow not getting away from her even though he'd left the house. What the hell was that about, anyway? "Her name's Shayna Curtis. She's got a new job as a staff photographer at the *Washington Gazette*. I've known her since she was a teenager, though it's not like I know her all that well. And that's everything there is to know. Okay?"

Although, even as he uttered the words, some part of him felt like he knew her better than his description let on...

But Billy couldn't really think about that when the debate on whether to keep digging was plain on Sean's face.

"Working on any interesting cases?" Mo said, throwing Billy a lifeline out of the conversation.

He happily grasped it. "The main thing on my plate is a civil investigation into suspected hidden assets, and I'm not finding the evidence they need for this trial. I'm going to give it maybe two more days before I deliver the bad news. And then I have a bunch of background checks to work through."

"At least you get to be your own boss," Sean said. "Firehouse is nearly as hierarchical as the damn Navy."

Which begged the question that they'd all asked at one time or another and never gotten a straight answer to—why Riddick had left the Navy before putting in his twenty only to get out and do the same job. The guy always played it off like he'd just gotten tired of the military, but people didn't end up in the Warrior Fight Club if they'd well handled the transition to civilian life. That was part of what WFC was all about.

Most of the people who ended up there—both men and women—did so because they had injuries, mental health struggles, anger-management issues, or other problems reentering the real world. Because the thing was that the real world did *not* feel very fucking real after being in the middle of the shit in Iraq or Afghanistan. Or in the case of Spec Ops teams like the Rangers, in a whole host of other places that the U.S. would never admit.

Mo sucked some chili off his thumb and nailed Sean with a stare. "You wouldn't know what to do with yourself if you weren't risking getting crispy every damn day."

Sean shrugged and nodded. "Prolly." He swallowed a bite of

his dog, grabbed his beer bottle, and threw a questioning glance at Billy. "You like being a P.I.?"

The *other* topic it seemed like all of Billy's thoughts and conversations led to lately. And he didn't have any more clarity on it than he had all the other times a similar question had bounced around in his noggin.

"There are things I like about it. It's flexible. It's not the same thing every day. The structure of it is a lot like running an op. A really fucking watered-down op, but still..." Now Billy was the one shrugging. "And it pays the bills."

But as the conversation turned to how the matches had gone down at Saturday's WFC training and Noah's Halloween party and how much the younger man had changed since he'd first joined the club, Billy couldn't shake Sean's question. Nor his own lackluster answer.

Was paying the bills all he really wanted to do with his life? When he had it to live and so many others didn't?

SHAYNA WAS SO excited about her first day at work that she started waking up at four AM and checking the clock to see if it was time to get up. She finally gave up on the whole project of sleeping around 5:30, a full half hour before her alarm was set to go off.

But she didn't even care. Because she was chomping at the bit.

She showered and dressed in a pair of comfortable gray dress pants, a smart white button-down shirt, and a pair of dressy ballet flats, then she grabbed her folder of personnel papers, swallowed down some cereal, and packed a lunch. Billy hadn't stirred during that whole time, so Shayna jotted off a quick note.

Hey Billy—off to work! Have a good day! –Shay

For a minute she second-guessed leaving it. Last night after she'd turned down his offer for dinner, she'd started feeling a little bad about her reaction to his seeing her photos. But when she'd went to find him to suggest they make dinner after all, he was gone. She hadn't heard him leave, and he hadn't said good-bye. And she couldn't help but think that maybe she'd...what? Hurt his feelings? Or something? She didn't know.

She'd spent the rest of the evening alternating between excitement over going to her new job this morning and regret that she'd worn so much of her emotion on her sleeve during that conversation with Billy.

She'd just felt exposed and even a little cornered by his insights into her work, like she might have to explain to him why she'd been in the cemetery and taken the shots in the first place. And that would lead to conversations she didn't really want to have with him.

Or with anybody. Hell, even with herself, truth be told.

Not giving herself another moment for the ridiculous debate, she left the note and headed out the door.

It was way earlier than she needed to go, but she wanted extra time to find her way on public transportation and to scope out the neighborhood around the paper's offices. She was half way down the block to the bus stop when she heard her name.

"Good morning, Miss Shayna."

She recognized Reuben's voice right away, and it lit a smile on her face. "Oh, hi, Reuben," she said, finding him and his wiggly dog sitting on his front porch. "How are you and Ziggy this morning?"

"We're moving a little slow, but we're all right. You heading off to that new job?"

She nodded as she came to a stop in front of his gate. "First day."

"You'll knock 'em dead."

"From your lips, Reuben," she said with a grin.

He pointed skyward. "He's listening. Don't you doubt it."

"I'll take all the help I can get." She threw him a wave. "Have a good day."

"You, too, now," Reuben said. Ziggy barked, and she heard the man tell him, "You settle down now. Shayna will give you a pet when she has more time."

The conversation was just the pick-me-up she needed to shake off the last of the weirdness she felt over what'd happened last night. It wasn't like she really knew Reuben, but there was something about his warmth of character that made him feel almost fatherly.

It occurred to her how much she missed that feeling. And to the extent she didn't have it as much anymore, it was her own fault. She knew that.

Her parents had never once blamed her for Dylan's death. Well, not out loud. But she feared that they did, down deep. And she knew for a fact that Dylan's fiancé, Abby, blamed her.

Rather than chance seeing it in their eyes or hearing it in their voices, she'd made herself a scarce during the past two years. Oh, she called and emailed and texted from time to time. And she'd gone home for Thanksgiving and Christmas even though those had been brutal in highlighting how many empty chairs her parents had around their table these days. But all of that represented the bare minimum compared to how much she'd once visited and talked to them.

But today was *not* the day for such thoughts.

Today was the day for fresh starts and knocking 'em dead.

Nine hours later and she wasn't sure how much of the latter she'd had a chance to do, but it'd only taken this one day to prove that she'd made the right decision—in coming to DC, in shifting the focus of her career, and in taking this job.

Even though a lot of the day had been spent in completing forms and watching training films and in ten-second introductions with about a hundred people, just being in the *Gazette's* offices had been thrilling. The low buzz of the news room. The occasional bursts of frenetic energy in the hallways. The framed newspapers that hung everywhere showing off the headlines of some of the biggest stories that the *Gazette* had broken.

Just the whole vibe of becoming part of a century-old tradition at this paper. It all thrilled her.

As did the hope that she might make her own mark by helping shed light on the world in which they all lived. The good and the bad and the beautiful and the painful of it.

It sounded almost Pollyannaish to think she could make a difference, but that's how it was for most people interested in reporting the news. At least that she'd ever met. All the way back to J school, she'd been surrounded by people who, for the most part, possessed a real purity of cause and purpose.

It had been such a good, energizing day that she felt like she nearly floated home, despite how crowded the metro had been and that she'd just barely missed one bus and the next one had been packed as tight as a can of sardines.

Reuben's stoop was empty as she made her way up Farragut Place. As was her house.

"Billy?" she called up the stairs. Nothing.

Will you be home for dinner? She shot off the text then went upstairs to change out of her work clothes.

Wearing a tank top and a pair of shorts, she dropped onto her bed, popped open her laptop, and posted the obligatory first-day-of-work update on Facebook. Then she went to Ryan's page to see if he'd posted any pictures from his deployment lately, but there was nothing new.

So Shayna opened up her email, because she was *dying* to tell someone about her day.

Hey Ryan! Just finished my first day of work at the Gazette. *It was mostly personnel and orientation stuff, but I can already tell that I'm going to like it here. Which means I owe you a couple of big thank yous, first for encouraging me to take the chance to move to DC by myself. And second for twisting Billy's arm to get him to let me stay here. His place is nice and he's cool, so I think this will work out fine until I can find some roommates and/or a place of my own. Except you might have warned the poor guy that I'm a slob!*

Her fingers froze on the keyboard as a dozen other comments flitted through her mind.

Like, *Billy's still as lickable as I remember, so thanks a bunch!*

Or, *He's already seen me naked but you don't have to shoot him because it was totally an accident and I'm pretty sure he only sees me as your "kid sister"!*

Or, *Did you tell him that Dylan's death was my fault?*

Yeah. No. None of that was happening.

So instead Shayna wrote: *Anyway, just wanted to share how excited I am after today. Wish you were here so I could tell you over a couple of burgers and steal all your fries. Shoot me a message when you can and TAKE CARE OF YOURSELF, YA SHITNUBBIN!* ;) *xx Shayna*

She hit the *Send* button with a snicker, because insults were pretty much a Curtis family tradition. She couldn't wait to see what Ryan would send back, though she knew it would probably be a couple of days before her brother saw the message. He wrote as often as he could, but it wasn't like he was free to sit around online all day. So Shayna cherished every update and note he was able to send.

After all that, she'd hoped to have heard back from Billy, but he still hadn't answered her text. The thought of eating dinner alone tonight felt like a total bummer, but it wasn't like she knew a lot of people here yet.

Except there was someone she knew at least a little...

Which gave her a possibly great idea.

She rushed down to the kitchen, decided to make some barbecue chicken breasts, baked beans, and a salad of diced tomatoes, cucumbers, bell peppers, and onions in balsamic vinaigrette. The first step was to season the chicken, so she whipped up a quick marinade, put it and the chicken in a sealed bag in the fridge, and then she made sure to clean up after herself. When she had that much done, Shayna grabbed her keys and headed down the street.

Her belly did a little flip as she let herself into Reuben's yard through the metal gate and approached his door. Even if he wasn't interested in joining her, surely he wouldn't mind the invitation. Right?

On a deep breath, she knocked.

Ziggy let out a bark immediately, and she could almost hear him dancing around on the other side of the door as Reuben's voice filtered through to her.

"Hold your britches, Zig. I'm coming." The door opened wide, and the man's smile was immediate. "Why, Shayna. Nice to see you. Everything all right?"

She nodded. "I wondered if you'd like to join me at my place for dinner tonight?"

"Well, yeah. Yes, I would," he said, his tone surprised but pleased.

"It's nothing fancy, but I'd love the company." She crouched to pet Ziggy and nearly melted when the dog pushed its big blocky head into her hand. "Dinner will be ready in about an hour but feel free to come over any time."

"You better believe I will."

"Great." She gave Reuben the house number and scrunched

Zig's face one last time. "See you soon," she said, tracing her steps back to her place.

Billy still hadn't responded to her text, but she'd make enough of everything for him to have later if he wanted.

She preheated the oven and gathered the rest of what she needed, then set about chopping the veggies for the salad. Finally, she placed the marinated chicken on a cookie sheet and slipped it in to bake.

Of course, she'd made a disaster of Billy's kitchen in the process of doing all this. How did he manage to keep everything so spotless while he cooked? It was beyond her, but she dove into cleaning it all up so she could set the table.

Except, Billy didn't have a table. He just had the breakfast bar with the high bar stools. And Shayna had no idea if the height of those stools would pose too great a challenge for Reuben's leg.

Which was when she remembered that there was a black metal table and chairs out on the patio. It was covered with enough dust and sticks and leaves to suggest that Billy didn't use it very often, so it was a bit of a project for Shay to scrub it all down, but once she laid out a couple of hand towels as place-mats and set the table, it looked rather festive. Which fit her mood perfectly.

She had just enough time to baste the chicken with barbecue sauce and slide it back into the oven when Reuben knocked at the door.

Over the course of their meal, Shayna found herself *so glad* she'd invited the man over.

His stories were humorous and interesting and awe-inspiring by turn. As a boy, he remembered riding on streetcars the very last day they'd operated in the city and recalled hearing Martin Luther King, Jr. giving his "I Have a Dream" speech at the Lincoln Memorial. He'd served in the Marine Corps during the Vietnam War and attended the opening ceremony for the Vietnam Memorial with other survivors from his unit. And he and his wife had raised two daughters of whom the man was obviously immensely proud.

She laughed and ate too much and delighted in Reuben's enjoyment of her cooking.

Shayna realized that she never would've guessed half the amazing things that Reuben had seen and done just by looking at who he was now. And wasn't that true of everyone? Unless you were the one to say hello or extend the invitation or share a piece of yourself first, you might never know what another person experienced or had to offer.

"Now tell me about your family, Shayna. You have any around here?" Reuben asked.

And you might never know what another person might be hiding either. Like Shayna was. Hiding her hurt and her shame.

She managed a smile. "My parents live in New York, where I grew up, and my older brother, Ryan, is an Army Ranger. He's deployed in Iraq right now." She felt the omission of Dylan's name from her recounting of her family story like a weight on her chest, and she hated herself a little in that moment. So maybe that was why she added something she rarely said out loud anymore, "And I had a middle brother named Dylan who died in a car crash two years ago."

"I'm sorry to hear that," Reuben said, just as Shayna caught movement from the corner of her eye.

Billy stood in the open doorway, freaking gorgeous in a pair of black dress pants, a white dress shirt with the sleeves cuffed around his forearms, and a blue tie loosened around his neck. And had a chunky watch ever looked so sexy on a man before? Wow.

"Oh, hey," she managed, even as heat filtered into her cheeks. For ogling him. And for the fact that he'd probably just overheard her talking about Dylan. "Are you hungry? You should come join." She could almost see his indecision as he hovered on the threshold. "Reuben, let me introduce you to my roommate, Billy. He actually owns the house and is kind enough to let me stay for a while."

That ended Billy's indecisiveness. He came out and extended a hand to the older man, who moved to rise. "Don't get up. Please. Nice to meet you, Reuben."

"Same to you, Billy." They shook.

"Come sit," she said, looking up at Billy. "I'll make you a plate. Reuben lives a few houses down and was in the military, too. You guys have lots in common."

The moment Billy nodded, Reuben took over. "What branch did you serve in?" he asked Billy as Shayna slipped inside.

It only took her a few minutes to get everything she needed, and when she came out, the two men were deep in conversation about their service. She settled a plate, cup of water, and silverware on the table in front of Billy.

He glanced up at her, and there was an intensity to his gaze that she didn't understand. "Thanks, Shayna."

"So enough about us," Reuben said, grinning at her as she sat down again. "How was your first day at work?"

The question had her grinning, too. "It was really good," she said. "I mean, it was all about getting oriented, of course, but just walking the halls of one of the biggest newspapers in the country and knowing I'm now a part of it was surreal. As a new staff photographer, I'll get assigned to community-interest stories at first, which I think will be a great way to get to know the city."

"That sounds exciting, young lady. Good for you."

"And I get my press credentials tomorrow, which is going to make it all feel real."

Reuben chuckled. "You're about to bounce right out of that seat."

Billy polished off his chicken and gave her a smile. "You really are."

Shayna laughed. "I know, I can't help it."

Shaking his head, Billy's expression was almost proud as he looked at her. "You don't have to help it. Don't change a thing about it. You'll bring that enthusiasm to every story you're a part of and people will see it through your work."

She nodded, moved because that had been such an incredibly sweet thing to say. "I hope I can do just that." Shay cleared her throat, suddenly uncomfortable with all the focus being on her. "Who wants seconds?"

Reuben waved a hand over his empty plate as Billy polished off the last of his dinner. "It was fantastic, but I'm stuffed," their neighbor said. He peered upward at the darkening sky. "And I suppose I should be getting back. My oldest daughter usually calls me around eight o'clock to check in on her old man."

"Aw, that's sweet," Shayna said. "Let me pack you some leftovers to take home."

"No, no," Reuben said, rising with the help of the table and his cane. "That's not necessary. This beautiful meal and even better company was all I need."

"Any time," she said, as she and Billy followed the man inside. At the front door, he gave them both a wave. "Take care now."

"Bye," Shayna said, watching at the door for several long minutes until she saw him turn into his own yard, then she closed the door. "He's such a nice man."

Suddenly, she felt heat at her back. The hair rose up all down her neck and she nearly shivered.

"And you're an incredibly nice woman," came Billy's voice in her ear. It took everything she had to resist leaning back against him, even though the pull to do so was beyond anything she'd ever felt in her life.

Did she feel this way because she'd had a crush on him when she was younger? Because he'd once seemed so unattainable and now, just maybe, he wasn't?

"Befriending Reuben, making such a great dinner..." His words trailed off, though she had the strongest feeling that something more hung on the end of his tongue.

Shayna really wanted to know what it was.

She turned, bringing them chest to chest. He was so close that she had to tilt her head back to meet his gaze. "I just wanted to do something a little special after I'd had such a good day."

He nodded, staring at her with a red-hot intensity that made her heart beat faster. "Special." His gaze swept over her face. "Definitely." Billy swallowed hard, and the tortured sound of it combined with his words and that look shot need throughout her veins.

Need of the *I-want-this-man* kind.

"I'm sorry I didn't return your text," he said. "I wasn't sure how the end of my day was going to go."

"It's okay—"

"No." He shook his head. "I shouldn't have ignored it. It's just...you...do you..." He pressed his lips into a tight line and made a noise deep in his throat.

Both of which drew her gaze to his mouth. She wasn't sure what was happening here, or what he was trying to say, but she knew what she *wanted* to happen.

Suddenly she was dying for it. To feel him. To touch him. To kiss him.

She'd been rocking those feelings since the intense conversation they'd had at the breakfast bar. She still wasn't sure how she'd held back from hugging him after all he'd shared with her. Now, she couldn't hold back. And didn't want to.

Shayna put her hands on his chest.

His eyes closed as if the gesture almost pained him. "Shayna."

She came a half step closer, and it was enough to learn that he was rock hard against her belly. A whimper spilled from her lips as she pushed up onto tiptoes, her hands smoothing up toward his shoulders.

And then his eyes were open and trained on hers, a war roiling in their dark depths.

Through his shirt, she felt the edge of a bandage under her palm. She pulled back her hand, not wanting to hurt him. "I'm sorry," she whispered.

The next thing Shayna knew, Billy grasped and pushed her against the wall behind the door. He kissed her full on the mouth. It only took her brain the beat of one second to realize that he'd given her exactly what she wanted and to kiss him back.

And dear *God*, the way this man kissed. Like he'd been *starving* for it. His hands were holding her face and his body was pinning her to the wall and his tongue was tasting her mouth like he was desperate for her.

"You can touch me, damnit," he gritted out around the edge of a kiss. She buried her fingers in his hair, and he groaned.

She moaned at the scorching intensity of the kiss. Her head spun and her pulse raced and her body absolutely bloomed with arousal. He ground that delicious hardness against her belly and she almost cried to feel it a few inches lower. And when his hands trailed down her body and one grasped at the curve of her ass, she lifted her leg around his hip.

Billy's cock hit her right where she needed him most.

Shayna arched her head back against the wall on a cry.

"Jesus," he said, still all over her. "We should stop this."

"Don't stop," she said, her voice gritty with need.

"Fuck, Shayna." His fingertips dug into the bare skin of her thigh where he held her to him. "We gotta stop this."

"Why?" She pulled her head out of the haze of lust and forced herself to look at him.

His eyes were pure dark fire, but his expression was tormented, torn, uncertain. "Because I'm about thirty seconds from burying myself inside you."

She was a hundred per cent sure that no one had ever said anything so sexy to her in her entire life. And she wasn't any virgin. "That's what I was hoping you might do, Billy."

Hand on the wall above her shoulder, he pushed himself away from her. "Coming home to dinner on the table and a friendly face that was happy to see me, to friendship and company... I don't think this house has ever felt so much like a home before."

His words unleashed a warmth inside her chest. "That's good. I'm glad. But I don't see why that—"

"I don't want to take advantage of you or your friendship because I'm such a lonely fucking misfit that I take more than what's mine to have."

An ache shot through that warmth, because the thought of him being *lonely* nearly slayed her. On top of the pain he'd revealed to her yesterday. The military required so many sacrifices about which people never even guessed. "You're not taking. I'm giving."

"Well, you shouldn't," Billy said, his tone tight. And was that regret, too? "Not to me. I'm sorry."

Another step, and his hand dropped from the wall.

"Leave the dishes. You cooked, so I'll do them later."

And another until that ache became a widening chasm inside her.

"Thank you for dinner."

Shayna couldn't say a word. Stunned and confused, she was

still pressed up against the wall and nearly aroused out of her mind. And then he turned away and went upstairs. The *click* of his bedroom door closing was quiet but final.

She'd just lived out a long-held fantasy in being kissed by Billy Parrish. It was more than she'd ever imagined it would be —hot and thrilling and so damn sexy.

Except, apparently, that he regretted it.

CHAPTER SIX

So FUCKING MUCH for keeping his distance and maintaining his cool.

Billy could not believe how bad he'd crossed the line with Shay.

From the moment he'd seen the note from her on his kitchen counter this morning, pot of coffee ready and waiting and fragrant in the air, his head had been a little fucked.

As if it wasn't enough that she was funny and cool and interesting, and that she somehow made him feel safe enough to say shit he normally wouldn't, *and* that he'd seen her naked and couldn't stop remembering how gorgeous she was—nope, couldn't forget that. The coffee and that damn note made him realize something he'd long known but never really dwelt on before.

He was really fucking lonely.

When you'd spent your entire adult life living in close quarters with a bunch of other men in your unit, *so close* in friendship and purpose that you thought of one another as brothers, getting out of the military and living alone was an unexpectedly devastating blow.

And here Billy had thought it would be nice to have some privacy and quiet, to not have to listen to his asshole brothers snore and bitch and Skype with their loved ones back home. It was possible he'd never been more wrong.

So coming home to dinner and people and conversation, not to mention how enthusiastic and passionate Shayna had been in talking about her job...it all made him feel good in a way he hadn't in so long. So long that it'd fucked with his head.

Clearly.

For just a split second, he'd let himself imagine that that could be his life. And he'd said and done things he never should've allowed.

Which was why he didn't step foot out of his room the rest of the night until he heard her go to bed. And then he waited another fifteen minutes just to be sure.

He'd never really noticed before how quietly the stone treads allowed him to move down the steps, but he was glad for it as he made for the kitchen to clean up from dinner.

Downstairs, he hit the lights for the kitchen and stopped short.

Everything was clean. The dishes that had been in the sink and on the counter were gone. The counter and stove top had been scrubbed down. The dishwasher had been run. As if the whole dinner had never happened.

Billy was torn between gratitude that she'd taken care of his space just as he would, and...something that felt a whole lot like regret that there was nothing left to remind him how nice their evening had been. Until he'd gone and ruined it.

And he *had* ruined it.

Because, Christ, he could still picture her pressed up against the living room wall. Her hair mussed from his hands, her lips red from the hunger of his kisses, a flush high in her cheeks, and a lust-drunk softness to the cast of her eyes when she'd offered herself to him.

He wasn't sure how the hell he'd pulled himself away.

He wasn't sure how he'd ever forget the way she'd looked, the sound of her moan, or that she'd wanted him.

And he also wasn't sure how she was going to forgive him—first for taking advantage, and second for walking away. Both had been dickish in their own way. He just hoped he hadn't gone and made her feel uncomfortable living here.

It was one big fucking mess of his own making. And if Ryan ever found out about any of it, he'd have Billy's head. And Billy wouldn't blame him.

He scrubbed his hands through his hair and smacked off the lights. His body felt almost heavy as he hit the upstairs hallway.

A high-pitched noise caught his ear.

Billy froze and cocked his head.

There it was again. Was that...crying? Oh, Jesus, had he made her cry?

His gaze swung to Shayna's door.

He heard it again. Prickles ran down his spine. God, he had.

Frowning at her door, he went closer. And closer. Until he was standing right outside of it, his fist poised to knock.

Which was close enough to know that it wasn't crying, it was *moaning*. And it wasn't Shayna. He was hearing some-thing...something she was watching.

Something with rhythmic moans and a man's rough, commanding voice.

Billy swallowed thickly against the wave of white-hot lust that slammed into him. His cock ached and his ears strained. Because Shayna was apparently watching porn.

Just a few hours after they'd made out. When she'd made it clear she wanted more. And he'd turned her down.

And because Billy had seen Shayna naked *and* seen her

aroused, he could too fucking easily imagine what she might look like right now. Laid out on her bed much as she'd been plastered against the wall. Pink nipples erect and those red-brown curls between her legs wet as her hand worked at her clit.

He released a harsh breath and fisted his hands against the urge to touch himself. Or knock. Or open the door.

He willed himself to leave, but his feet were suddenly cemented to the floor. And then *finally* he forced himself to step away—just like he had before.

The floor creaked under his foot, just the littlest bit.

Nearly holding his breath, Billy froze. Shayna's room went quiet.

Son of a fuck.

Billy Parrish had jumped out of perfectly good airplanes and faced down terrorists who wanted nothing more than to see him dead, but at that moment, the idea that Shayna might find him standing there had a really goddamned high pucker factor. Because whether she was outraged that he was invading her privacy *or* came at him with more of that invitation in her eyes and on her lips, it would be bad.

So he held still. And prayed that door did *not* open.

After a few seconds, the sounds started again, although softer now, and Billy high-tailed it out of that hallway and closed himself inside his room like his life depended on it.

On a harsh exhale, he *thunked* his head against the molding next to his door.

Which did nothing to ratchet down his arousal. Or keep him from ripping open his button-fly. Or from taking the aching length of his cock in hand.

Billy leaned his other forearm against his door, rested his head against it, and gave his erection one tight stroke up and down.

His teeth clenched against how fucking good it felt.

And as his eyes fell closed on the next stroke, he told himself not to do it—not to picture it. But that was the thing about your brain. Trying *not* to think about something was the surest way to make sure it was *all* you could think about.

Which was why Shayna Curtis was the only goddamned thing he could see.

And finally he couldn't do anything but give in to the urgent need. He jacked himself on tight, demanding, almost punishing strokes. Choking his root to hold back the orgasm that already threatened. Gritting his teeth every time his palm twisted around the fat head of his dick. Thrusting his hips forward so that he was fucking his hand.

It might've been perverted that he was so damn turned on by the knowledge that she was masturbating at the other end of the hallway. And without question it was a million per cent inappropriate that he was getting himself off on that fact.

But Jesus fucking Christ, it was the hottest thing he'd experienced in a long-ass time.

And that was no slight whatsoever to the other partners he'd had. Billy didn't need sex to mean something to have a helluva good time—and to make sure his lovers did, too. But there was just something about knowing that they were both so turned on by what'd happened earlier that they *had* to come.

Was she picturing him, too?

The question shot sensation down his spine and into his balls.

And then he imagined himself leaning against *her* door instead of his own, and his orgasm nailed him in the back and shot into his hand and against the door. On a strangled shout, Billy stroked his cock through it, making a mess of himself and the door and the fly of his jeans. But all of that was really damn hard to care about when his head went spinny and his heart threatened to beat the fuck out of his chest.

Jesus.

Jesus fucknugget.

Yes, Shayna, for fucking sure.

Still braced against the door, Billy blew out a long, shuddering breath and admitted the obvious. "This woman is so far under my fucking skin."

He wasn't sure how that had happened in a few days' time, but there wasn't any question about it. That much was clear.

And if he wanted to do right by her and by the best friend who'd asked him to take care of her, Billy was going to have to steer clear of her until he got his head screwed on tight again. Both of them.

Which was why, after he cleaned up, he logged into his email, opened the message from a new prospective client that had hit his inbox earlier that afternoon, and agreed to a meeting to talk about the marital infidelity surveillance work she wanted to hire him to do.

If he had to stay out of his house for a few days to get his shit together, he fucking would.

"Hey, Shayna. Some of us are going out after work. Would you like to come?" Havana Jones asked.

Shayna looked away from the photo editing project she'd been assigned, surprised to see that it was already nearly five o'clock. "Wow, where did the day go already?" she said, smiling at the woman who was quickly becoming one of her favorite people at work.

Havana had worked for the paper's graphic arts department for about nine months and always had such a warm smile and a big laugh that she immediately put you at ease. Plus the fact that she'd grown up and gone to college in DC meant that she knew all the best places to go.

"I don't even know, but it's a good thing when time at your job flies by." Havana leaned her hip against the desk. "So, you in?"

"I'd love to join. Thanks. When did you want to go?" Shayna asked, wondering if she could finish her work on the two remaining photographs.

She'd been assigned to the team of news editor, Joe Daniels, and picture editor, Rose Kim, and these photos were part of her second editing assignment for her new bosses. This particular community feature wasn't running until next week, so she had a few days to finish them. Still, it would be good to get in the habit of working ahead of deadline.

"Maybe half an hour? I'm gonna round up some other folks and then we can officially celebrate the fact that it's Friday." Havana's tight black curls moved as she rounded Shay's desk.

"Sounds good," Shayna said, excited to be getting to know people better and to make some friends. Especially since it'd been so quiet around her house all week. Billy had taken some surveillance job that necessitated he work nights, which meant that their schedules were complete opposites.

She hadn't seen him for more than five minutes since The. Kiss.

Oh, man, the kiss.

A kiss that had *literally* been the stuff of which dreams were made. Because she couldn't stop thinking about it, even when she was asleep. And when she was awake, just the memory of how good it'd been was enough to turn her on, which was probably why she'd gotten herself off thinking about it—and him— three times in the past five days.

It was as if, with just one hit of him, she'd become an addict, incapable of thinking about or wanting anything else. It was bad.

But, on the plus side, at least there hadn't been much opportunity for things to be weird between her and Billy, who no doubt had long forgotten what'd happened. The guy was older, a hero with a Purple Heart, a world traveler, and hot as hell. Shay wouldn't be surprised if their little moment ranked *way* down his list of hottest-things-that'd-ever-happened.

Meanwhile, despite the fact that she'd had more than a few boyfriends and two no-strings-attached, on-again/off-again fuck buddies in her day, her up-against-the-wall make-out session with Billy ranked somewhere close to the top of hers.

Le sigh.

"Stop thinking of the stupid fuckstick, Shay," she whispered to herself. But, then, of course, She. Could. Only. Think. About. Billy's. Fuck. Stick. For. Fuck's. Sake.

On a sigh, she dropped her head forward and heaved a deep breath.

In her mind's eye, she saw that old Seinfeld episode. *No fucksticks for you! Come back one year!*

And that was precisely when she knew her Friday night was going to require alcohol. Copious amounts of alcohol. *All. The. Alcohol.*

An hour later, she and five other new and newish *Gazette* staff members crowded around a high-boy table in a bar a few blocks from the office. The place was popular and the music was loud, so they were all leaning close just to be able to hear one another.

"To surviving your orientation week," Havana said, raising her glass.

Shayna joined the others in raising her strawberry mojito and clinking. "Here, here," she said, everyone laughing and joking.

Leah Scott, Malik Morrison, and Rob Cho were among the other newbies who had started the week with Shayna, and of them, only Rob had been assigned to her team. So it was good to have the chance to spend more time with them out.

"Did you all hear that reporter in the newsroom earlier?" Leah asked. Petite with a short, pixie-like haircut, she was loud and funny and talked non-stop, and was one of the new reporters.

"Who? Maxwell?" Bran Morgan asked. Shayna had just met him on the way to the bar, and all she knew of him was that he was a sports reporter.

"I think so," Leah said. "Short, bald guy."

Next to her, Rob pushed up black glasses that matched his short hair. "Yeah, that's him. I met him yesterday."

Bran nodded. "That's Maxwell. Was he shouting?"

Leah's blue eyes went wide. "Yeah, how'd you—"

"Maxwell always shouts," both Havana and Bran said at the same time before laughing.

Bran grinned. "One time I heard him yell, "I'm not shouting! I'm saying things loudly!' in the middle of a meeting. And everyone in the newsroom tried not to laugh."

"I remember that," Havana agreed. "Do you remember the time that Chief asked him if he was on drugs and he yelled, 'You and I both know I don't make enough money to take drugs!'"

Everyone laughed, and Shayna knew that the stories were good-natured because Maxwell was also one of the reporters that all the younger journalists revered for how long he'd been in the business and how many big stories he'd broken. He held the byline on more than one of the framed stories around the office.

"But, let's be real," Havana said with a smirk, "with the amount of coffee and cigarettes most of the reporters have in their system, and news breaking every other minute, it's a wonder there's not more screaming, shouting, and general madness."

"And alcohol, too?" Shayna asked, raising her glass again, and just about needing another.

Hannah clinked with her and nodded. "Absolutely. Drinking, smoking, and digging up dirt on people. That's pretty much what journalists do."

Laughing, Shayna nodded. "Well, I don't smoke, but otherwise I'm right on track," she said as she waved down the waiter and indicated that she wanted another.

"I'll have another, too," Malik said from where he stood right beside her. A good-looking man with warm brown skin and striking hazel eyes, he was a new reporter for the business and financial section who was also said to be scary smart. "Where are you from, Shayna?"

"New York," she said.

"The city?" he asked, leaning in.

"Upstate. Near Albany."

He nodded. "Ah, I grew up in the city. Then I worked on Wall Street for a couple years, but I never made it up to Albany," he said.

"So how did you make the transition from Wall Street to journalism?" she asked, curious since she'd made a similar shift.

Malik's smile was legitimately *beautiful* as he nodded and spoke. "The longer I worked in the financial sector, the more clear it became that money was at the heart of nearly every story. Politics. Government. Business. Culture. Hell, even sports. And I just got less interested in growing other people's bank accounts and more interested in telling stories that can be hard to tell and complicated for a lot of people to understand."

"It's not really at the same level, but I left working for a museum where I photographed and digitized the collections because I felt like I wanted to capture history in the making rather than preserve the existing record," she said, adding a thanks to the waiter as he dropped off their drinks.

Malik raised his beer. "I hear you. To telling all the stories."

Shayna grinned and toasted. "I'll drink to that."

Bran leaned in. "Enjoy the idea of the noble grandeur of the profession while you can because as soon as people see your first byline or photo credit, they'll be all like, let me show you the incredibly important pothole on my street. It's an outrage!" They all laughed.

And that was the way the rest of the evening went. Havana and Bran told war stories from around the office, while the rest of them hung on every word and got to know each other over a constant flow of drinks and more than a few fried appetizers.

By the time the party broke up, it was nearly eleven o'clock and Shayna was buzzing enough to feel warm and fuzzy but not so much that she was couldn't handle herself.

"You gonna be okay getting home?" Havana asked her when they spilled out onto the sidewalk into the muggy September night.

"Yeah, but I'm not attempting the metro and bus. Uber will provide my chariot," she said, pulling out her phone and swiping to find the app.

"Where do you live? Maybe we could split one," Malik said. When they worked it out, they found it made sense.

"There's one only four minutes away," she said. "Perfect." The two of them said good-bye to the others, who left them to wait. "I need to spend some time learning my way around the city so I have my bearings and feel comfortable getting around on the metro."

"The subway here is pretty easy to figure out. Not as many lines or stops as in New York." He stepped out into the street. "This is us, I think."

The minivan matching the info in the app stopped in front

of them, and they got in and greeted the driver. They made small talk about their plans for the weekend, and Malik was so easy to talk to that it made the fifteen-minute drive to her house go quickly.

"This is me," she said when they pulled to the curb. She did a double take at the house. Lights were on inside. If that meant Billy was home, it was his first night in the house all week. She smiled back at Malik. "Thanks for sharing the ride."

He nodded. "Any time. If, uh, if you want company exploring the city at any point, shoot me a text."

Shayna grinned. "I'll do that. Have a good weekend." She waved as she got out, then turned to watch the minivan pull away. She'd had a truly good time at the bar and felt pretty damn good about finishing out her first week at her dream job, so it was possible she floated to the door. Or maybe that was the alcohol.

Either way, she was having one of those rare moments—especially given her past two years—where she felt a little like she was on top of the world. Invincible. Strong. Ready for anything.

She stopped short just inside the door. Ready for anything except for Billy to be sitting on the couch staring at her.

CHAPTER SEVEN

"Hey. Long time no see," Shayna said. It wasn't that a man sitting on his couch was odd, it was that *Billy* sitting on his couch was odd. Granted, she'd only lived in his house for a week, but not once during that whole time had she seen him use his living room at all.

"Hey," he said, just that one syllable sounding bone tired.

Which took a little of her focus off how damn hot he was even in a pair of beat-up jeans, hems frayed around bare feet propped up on the coffee table, an old concert T-shirt, and more than a day's worth of scruff on his jaw. Not to mention the finger-raked mess of his hair.

"Tough week?" She closed the door behind her and promptly kicked off her shoes. When Billy's gaze tracked the movement, she scooped them right back up, stumbling a bit as she did so. Damn you, delicious rum. "I'll take them up to my room, I promise," she said, placing them on one of the stair treads so she wouldn't forget.

He scrubbed his hands over his face. "Don't worry about it."

It hadn't escaped her notice that he hadn't answered her

question, but she didn't push. Instead she padded into the kitchen.

"Want anything?" she asked as she filled a glass with water. Shayna stood at the counter and chugged half of it. She didn't drink that often and hoped to avoid feeling bad from indulging in the morning.

On a sigh, he pulled himself off the couch and joined her at the counter, his hands heavily braced upon the granite. "I was just trying to rouse myself to get some food."

"Sit."

He looked at her.

"Sit. I'll make you something. What do you want?" She emptied her glass on another long drink just to have something to do. Because he was staring at her. And Shayna couldn't decide what the stare meant.

"A sandwich?" he finally said.

Satisfaction flooded through her. "Consider it done. Except you're still not sitting."

"Yes, ma'am," he said, dropping into one of the bar stools. "You go out tonight?"

Shayna nodded as she started pulling things out of the fridge. "Yeah, with some people from work. Seems like it's a good group."

"I admire you. The way you've hit the ground running here."

She nearly dropped the squeeze bottle of mustard to the floor. He *admired* her? It was a totally casual compliment, obviously, but after the past couple of years of putting herself down —and believing everyone who knew her was secretly doing it, too—it still meant a lot to her.

"Wow. Um. That's a really nice thing to say. But at best I'm walking fast, not running. After all, I'm crashing in your office and I still don't really know my way around very well."

He shook his head. "Power-walking, then."

She chuckled and put the finishing touches on his sandwich, a turkey and cheese on rye with lettuce, pickles, and mustard. She placed the plate in front of him. "Chips or anything?"

He reached for the sandwich. "No, thank you. This is already about ninety-nine per cent more than I was up to doing."

His words made her wonder once again what had made it such a tough week for him, because he seemed completely mowed over. But he hadn't answered the first time she'd asked, and it seemed pushy to ask again.

Instead, she made quick work of cleaning up, then pulled out her cell to scroll through her social media as she stood at the counter. Which was when she saw that Ryan had finally returned her email. She nearly gasped as she rushed to open it.

"Everything okay?" Billy asked.

Grinning, Shayna nodded. "Yeah. Ryan wrote me." She had to force her eyes not to rush over the words.

Hey Shay. Shitnubbin is solid B- material. You can do better, squirt.

She grinned at his use of the million-year-old nickname. As a kid she'd hated it, but it didn't bother her so much anymore. Shayna would gladly take any and all teasing her brothers had ever done if it would bring her other brother back again...

Focus. Right. She mentally shoved the thoughts back into the corner where they lived, always looming just on the edge of consciousness.

I'm glad you're liking the job, but you don't owe me a thing. You did this all on your own. All I did was tell you what you already knew. And Billy's arm didn't take any twisting. Though if he gives you any trouble, tell him I'll kill him in his sleep.

She sniggered and grinned at Billy. "He says if you give me

any trouble, he'll kill you in your sleep. So, that's a hello, I guess?"

He smirked around a bite. "Pretty much."

Seriously though, take your time finding a place. You have a home there as long as you need it, trust me. I'd rather you find the right situation then rush into something with a roommate that doesn't work out or a place that isn't safe. You don't need that kind of headache. And get Billy to run a background check on any potential roommates, will ya?

She rolled her eyes as she talked to herself. "I don't think so."

"What?" Billy asked.

"Nothing. He's being stupid."

"Highly doubt that."

Now she was the one smirking. "Ryan is capable of massive amounts of stupid. Trust me. He wants me to have background checks done on potential roommates."

Billy's expression grew thoughtful. "I can do that."

She rolled her eyes again. "Omigod stahhhp."

He chuckled and shrugged. "Makes sense to me."

"Well *there's* a big surprise, Ranger Parrish." She continued on:

It's hot as balls here and I've got sand in places no one fucking wants sand. Otherwise, everything's good. Keeping busy and doing the job. Looks like we're still on track for getting home before Thanksgiving. Fingers crossed. I'm glad you're excited about your new job, Shayna. You deserve it. After everything.

A stinging sensation unexpectedly burned against the backs of Shay's eyes. With those two words, Ryan had said so freaking much. More than they hardly ever even broached, as if talking about Dylan—and her role in his death—was a poison that neither of them wanted to drink. She blinked fast to force the threatening tears away as she read the rest.

Kick ass. Take names. And get up the next day and do it all again. Just, next time, don't make me think of real burgers and fries, crotchfruit. All we have is mystery meat you know.

Take care, Shay. More soon. It's good to hear from you when I'm over here so stay in touch. Ry

Not even the awesomeness of *crotchfruit* could fully chase away the impact of *After everything*. Shayna filled her water glass again and took a big drink just to have something else to focus on.

Finished with his dinner, Billy came around to the sink to rinse his plate and the knife she'd used to cut his sandwich.

Then they stood there. Facing each other. An arm's reach apart. Just looking.

And, for her, once again wanting...

Obviously, the desire was all on her side. But she'd been there, done that, and had the sexual frustration to prove it.

And the last thing she wanted was for it to get weird between them again. Despite how good she'd been feeling just minutes before, she felt fragile now. Vulnerable. She couldn't handle weird. Or another rejection.

So Shayna stepped away, using the excuse of dumping out the rest of her water and putting the glass in the dishwasher. "What are you up to this weekend?" she asked, needing something to break the weighted silence between them.

"Uh..." He raked his hands through the sexy mess of his dark blond hair, causing one piece in the front to stick up at a comical angle. "Just the gym tomorrow, I guess."

She bit back a smile. And crossed her arms so she wasn't tempted to fix his hair. "Oh, yeah? Do you like your place? Is it nice?" she asked.

Finding a gym was definitely on her to-do list. The break room at work always had a tray of cookies or a box of donuts just sitting available, and it seemed like every editorial assistant had a jar of candy on their desk. Shayna had happily partaken on more than one occasion, but that situation could go on only so long if all she was doing was sitting around on her butt.

Billy cocked his head as he peered at her. "Yeah. Place is only a few years old. Big, clean, lots of equipment. Their specialty is MMA training, but there's a regular gym part, too."

MMA training sounded interesting...and like there'd be a nice view to watch while on the elliptical... "Any chance I could tag along to check it out?" she asked.

And immediately regretted it. Because Billy's face went through an almost funny number of expressions, most of which she couldn't read. Though, collectively, they seemed to say *hell no.*

"You know what, scratch that."

Way to keep from doing something that might end in rejection, Shayna. Really. Super smooth. You're such a twatermelon sometimes.

"I didn't say anything." He held up his hands like he was confused.

She gave a rueful chuckle. "You didn't have to. And I get it. Really."

He came closer. "No, Shay, really. I, uh, it's just that I don't go there just for regular work outs. I belong to a club that meets there."

"What kind of club?"

Billy shrugged with one big shoulder. "A fight club."

"A *fight* club?" she said, immediately picturing Edward Norton and Brad Pitt fighting in the dark basement of a sketchy bar. "I thought the first rule of fight club was that you didn't talk about fight club?"

He gave her a look. "You're picturing Edward Norton right now, aren't you?"

She smirked. "And Brad Pitt."

"Uh huh. Not that kind of fight club. It's a, uh..." He twisted his lips, like he couldn't figure out how to describe it. Or didn't want to. And then the words rushed out. "It's called Warrior Fight Club. Our first rule is that all the members are vets."

That was...not what Shayna expected. "So it's a club where veterans fight each other?" Wait 'til Ryan got a load of that!

Billy unleashed a tired-sounding breath. "No. I mean, we do mixed-martial-arts training and sparring, but it's not really about the fighting."

Shayna opened her mouth, but no question came out. Because it really sounded like he'd just described fighting...

He braced his hands against the counter and nailed her with a stare. "It's a place for veterans to get help transitioning to civilian life."

Oh. *Oh.* Why did that sound like therapy? No way she was voicing that word, though, not with the almost challenging way Billy was looking at her. Gaze hard. Eyebrow arched. Jaw muscle ticking as if he was clenching his teeth. It was actually kinda freaking hot.

Screw kinda.

"That sounds awesome," she said. Because it did. Anything that acknowledged and helped veterans after they'd sacrificed so much was good in her book. Billy stared at her for another long stretch. "What?"

"Nothing," he said in that way people used when they actually had a lot they were thinking of saying.

"Okey dokey." She took the long way around the island so that she didn't have to squeeze between him and the counter. "Well, good night, Billy. I hope you can get some sleep. You look beat."

She made for the steps without waiting for him to reply. At the bottom of the staircase, she gathered her shoes just like she'd promised, and then she headed up.

She'd made it three steps before he called her name. "Shay. Wait."

THE WORDS CAME out of Billy's mouth before he even thought to say them. As if keeping Shayna around had been pure instinct.

And maybe it had been, because despite staying away from her all week, just one night in her presence had him craving more of her. Her humor. Her sarcasm. Her easy acceptance.

Maybe it was because of how little sleep he'd had all week. Or because doing his job well had meant delivering to his client the terrible news of her husband's infidelity. Or because his surveillance work had required a lot of hours of sitting in his car —and the constant press of his back against the seat had awakened the phantom pain of long-ago fried nerves that he sometimes felt something fierce. All of which had him feeling exhausted.

Billy sighed and crossed the room to the staircase. "Come with me. Tomorrow, I mean."

From where she stood on the fourth step, Shayna frowned. "Dude, it's okay."

He shook his head. "I want you to come."

Her frown deepened. "Why? It's not a big deal. Really."

Why *did* he want her to come? When just moments before he'd felt so ambivalent and even a little embarrassed about it?

Billy didn't have to think long on the answer—because she'd reacted as if WFC was not only perfectly normal, but really cool. And it was. But it was also fucking therapy of a sort, even though the format was something way different than sitting on a couch and spilling your emotional guts.

He needed to make up for hurting her feelings—and he

knew he'd done just that. The expressiveness of her face made her an open book. And telling the truth was the best way to make up for it. He knew that, too.

"I was fucking embarrassed about what you'd think. That's why I hesitated when you asked. Not because I didn't want you to come. Besides, you could meet some of my friends." Unusual heat rushed into Billy's face, and he dropped his chin to his chest.

Shay made her way down to him until he was staring at her bare feet and her bright red toenails. "Did you think I'd tease you or something?" she asked, her voice neutral.

He forced himself to lift his chin and meet her gaze. "You do like to bust my balls."

"Not about this. Never about this." Her expression was so fucking earnest, and her face was even more beautiful.

He nodded, feeling the truth of her words down deep. After all, she'd seen his scars and heard him talk about how hard it was to come home from deployment and been nothing but cool about that, too. "So. will you come?"

Her smile answered before her words did. "Yeah. Sounds fun. I'd like to come. But I promise I'll stay out of your hair."

"You don't have to stay out of my hair, Shayna."

"Oh, good, because this is driving me crazy," she said, her fingers suddenly combing through his hair. "You made it stand up funny."

Billy could've fucking purred. If he did things like purr, which he fucking didn't. But her nails felt damn amazing against his scalp. He would've closed his eyes at the goodness of it if it weren't for watching the satisfaction shaping her pretty face as she touched him.

"There," she said, her smile turning a little shy. She cleared her throat. "So, uh, okay then. What time do we need to leave?"

CHAPTER EIGHT

THERE WAS one fatal flaw in his plan to bring Shayna to Full Contact—Billy hadn't given any thought to how she might look in her workout clothes.

And, Jesus, how goddamned sexy she looked in her workout clothes.

Short spandex shorts hugged her curvy ass, and the cut-outs on the back of her sports bra and tank top revealed some of her ink. With her red curls up in a ponytail, she managed to look both cute and sexy at the same time—and it was a killer fucking combination.

None of which he had any business noticing.

But what made it even more appealing was how obviously excited she was to be going to the gym with him. Her enthusiasm and gratitude hit him right in the chest, as if he'd given her the moon instead of an invite to come meet his friends. She'd kept up a nearly running commentary the whole car ride there, only pausing to ask Billy questions—about the gym, about his surveillance work, about WFC.

"How long have you belonged?" was her most recent question, and Billy could feel her eyes on him.

He was glad that driving gave him an excuse not to face her while they talked. "A few years," he said. "I joined not too long after I got home, even though I couldn't spar at first because my back wasn't healed enough."

"Does it, um, is it okay...I mean, does it hurt now to get hit where your scarring is?" she asked.

Billy did look at her then. He didn't love focusing on his injuries, but he had to admit that he respected how Shayna tackled the subject head-on, even if she was a little uncomfortable asking. Sure enough, her cheeks were pink. But he found only curiosity in her eyes, and maybe a little concern. No pity. Thank fuck. "Sometimes," he admitted.

And even though that one word was all kinds of vague, he'd said more to her in those two syllables than he'd said to his friends in WFC—or to Coach Mack who led the club.

Sometimes...as in, sometimes it triggered a temporary worsening of the phantom pain of the kind that he'd had all this past week—and still had even as his ass sat behind that steering wheel, a sensation that ranged from an uncomfortable feeling of pins and needles to a nearly intolerable electrical burning.

And, *sometimes*...as in, his inability to fully feel there meant that he occasionally took hits or kicks to his ribs on the right side without realizing that he'd been injured. Usually when that happened, he'd find big black bruises covering his side the next morning. Once, though, a pinch he felt when he took deep breaths sent him to his doc's, where he learned he had a broken rib.

He hadn't admitted that to Coach or the others back then, and he didn't tell her any of that now.

Her gaze narrowed. "'Sometimes' doesn't sound good."

Billy shrugged, even though he respected her skepticism. Because she wasn't wrong.

"The benefits outweigh the occasional risks." She didn't

respond to that, but he could almost hear her brain chewing on the topic, so he didn't make her ask. "Which, for me, include blowing off the steam that always seems to be building up in my head. I...I just get to the point where I feel like, if I don't release it, it'll just...I don't know, consume me."

It was a nearly stunning admission, and he wasn't sure why the fuck he'd made it.

Luckily, they'd arrived. Better yet, there was a possibly god-sent parking place available on the street in front of the gym.

Shayna wasn't deterred by the fact that they'd made it to their destination. "What is 'it'?" she asked in a quiet voice as he parallel parked.

Guilt. It's guilt.

He didn't give that answer out loud, of course, even though he heard her loud and clear. Instead of answering, he parked, killed the engine, and pulled the key from the ignition. Billy's stomach tied in knots as he turned to her with the lie of 'I don't know' on his tongue.

But then he saw her expression. And for just a second, he felt like he was looking into a mirror.

Shattered. Ashamed. Guilt-ridden. That's how he would've described what he saw on her face.

Billy's heart tripped into a shocked sprint.

Shayna looked away. And he would've done almost anything to make her look at him again, because he'd never seen another person so reflect how he felt. Why had she looked that way? He didn't know, but the only thing he could think to do to find out was to answer her honestly.

"It's guilt," he said, nearly holding his breath.

Finally, those blue eyes swung back to his. The shattered shame and grief was gone from her expression, but it was there in those eyes. As if the mask she'd donned wasn't quite big enough to cover everything she felt. "Yeah," she whispered. "Me, too."

Billy frowned, her words ricocheting through him. "What do you have—"

Knock, knock.

"Jesus," he bit out, nearly jumping out of his skin. He looked to his left to see Sean and Mo standing on the sidewalk grinning like idiots. "My friends, such as they are."

Shayna managed a chuckle, and there was a lot of relief in the sound of it. "Well, let's do this." She reached for the door handle, but Billy grasped her arm. When she peered back at him, he nailed her with a stare. "Can we pick this up later?"

She swallowed hard. "Maybe?"

He arched a brow, recognizing his own avoidance in her answer.

Her gaze nearly pleaded. "Your friends—"

"Can wait. Shay—"

"Okay. Later."

Billy wasn't sure why he'd pushed her. It wasn't like he discussed this shit, like, ever.

But the idea that she might feel something similar made him need to know. Out of morbid curiosity. Out of a need to not just know but *feel* that he wasn't alone. Out of gut-deep concern for her. Because Billy had survived something he shouldn't have, while better men had died. He deserved the guilt he carried. He'd earned it.

"Okay," he said with a nod.

She pasted on a smile and pushed out of the car.

What could Shayna possibly have experienced to make her feel anything similar?

The only tragedy he was aware of in her family was the death of her brother, Dylan, two years before. But he'd been killed by a drunk driver, and Shayna had been hurt in the accident, too. Billy and Ryan had been on deployment when it happened, and Ry had been gutted by the news but relieved as all hell that Shayna had survived, especially when his parents told him the cops said it was a miracle she hadn't been hurt worse.

Of course, there was a lot about Shayna's life Billy didn't know. He really hoped she gave him the chance to change that.

"Hi," Shayna mouthed as she rounded the hood of his car and reached to shake Mo's hand.

Billy hauled himself out of the car. God only knew what his friends might say to her.

"So, this is the famous Shayna," Mo was saying. Case in point. Billy wanted to beat him about the head and shoulders.

"Uh oh. Why am I famous?" she asked with a hesitant smile as her gaze swung from his asshole friend to him.

"Because you broke into his house," Sean said, grinning like a shithead. "And he pulled his gun on you."

Her eyes went wide, and he saw the question there. *Did you tell them you saw me naked?* Billy gave a single head shake and willed her to understand that he hadn't told them anything else.

Finally, she grinned, and he hoped that meant the message got through. "That was me," she said. "He was late, though, so I didn't have much of a choice. Did he recount that part of the story?"

The guys laughed, and suddenly it was as if the three of them had known each other forever with how easily they fell in and got along. Billy followed them inside, not minding being the odd man out so much when he heard Shayna laugh at his friends' antics.

The three men signed in on the clipboard on the counter, and then Billy made arrangements for Shayna's seven-day visitor's pass. When she was done filling out her paperwork, they went down one level to a large rectangular gym space. Blue mats covered the open part of the floor, and two eight-sided cages dominated the far end of the space. A few people had already arrived and were spread out on the mats, stretching and talking. Tara and Dani waved, and Billy threw a wave back.

Sean winked at them. Well, probably mostly at Dani. No doubt because it would irritate her and, sure enough, she flipped him the bird. It'd been that way between the two of them the whole time Billy had belonged to WFC. He wasn't sure if it was actual hatred or foreplay.

"Don't be an asshole," Mo said to Sean as he eyeballed the exchange.

"I gotta be me," Sean said, winking at Shayna.

She chuckled. "Oh, I see. So you're the one who lives to get under other people's skin."

Sean's expression went total *who me?*

"She's got your number, Riddick," Billy said.

"Uh huh," Mo said, chuckling.

"I thought we were friends, Shayna," the guy said, making her laugh again.

They dumped their belongings onto the benches at the side of the room, and Billy took the opportunity to introduce Shayna to a few more people as they arrived—Coach Mack, Leo, Colby, and Noah among them.

"Heard a lot about you, Shayna. Nice to meet you," Noah said.

"Have you now?" Shayna said, giving Noah a sweet smile that turned suspicious as she directed it at Billy.

Noah laughed—and it was a helluva different look on the guy. The former Marine had worked his ass off to get better, and seeing him had Billy thinking of the conversation he and Shayna had nearly had in his car. A conversation about grief and shame and survivor's guilt. Well, at least, that was the source of his own guilt.

Now, seeing how much Noah had changed held a mirror up in front of Billy, making him face the reality that he hadn't done all the hard work he had to do on himself yet, had he?

Which made him more than a little bit of a hypocrite, given how Billy had once pushed Noah to confront his demons.

"Don't worry," Noah said. "Everything I heard was great."

Shayna grinned. "Well that's good. Nice to meet you, too, Noah."

"Okay, let's warm up," Colby was saying from the front of the room.

Billy turned to Shay. "That's my cue. We'll be done in about 90 minutes or so."

She nodded and hiked her small gym bag up on her shoulder. "Sounds good. I saw the cardio machines on our way in." She retraced her steps across the training space, and Billy watched her go as he found a spot out on the mats.

"She's a fucking cutie," Sean said. "No wonder you're into her."

"What?" Billy pulled a face. "I'm—" *Not into her.*

At least, those were the words he'd meant to say. But they wouldn't come. They wouldn't pass between his lips. Because they weren't true, were they? He'd been into her almost from day one. Hell, minute one. When she'd had a gun pulled on her, dropped her towel, and proceeded to make jokes about it.

"I'm not after her, Riddick."

Sean held up his hands as Colby guided them through a variety of stretches. "Whatever you say, man."

Billy forced himself to think about the stretches, his breathing, how his beat-to-hell body felt as he forced it to move. Truth was, he felt like shit. Clearly his body was registering its protest that nearly a week with little sleep and almost no horizontal time in an actual bed was all kinds of unsatisfactory.

To be thirty-three and feel this fucking old was a bitch. But he was never going to be the man he'd been before, was he? At this point, that wasn't really a newsflash, though it was never fun having that reality driven home in yet another new way...

That was one of the reasons he made a point of attending WFC almost religiously. People here got it. They lived it. Many of them had it worse.

The day he'd met Noah, Billy had asked him what his damage was. It wasn't a question of whether someone here was damaged in some way, it was a matter of *how* damaged they were. And in what ways.

Because war...hell...war damaged you even if your body came back whole. There was absolutely no way to experience crisis, trauma, and violence—or even the threat of it—without it changing the way you viewed the world.

PTSD didn't just happen to those who'd been physically injured, it could happen to anybody whose situation constantly forced them to confront the fragility of life and the capriciousness of death. As all soldiers had to do. That fragility, that capriciousness...it became a warrior's *reality*. And most civilians' real world where everyone was safe and people were good and you could protect the ones you loved—*that* became the fantasy world.

Even if you had enough insight into your own head to know your thinking wasn't fully rational, there was no convincing a central nervous system that'd been trained to survive threats that those threats were now gone.

So the veterans who came to WFC were scarred, all right. In ways that were both visible and invisible. For Billy, it was some of both. His PTSD was nowhere near as bad as some, but he still had nightmares and that nearly suffocating survivor's guilt, and he didn't fucking like fire. No big surprise there.

All of which had him thinking about Shayna again. What

was *her* damage? And fuck, it killed him to think she had any at all.

"All right," Hawk said, taking over the lead when they finished stretching. "Everyone into child's pose." Yoga as part of WFC had seemed strange to Billy at first but was old hat to him now, and he had even occasionally worked on some more demanding yoga positions on his own time to stretch out his stubborn scar tissue.

The point of WFC wasn't to teach you to fight, it was to provide an emotional outlet, offer community, and teach people to think, not just react, in stressful situations. It put club members in a controlled situation of being attacked, and through the rigor and training of various mixed martial arts, made you realize the value of using your head before you used your hands.

As with so fucking much else, fighting was a head game. And yoga helped teach all of them how to slow down, take a breath, and *think*.

Billy breathed into the position and, face to the mat, let his grimace show when he felt the pull at his muscles and back.

Because *fuck*. He was raw in all kinds of ways, wasn't he?

After moving through a few more poses, they got paired off to practice technical skills. And because they were pretty evenly matched, Coach put Billy and Noah together to run through kicking drills.

"Start with handshakes," Coach yelled as people began putting on their shin guards and spreading out over the mats.

"You can go first," Billy offered, squaring off in front of Noah.

The guy went from zero to focused in no time flat, assuming a fighting stance—hands up, elbows close, lead leg forward. This drill was meant to improve accuracy of the roundhouse kick, which meant that Noah directed his leg in a controlled slow-mo against Billy's ribs, and Billy caught it so the other man could assess where the 'hit' had landed. Noah did a number of handshakes with his right leg against Billy's left side, and then he switched.

On the fifth practice kick against his scarred right side, Noah's foot landed with a little more pressure. Billy sucked in a breath through his teeth.

"Shit, man. What happened?" Noah asked.

Billy rolled his shoulders. "Nothing. You're good." He gestured for him to keep going.

Noah crossed his arms and nailed him with a dark-eyed stare. "You gonna bullshit a bullshitter?"

"I'm just achy. Pulled a week of surveillance and haven't seen a real bed all week until last night. I'm good. Let's go."

Eyes narrowed, Noah didn't push him, but the roundhouse kicks that followed were so controlled that the guy stopped his rotation before his shin came anywhere near Billy's body.

Billy might've been impressed given the guy's occasional equilibrium problems, a consequence of his TBI, but he was too fucking annoyed at the limitations of his *own* body at the moment.

So, gritting his teeth, Billy glared. "Cortez, if you don't take off the kid gloves, I'll take them off for you."

"Uh huh. Try it, old man," Noah retorted. The fucker. Like their six-year age difference was that big.

On the next kick, Billy grasped Noah's leg in a tight hold against his ribs and twisted.

Noah nearly got knocked off balance. But on a surprised laugh, he caught himself by rotating his upper body in a move that resembled the body kick mobility drills they sometimes did. "Okay, asshole."

"Not too old after all." He allowed Noah to twist his leg back to the roundhouse position and released him.

"Somebody has a fucking bee in his bonnet today," Noah said as they switched so that Billy was the one practicing his kicks.

After the admittedly assholish stunt he'd just pulled, he remained on alert for Noah to catch him off guard next. But the guy let Billy do his thing, practicing a dozen kicks on each side. At first, every movement took a concerted effort, but the more he got his blood flowing, the better he started to feel.

Ah, adrenaline, my old friend.

"Okay," Coach called as he walked around, surveying everyone's form. "Kick attack and footwork drill. Round kicks only to the legs. No other strikes or targets are permitted. No checking the kicks either—your only defense is evasive footwork."

Noah grinned, and Billy smirked and said, "Bring it, jarhead."

"You're just sad you *Ain't a Real Marine Yet,*" he retorted with one of the most tired taunts in the book.

Billy took up his fighting stance as they squared off. "How many years did it take you to learn how to spell 'army'? Wouldn't want you to hurt yourself."

Noah surged at him with a kick that Billy dodged. They were both fast on their feet, which served to push both of them harder, faster. Billy rounded with a kick that caught the outside of Noah's knee. The key was to stay agile and evasive, but to remain close enough that he could quickly counterattack when he saw opportunities.

They'd been at it for a few minutes when Coach Mack came by. "Don't drop your guard, Noah. Hands and eyes up even though you're not punching or needing to protect your head. Make it a habit."

Noah nodded and tightened up his stance, then he came at Billy with a vengeance.

"Good," Coach said, clapping. "That's what I want to see."

Another ten minutes of the fast footwork had both of them breathing harder.

"Take a break and then we'll run the tag team grappling match drill," Coach called out.

"Nice work," Billy said, offering his hand to Noah.

The guy nodded and clasped hands with him. "You too." But when Billy went to let go, Noah held on. "I feel like something's going on with you." He let the words hang there for a moment before he continued. "You were there for me in some of my darkest fucking moments, Parrish. I want you to know I'm here. Just say the word."

Billy gave him a single nod. He appreciated the sentiment. A lot.

And, begrudgingly, he even appreciated the fact that Noah was pushing him when Billy had made it pretty clear that he wasn't into sharing. The two of them had gotten close over the past few months, but it was the first time that Billy had really felt the kind of brotherhood with the guy that he'd had with his Ranger brothers.

Christ, how he fucking missed having it.

But as powerful as that revelation was—and it was—there was only one person who Billy had the slightest interest in opening up to. Shayna Curtis. Mostly because he wanted her to open up in return.

He just needed another chance to pin her down.

CHAPTER NINE

AFTER FORTY-FIVE MINUTES on the elliptical, Shayna was drenched in sweat and her legs were noodles. Yet, despite the good work-out, her internal voice still hadn't stopped screaming, *Why in the world did you tell Billy you felt guilty, you freaking cockburger?!*

So much for exercise instilling any sort of peaceful calm...

On a sigh, she wiped down her machine and then toweled off her face. When she wasn't berating herself, it was only because the memory of Billy's voice intruded.

"Can we pick this up later?"

This. Meaning their conversation about the guilt that built up inside both of them, apparently. And probably also meaning the question Billy had tried to voice when they'd been interrupted by his friends.

"What do you have—" To feel guilty about... She knew without question that those were the words he'd intended to say.

Which meant that there was a one-hundred-per-cent chance that if she kept her word to resume their conversation, she would have to talk about the night Dylan died. And that Shayna really didn't want to do.

No part of a fresh start involved telling the people new to her life about her biggest, worst, and most unforgivable failings.

Shayna didn't want Billy looking at her with disappointment or accusation in his eyes. And she also didn't want him telling Ryan anything she might say if she were foolish enough to give into such a conversation.

Refilling her bottle at the water cooler, Shayna muttered, "Why didn't you keep your mouth shut?" It might've been the tenth time she'd asked herself that question, but that repetition was more out of a stunned shock at herself than from a lack of understanding.

She *knew* why.

What Billy had said about being consumed by the emotions inside him had so perfectly described how she sometimes felt. It sounded like MMA training was his outlet when those emotions became overwhelming. For her, photography was the most effective thing to allow her concentrate on something beyond herself. And that moment of relating to Billy's words...had pulled the admission from her before she'd fully thought through the consequences of making it.

Now Billy wanted to talk further.

As Shayna headed down to the locker rooms, her stomach went on a nauseous loop-the-loop at the thought of it.

And then she saw Billy through the windows to the gym with the fighting rings where his club met. He was on his knees facing another fighter—a woman with a long black braid—while a bigger group knelt around the two of them. Shay had just enough time to appreciate that the club included women veterans before the woman attacked him.

For a long moment, they grappled with each other until Billy managed to flip the woman and pin her to the ground.

Three visceral reactions rocked through Shayna.

An almost animalistic appreciation of Billy's brute strength.

Arousal at the memory of Billy pinning her against the wall.

And jealousy that another woman was experiencing the feeling of the weight of his body instead of her.

Shayna's heart tripped into a sprint as she stood there, slack-jawed and wanting...

Suddenly, Billy sprang into a kneeling position again as the woman got up and moved to the outer ring of people, and it was clear that some sort of trash-talk being thrown between them from the looks on their faces and the way the others were laughing and clapping.

And then Mo moved into the center with Billy. As big as Billy was, Mo...Mo was like a *mountain*. His ready smile and deep laugh had earlier put Shayna at ease and allayed any concerns she'd had that she might be invading a space where she wasn't wanted. But now Mo looked nothing short of intimidating as he stared Billy down.

The men seemed to lunge at the same time. They slammed into each other and worked to pull each other flat to the ground, and then finally they both went down. Shayna couldn't see who had the advantage around those cheering the two men on, and she realized that she was straining and moving to the side to get a better view.

Whatever was going on, it was much longer before the fighters traded out, and this time it was Billy coming out of the center to join those on the side. A few of his teammates shook his hand before he moved outside of the group to grab his water bottle. And then he tilted his head way back to take a long drink.

And, holy mother of sweaty hot men, Billy Parrish was freaking gorgeous.

Muscles glistening. Shorts hanging dangerously low on his lean hips. Dark blond hair made even darker from sweat. Even the fingerless black gloves he wore were sexy as fuck. His Adam's apple bobbed as he drank.

Shayna swallowed hard herself.

He wiped his mouth on the back of his glove and capped the bottle again, and then he did a double take as he noticed her standing in the window.

Heat absolutely *roared* over Shayna at having been caught so blatantly ogling him. And there was a smugness to the almost-smile he wore. But he gave her a little wave and nodded his head as if to invite her inside.

The gesture should not have made any part of her feel gooey, but it seemed her crush on her brother's best friend had resurrected enough to indeed cause gooeyness. Whether she wanted that to happen or not.

She went inside and sat on one of the benches, giving her a much better view of the wrestling matches. And now she was close enough that she could see that the fighters only switched out when someone gave up and tapped on the floor or reached a teammate's hand off the edge of the mat to tag out. A few more changes happened, and then Sean was in the ring up against Noah.

The looks on the men's faces proved that it was all good-natured competition even as they trash-talked each other and Noah managed to throw Sean off balance and knock him down. And then it was several long minutes of watching the two of them try to gain the upper hand by getting each other in armlocks and chokeholds.

On a roar and a sudden surge of muscle, Noah managed to tag out. And then the woman with the long black ponytail who had fought Billy earlier was in again.

"Come on, Dani. You got this," Noah said, clapping his hands.

Shayna internally cheered Dani on, too. First, because she was one of only three women in the room, and that seemed to take a certain kind of bravery all by itself.

Second, because the woman was pretty badass, not showing the slightest bit of uncertainty or restraint as she went after Sean with possibly even more aggression than that she'd used against Billy.

And, third, Shay cheered for her because she remembered how Sean had blown Dani a kiss when they'd come in, and the woman had responded by giving the guy the finger. So there was obviously some sort of history between them. And, nice as he'd been, Sean seemed like the kind of guy who could use having his ego knocked down a notch or two every once in a while. Just for the sheer fun of it.

It was clear that the rest of the club thought egging the two of them on was fun, because the volume of the clapping, laughing, and trash-talk escalated with each passing minute that they wrestled. Dani was so quick and flexible that she kept escaping Sean's efforts to pin her, and the guy was nearly growling as he finally managed to flip her face-down against the mat, his greater bulk on top of her.

"Tap out, Daniela," he bit out.

"Screw you, Riddick," she said, the light brown skin of her face going red as she twisted to get out from under him.

"Come on, D. I got you. Admit it," he said, his muscles seriously straining as he held her.

As Shayna watched the two of them fight, she wondered if she was the only one who found their antagonism weirdly hot. She almost suspected that something must've happened between them at some point to generate the kind of explosive chemistry they seemed to give off.

"Damnit," Dani finally said, her hand smacking against the mat.

To his credit, Sean didn't gloat. He got off of her in a flash and offered a hand up, which she begrudgingly took. And then they shook before Dani stepped out and Noah and Mo gave her a pep talk as Sean took on a fighter Shay didn't know.

Finally, the coach blew his whistle and gathered everyone around. "Good work today. I'm ending things early because my wife's parents are in town and I promised I'd make it for dinner."

The amount of razzing that statement generated made Shayna laugh—not to mention a little envious, because it was clear how much everyone here liked and supported each other. Shay wanted a community like that for herself. Given how much fun she'd had the night before at the bar, maybe it'd be in the cards for her, too.

As the group broke up, Shayna rose. She felt a little conspicuous standing there like she was waiting on Billy, and she certainly didn't want to cramp his style. But he came right over to her anyway, a couple of the other guys in tow.

"A group of us usually goes out for dinner and drinks after," he said. "You good with that or you want me to run you home first?"

"No, don't go home, Shayna," Sean said. "Hang out with us."

"I second that," Mo said, making her grin.

Before she had a chance to answer, two of the women joined their group. "We're just gonna grab a quick shower and then we'll be ready," Dani said. "What's the plan?"

"I'm game to join," Shayna said to Billy as the conversation turned to debating the pros and cons of several restaurants.

Billy winked. "Good. I'm glad."

Annnnd more goo.

God, her inner fourteen-year-old was present and accounted for, wasn't she?

When Dani and the other woman stepped away and left it

to the men to decide on a place, Shay followed. "I'm going to clean up, too," she called to Billy.

He nodded and gave her a quick once-over that made her belly flip.

At the door to the locker room, Dani made introductions. "I'm Dani England and this is Tara Hunter," she said, gesturing to the brown-haired woman with a prominent scar on her neck.

"Hey, I'm Shayna Curtis. Billy's roommate. Well, temporarily," she said as they all found spots along the bench that ran between two rows of gray metal lockers.

"Why temporarily?" Tara asked as she shucked her tank top and fished a little zipper bag of shower supplies from her duffle.

"I just recently moved to D.C. for a new job. Billy's one of my brother's best friends, so they arranged a place for me to crash until I find something permanent."

Dani's eyebrows lifted. "Your brother's a Ranger too, then?"

Shayna nodded and gathered her soap and shampoo. "Deployed to Iraq right now."

"Or somewhere," Dani said with a knowing smile. "I was in the Army for eight years myself. Nurse."

"Wow. Thank you for that," Shayna said. And then she quickly added, "I don't mean that in the sort of generic *thank you for your service* way I know you probably often get. I mean that people like you were there for people like my brother, and I really appreciate that."

Dani gave her an appraising glance and nodded. "I'm out now," she said stepping into one of the shower stalls. "Still nursing, though."

"What's your new job?" Tara asked Shay as she stripped down and wrapped her pin-up curves in a towel.

"I'm a photographer for the *Washington Gazette*." Shayna supposed she ought to start thinking of herself as a photojournalist, but that seemed grander than her experience had yet justified.

Tara's eyes lit up. "Ever do any underwater photography?"

"No," Shayna said, intrigued by the question as she headed to one of the stalls. "Have you?"

The woman nodded as she gathered more of her things. "I work in commercial diving, and we often use video and still photography to get a full picture of what's going on beneath the water's surface on a project."

Shay hung her towel on a hook. "I am kind of a photography nut so now I have to know everything about that."

Tara laughed as they both stepped into their respective stalls. "That can be arranged."

The hot water felt great as it rained down against Shay's tired body, but then she had a funny thought. "Uh, oh, Tara, wait. Does your diving job by any chance mean we're going to be on opposite sides of the Army-Navy game come football season?" Shay called out over the sound of the running water.

"Go Navy," Tara said, amusement plain in her voice.

Shayna chuckled. "My brother played Army football."

"Oh, no, so what you're telling me is that you're hardcore?" Tara asked.

"I mean, a little?" Shay said, grinning as she washed her hair. And if she thought she could really get to like these women, she *knew* she did after two hours of dinner and drinks at a nearby steakhouse.

Dani had an absolutely cutting sense of humor that had Shayna laughing all night, especially as Sean and Billy were often on the receiving ends of it. And Tara was the kind of wicked smart that made you sit back, shake your head, and wonder what you'd done with your life. She told the most interesting stories about things she'd seen during her years as a Navy diver and about where her travel as a commercial diver had taken her since.

And all the while, Shayna sat nearly plastered against Billy's side, because the restaurant had squeezed the seven of them into a booth that would've been more comfortable for four or five. Only the fact that Mo sat in a chair at the end of the booth made it work, but it was still a tight fit.

Shayna was *not* complaining.

Because Billy smelled like soap and a clean-scented aftershave and something that was all him—combined, they made up a mouthwatering scent that she wouldn't have minded drowning in. The whole night she'd been over-aware of the press of their thighs and the way they kept bumping arms until they'd finally broken down in laughter over how difficult it was to cut their steaks without elbowing each other in the face.

She only hoped that she wasn't giving off the same *I'm really freaking interested* vibes that Sean gave off every time he looked at Dani—especially when Dani wasn't looking back.

He probably thought he was being all chill about it, but the guy was about as subtle as a heart attack. She couldn't be the only one who saw it, could she? Not that Shayna blamed Sean at all, because Daniela looked absolutely beautiful. Between her long, glossy hair, a form-fitting black wrap shirt, and the almost delicate perfection of her facial features, the woman was truly stunning.

Billy turned to Shayna. "Are you having a good time?"

"Yes. Thanks for letting me tag along," she said.

He shook his head. "You're not tagging along. I wanted you here. And everyone wanted to meet you."

"It's true," Sean said. "Because it's not everyday someone gets a jump on a Ranger."

Billy threw the guy an unamused look, and Shayna laughed. "I wouldn't go that far," she said.

"Thank you," Billy said.

"Wait." Dani held out her hands and surveyed the lot of them. "I need this story from the beginning."

Which kicked off twenty minutes of her and Billy fighting to tell their versions of the story—sans all mention of her getting naked at the end of it, thank God—while everyone laughed and taunted Billy and high-fived Shayna.

Dani and Tara were totally on her side all the way, and that had Billy refusing to share the piece of cheesecake that he'd agreed to split with Shayna when they ordered it.

She tried to maneuver her fork around his arm, but he blocked her, making her laugh even as she pleaded for a bite. "Come on. It's not my fault that all your friends think it's funny that I broke into your house."

He smirked at her. "That isn't earning you any cheesecake."

"It's my cheesecake, too," she said, trying again.

He easily blocked her next attack. "Possession is nine-tenths of the law."

"Quit being a dickweasal," she said, laughing as she tried again.

He grinned and held the dessert plate further away. "Dick-weasal, am I?"

"Oh, do you prefer jizzmuffin?"

Mo's eyebrows went way up. "Listen to the genius coming out of this girl's mouth." Everyone laughed. "Is this also courtesy of your brother?"

"Brothers," Shayna said, not failing to claim Dylan, too. For once. "And yes. I had to be able to insult them back, didn't I?"

Grinning, Mo grabbed the plate from Billy's hand when he wasn't looking.

"Hey!" Billy said, a comically outraged expression on his sexy face.

"Creativity like that takes fuel, brother, that's all I'm saying." He handed the plate around Billy to Shayna.

About two-thirds of the cake was left, and Shayna promptly licked the whole top of it. "I licked it. It's mine now. Take that, assclown."

The whole table howled in laughter. Mo was actually crying.

And she thought Billy's expression had been comical before. His jaw dropped. "I can't believe you just did that."

She slid a big forkful of the sweet, creamy deliciousness into her mouth. "Oh, believe it," she said around the bite.

As he watched her, his gaze shifted. From outraged to playful to challenging. And she didn't think she was imagining more than a little heat in those dark eyes, either. "You think I'm put off by a pretty woman's tongue, Shayna Curtis?"

"Damn," Sean said. "It's getting a little X-rated up in here."

"Check, please," Noah called out, making everyone laugh again.

Meanwhile, Shayna nearly swallowed said tongue as she prayed to God that the heat lashing through her body didn't climb up her face. Because Billy was staring at her with an arched brow and a smug, expectant look in his eye. "No curses for me now?"

"So, so many," she managed, smiling despite herself and her arousal and the way her belly was flipping. Because there was no way to read what was happening just then but as flirtation. She put the plate between them. "Help yourself if you really want." She said the words looking him straight in the eyes, silently inviting him to interpret them however he wished.

Right in that moment, she was entirely open to him helping himself to *her*, too.

He took a big bite and made a point of closing his eyes and *mmm*ing.

The sound of Billy's moan seemed connected to something primal in Shayna. Because she was suddenly wet. Lordy.

And as they paid and said their good-byes, Shay had absolutely no idea what to think about their flirtation or whether to expect anything more to come. All she knew was that she'd probably say yes to anything Billy Parrish wanted from her.

Anything at all.

CHAPTER TEN

SHAYNA'S HEART was a bass drum in her chest as Billy parked his car around the corner from their place. The whole car ride home, they'd made small talk about dinner and laughed about Billy's friends and teased about the *great cheesecake incident.* On the surface, it all seemed like normal conversation.

But the car was absolutely vibrating with an underlying tension that had her body on edge and her mind racing.

It wasn't just some warm and fuzzies from the one glass of wine she'd had, either. While Billy *seemed* relaxed, his fist kept squeezing around the steering wheel. Sitting at red lights, he cracked his knuckles and rolled his shoulders. And when she sneaked glances at him, she noticed that his jaw ticked.

Once, he caught her looking, and the answering heat in his eyes appeared nothing short of hungry.

"I'll grab our bags from the trunk." He pushed out of the driver's seat.

"Okay," Shayna said, reaching down for her purse—which was when she noticed that it'd fallen over and a few things had spilled out. "Shit." She gathered the loose lipsticks and pens up, then felt around with her hand in the darkness to make sure she hadn't missed anything.

Next to her, the car door opened.

"You okay there?" Billy asked, his big body filling the breach.

She laughed. "Just dropped something." He held out his hand and helped her out. "Very chivalrous of you, Mr. Parrish. Unlike your earlier hoarding of the cheesecake." They both stepped aside to allow him to close the door, which had the unintended consequence of him damn near pinning her to the rear door.

Standing almost chest to chest, their gazes collided. And if Shayna's heart had beat hard before, now it downright pounded. Especially as his gaze ran over her face.

"I'm glad you were there today. With me. At fight club and after."

"Me, too." Shay hoped her voice didn't sound as breathy to him as it did to her own ears.

"You have a knack for making things fun." It was a sweet thing to say, and Shayna wasn't sure how to reply. But she couldn't have even if she'd had the words, because just then he tucked a few of her curls behind her ear. And then a second time when one sprung free again. Goosebumps rushed down her neck, sending a shiver through her whole body.

"I enjoyed your friends," she finally said.

His eyebrow arched. "Just my friends?"

Her stomach went on a loop-the-loop even as she batted her eyelashes and played coy. Because she still couldn't read the situation between them and it was driving her crazy. "Am I forgetting someone?"

Billy smirked and shook his head. On a rueful laugh, he stepped back, both of their gym bags in his hand. "Come on, let's go in."

She reached out a hand for her bag. "I can take that."

"It's no problem."

Not saying another word, they walked side by side around the corner. Down their street. Up his sidewalk. Billy unlocked the door and gestured for her to go first. She hit the lights for the living room, and he dropped their bags onto the living room floor next to the door.

She turned and frowned, because it wasn't like him to—

Billy's hands were suddenly in her hair and his forehead was against hers. "You drive me fucking crazy, Shayna."

"I-I do?" she asked, totally caught off guard but nearly euphoric at his words. "Good crazy, o-or—"

He nodded. "Good crazy. Even though, *fuck*. I should resist wanting you. I know I should."

"No, no you shouldn't," she said, nearly breathless. "Why should you?"

His eyes were dark fire as they bore into hers. "You're just starting out in life. Everything ahead of you, full of possibilities. But me...I'm a busted, used-up soldier without an army or a war. And I'm supposed to be looking out for you, not taking advantage of you."

Shayna didn't know what to respond to first. She hated that he saw himself that way. Shaking her head, she grasped at his wrists, holding him to her. "We had that conversation already. You can't take advantage of someone who wants what you're doing. And I...I do. God, you have to know how much I crushed on you when I was younger. Living with you has only made that stronger, Billy. Nothing about you looks busted or used-up to me. Nothing at *all*."

He came closer, close enough that they touched everywhere, and he searched her eyes. "Ryan wouldn't approve of this, of me."

The closeness made it clear just how turned on he was, and

the demanding press of his erection against her belly nearly stole her breath. "Ryan doesn't get a say..." Her words trailed off, because as much as she believed them in this moment, they resurrected a memory she didn't want to recall.

Of a time she'd uttered nearly those exact words to Dylan. And the consequences had been catastrophic.

"What do you want then?" Billy asked, pulling her from a lane of memories she didn't want to go down. "I don't want to assume, and I don't want you to feel pressured into anything because you live in my house. Jesus, just saying that makes me feel like a lecherous asshole."

"You're not. And I don't feel pressured. I just want you."

Suddenly, Billy's lips were on hers and his tongue was in her mouth and his hands tightened in her hair. She moaned at the suddenness of it, at the goodness of it.

He walked her backwards towards the steps. "Is this okay?"

"Yes," she whispered around the edge of a kiss.

His hands moved to her waist and went to the hem of her white tank top. "Can I see you?"

Shayna nodded, pulling away from their kisses only long enough for the shirt to pass over her head, leaving her standing there in a lacy white bra and her jeans. He dropped her top to the floor.

"So fucking beautiful. Can I touch you?"

"Yes," she whispered, sucking in a breath as he spread out his big hand against her throat and then dragged his fingers downward until he was cupping her breast.

He caught one of her bra straps and dragged it off her shoulder until he bared her nipple to his fingertips. He hauled an arm around her waist, bringing them closer even as he leaned down to kiss her exposed flesh. "Can I taste you?"

Jesus, those questions in that deep rasp were so freaking

sexy that she could hardly stand it. "Please." His tongue stroked over her nipple, once, twice. Her fingers wound into his hair, then tightened as his lips closed around the sensitive peak and sucked her into the heat of his mouth.

And after their dinner and their flirtation and the tension that had been building between them, Shayna felt herself get instantly wet between her legs.

"Oh, God," she rasped.

He unclasped her bra and dropped that to the floor, too.

When Billy lifted his face to hers, his expression was a total stunner. Eyes hot with lust. Tongue dragging against his bottom lip as if he were still tasting her. He arched a brow. "I want you in my bed."

Shayna's pulse raced so hard the room started to spin around her. "Yes."

He lifted her so that her legs surrounded his hips.

Clutching his neck, she threw her head back on a laugh. "You don't have to carry me."

He kissed her neck and started up. "I don't want to stop touching you."

She didn't want him to either.

Shay shivered as the kisses and licks and little nips continued until they were in the darkness of his room. He lowered her feet to the ground and reached to turn on the lamp on the nightstand. But true to his word, he kept one arm around her while he did it.

And then Billy was kissing her again. Her mouth. Her throat. Her chest. His tongue went to her breasts again, and then lower as he dropped to his knees. The scruff on his jaw made her chuckle as he dragged it against her stomach, and then his hands went to her fly and his gaze lifted to hers.

Holy crap, seeing him on his knees in front of her, eyes full of desire and hair a sexed-up mess, was like a dream she never knew she needed to have.

Shayna didn't make him ask this time, though. "Take them off," she whispered. She tugged at his sleeve. "Your shirt, too?"

Nodding, he pulled his shirt off in that one-handed way guys did, further mussing his dark-blond hair. Then he was all about undressing her, which he did like he was unwrapping a present, eager and impatient. The second her shoes and jeans were free from her feet, he held her by the hips and buried his face against her lower belly. She gasped and braced against his bare shoulders, making sure not to grab the nearly healed cut.

Billy kissed her through the satin of her panties, ripping a moan from her when his lips grazed her clit. "I need my mouth on you, Shayna. Lay down."

Words she would never, *ever* forget.

On a shaky breath, she sat on the edge of his bed and started to recline, and then he was on top of her, encouraging her to scoot back and laying her out.

His weight came down on top of her. The total freaking *pleasure* of that sensation floored her, and Shayna immediately clutched at his back. At his scars. Belatedly remembering, she pulled her left hand away.

"It's okay. It didn't hurt," he said, kissing and breathing into her ear. "I want you to touch me. Just maybe save your nails for my ass."

She grinned. "Duly noted."

He kissed his way down her curves again, lingering over every place that made her moan or squirm or roll her hips. Where her shoulder met her throat. Her nipples. Her hip bones. And then he pushed her thighs apart and settled his big shoulders in between like he was getting good and comfortable.

And Shayna had thought seeing him on his knees was sexy.

Nothing was freaking sexier than Billy Parrish's ravenous

expression as he lowered his face between her legs. He licked a firm drag of his tongue right over her clit. Her fingers immediately knotted in his hair.

"That's it," he said right against her most intimate flesh. "Let me know you like it."

"God, I do," she rasped.

He held her ass in his hands and tilted her hips so that her core was laid out right in front of his mouth. And then he dragged his rigid tongue through her wetness on a groan that made her even wetter.

"Billy." It was a plea. A request. An urgent, needful demand.

"I got you." And then he didn't tease. Didn't go slow. Didn't hold back.

Billy Parrish *feasted* on her.

He alternated between penetrating her with his tongue and sucking on her clit until she was moaning and arching and grinding against this face. And when he latched onto her clit again and worked his tongue over it in a succession of fast, tormenting flicks, she grasped the back of his head with one hand and held him there.

"Gonna...gonna c-come," she said as the orgasm shuddered through her so hard and so good that her thighs shook and her heart thundered and her hips couldn't help but ride his mouth in a series of instinctual thrusts.

And though he didn't stop licking her, his ravishment slowed and gentled. Dark eyes peered up her body as his torment drew her orgasm out.

"Stopstopstop," she finally pleaded.

He kissed the inside of her thigh and looked at her with a little smile playing around his wet lips. Smug and gorgeous. "I could eat you all fucking night."

"Jesus," she whispered, overwhelmed by how much she

suddenly felt in that moment. Not just intense sexual satisfaction, which she did, in spades. But also desired. And, even more, *cherished*.

She had no idea what to do with those feelings, or whether she was letting her emotions run too far from what this night with Billy might actually mean—after all, he'd said he wanted her. As in, desired her sexually. Not that he wanted a relationship with her.

So she made light of the moment. "I'd never survive it. But what a way to go..."

On a chuckle, Billy climbed onto the bed and sprawled out all along her side. He propped his head up on his hand and peered down at her, his expression one of hot masculine satisfaction. "I'm trained in CPR. I'd resuscitate you."

Shayna grinned. "Good to know."

He leaned his face against hers. "You're stronger than you look, though. I think you'd survive it." He kissed her then, and the sweet, sweet words played with more of what was happening in her chest.

Something bigger and more intense than her decade-old crush, that was for sure.

She turned onto her side, aligning their bodies in a way that allowed her to feel that he was still rock hard. Palming him through his jeans, she met his still-heated gaze. "Well, it's my turn anyway."

Something flashed behind his eyes. Something hesitant and unsure. For a moment, she was almost certain of it, and then it was gone again and there was just the sexy, naked desire he'd worn since they'd walked into the house.

So she wrote off what she thought she'd seen and pulled at the button to his fly.

Billy's hand grasped and stilled her wrist. "Don't."

"I MEAN, THERE'S NO RUSH," Billy said, a war raging inside himself. A war between what he wanted and what was right. Desire still stirred through his blood but making her come so damn beautifully was its own kind of satisfaction, and his arousal was at a low roar now compared to the frenzy of before.

Making her come could be enough. He could stop it here. Before he'd taken anything for himself. Or, at least, anything more.

They'd careened way the hell over the line—and that was on him. But there were other lines he could keep them from crossing. That he could keep *himself* from crossing.

Uncertainty flickered through Shayna's wide eyes, and he hated himself for it. He really did. But she brazened it out like the brave woman he was discovering her to be. "Can't blame a girl for being eager."

He chuffed out a laugh despite himself. "Is that so?"

She grinned as her hand unzipped his jeans and slipped into his open fly. Then under his boxers. Until she held his cock in the warmth of her grip.

"Fuck," he groaned, watching a new line get blurrier and blurrier until he could barely see it at all.

Don't was on the tip of his tongue again. *Say it, Parrish. Fucking do the right thing and say it.*

But all he did was close his eyes at the goodness of her touch. At the way she stroked him. Root to tip, root to tip. At the way her palm circled around his sensitive head. At the way her thumb found and spread the pre-come at his tip.

At the way she kissed down his chest, his pecs, his abs, her chin and her hair nuzzling his cock.

He fucking loved it. Of course, he did.

Billy ate up Shayna's desire for him like it was the air he needed to breathe. But that just proved he was a greedy, selfish, self-centered sonofabitch. There was so much she didn't know about him. So much he would never tell her either.

About how he thought others had deserved to live more than him. About how he sometimes wished he'd died in their places. About how he used sex and fighting to escape the pain of his guilt and his loneliness and his insecurity and his massive nerve damage from the burns.

And about how, once, he'd used his pain meds to escape that pain—too many of them. Enough that it'd left his mother to find him unconscious and apparently barely breathing.

In his heart of hearts, Billy *still* wasn't sure whether or not he'd done it on purpose. Or whether his intent had been more than a temporary escape. Either way, he'd nearly thrown away—carelessly—what some of his brothers had lost forever.

With that thought, the line he'd been struggling not to cross got a helluva lot clearer again.

He opened his mouth to put an end to this, except that was the exact moment that Shayna's mouth closed around his cock. Wet and hot and deep.

Billy nearly shouted at how good it felt. And in the wake of coming up against the mental edge of his greatest failings and his most shameful weaknesses, feeling anything good was a goddamned miracle.

He couldn't end it. He couldn't pull away. He couldn't avoid letting them cross the line. Again.

Instead, his hands went to the back of Shayna's head, resting there, at first, as her mouth moved over him again and again. Then urging her on with the slightest pressure. Her hair was so soft against his fingers and her mouth was so intense around his dick and her humming moans were so sweet in his ear.

"God, Shay, your fucking mouth," he gritted out as his hand fisted in her curls.

She pulled off long enough to gasp a breath. "Show me what you like, Billy," she rasped before taking him in deep again.

Her words shot sensation into his balls, and all he could do was obey. He drew his hips back and then rocked forward again, fucking her mouth in a long, slow in and out.

"Aw, yeah," he said, the words repeating with each torturous stroke. "Aw, yeah, Shay."

Gripping his hip in her hand, she moaned and opened her mouth wider, her tongue sticking out to just bathe his balls.

"Yes, take it deep," he rasped. "Roll onto your back." When she did, he kicked off his jeans and boxers and then braced himself atop her, knees next to her shoulders, his cock finding its way between her lips again. Except this time he had an absolutely mind-blowing view as he peered down and watched his length disappear inside her mouth. "Yes, take it."

Those sea-blue eyes flickered backward, towards him, and their gazes collided.

All at once, his orgasm was a freight train barreling down his spine and nailing him in the ass. His balls went tight and his hips jerked and he had just enough time to pull free of her heat as he yelled, "Christ, I'm coming."

His release shot through him in tormenting pulses that lashed at Shay's cheek, her throat, her lips. Which was when Billy realized that she held her mouth wide for it, her hand directing his head inside again. So she could drink him down.

Peering up at him once more, she licked at where he'd spilled on her cheek and, not quite able to reach it all, she swiped at it with a fingertip and drew his cum to her mouth. Her lips ovaled around the wet finger.

He wasn't sure if it was the eye contact when he felt so fucking raw. Or if it was the decadence of her willingness to not only swallow his cum but drink even what he'd spilled. Or if it was the way she hummed in pleasure as she did it.

All he knew was that it unleashed an absolute *roar* of possessiveness inside him.

One he had no goddamn right to feel.

CHAPTER ELEVEN

Shayna stretched out on the bed next to where Billy lay looking absolutely wrecked. After lusting over him for so long, she could barely believe what they'd just shared and how thrilling it'd been to make him fall apart. Or that she had the ability to look her fill of his naked body, sprawled out beside her like a freaking *god*.

Now, she wasn't sure what to do or how to play it.

Were they done? Would he want more?

In a delicious display of masculinity, his cock lay semi-erect against his hard belly. Jesus, he'd been a delicious and slightly overwhelming mouthful. And just that one thought made it clear that *she* was game for more if he was. Then again, she was the one with the possibly run-away feelings.

Not just possibly, Shay.

Er, right.

So then, should she instead act casual, say good night, and go back to her own room? Probably. She inhaled to attempt the latter when his gaze cut to her and he extended his arm.

"C'mere."

Shayna's heart did a little flip inside her chest. Because

snuggling with him hadn't been within any of the neighboring realms of possibilities in her mind. But she wasn't questioning it, either.

She moved into the nook along his body—head on his good shoulder, knee on his thigh, hand on his chest. And then he wrapped his arm tight around her shoulders and pulled her in that much closer. The sigh he released was one of pure satisfaction, and it made her smile.

He was warm and strong and being so sweet, and he held her there for long enough that her eyelids grew heavy. His breathing calmed and slowed, lulling her closer to sleep. Close enough that, when she heard his voice, she was sure she'd dreamed it.

Or, perhaps, "nightmared" it, given what her mind had conjured him saying.

Can we return to our earlier conversation?

Nice try, subconscious.

"Shay?" his voice came—again, apparently—at little more than a whisper. "Did you hear me?" His chin turned into her head as if he were peering down at her.

Her heart played a sudden thundering beat in her chest. Not dreaming after all. "What?" she asked, hoping maybe he'd think he'd awakened her and let it go. Because she didn't want to return to their conversation.

That was *not* the more she was game for.

His fingers drew a lazy circle on her ribs. "Can we return to what we were talking about this morning? In the car."

No. Nonono.

She didn't want to talk to him about why she felt guilty. Not after what they'd just done. Not after he'd managed to see her as a desirable woman and not just her brother's kid sister. And not when part of her hoped he could someday see her as even more than that.

This morning, she'd been impulsive and stupid, as if his words and demeanor had worked a spell on her. One that made her open up when she normally wouldn't. Even if that had been true, that spell was broken and her sense of self-preservation was back. In spades.

"I..." Swallowing hard, her mind raced for how to say no in a way that wasn't just a flat refusal. "*Now?*"

"Why not?"

"I, uh, don't know. Pretty tired." *Could you be anymore lame, Shay?*

Those circles continued against her side. "It's important," he whispered.

"Billy—"

"Tell me, Shayna." His voice was quiet, but there was an intensity there.

She didn't make him specify what he wanted to know, because his earlier question still rang in her head. *"What do you have"* ...*to feel guilty about?*

"I...I don't...not now."

"Why?" he asked, rolling them so that she was on her back, her head cradled by his arm. His dark eyes searched hers.

She felt...so freaking exposed.

It wasn't voicing the words that scared her, it was the consequences that followed. The horror and the disappointment and the accusation she'd see on his expression and in his eyes. How the way he looked at her would change. How what he learned would quash the potential of whatever this was between them before it had really even begun.

Shayna knew these were the consequences of telling her secret because she'd seen them all before. And not just in her parents' understandably darker moments. But from Dylan's fiancé, Abby. Who'd been one of Shayna's closest friends. Almost a sister, even.

But no more.

I hate you! You killed him and you ruined my whole life! Why couldn't it have been you?

Like Shay hadn't had the same damn thought.

Still, it had nearly killed her to hear those words from someone she'd loved after Shay had lost someone else she'd loved, and all while trying to hide just how much pain her broken arm, collar bone, and ankle caused her so her parents had one less thing to worry about.

From his visits to and stays at their house, Billy had known Dylan. And because Dylan was older than her and a guy, he'd hung out with Ryan and Billy during those stays. So Billy had a reason to care about what Shayna had done because he'd known the person she'd done it to.

A knot suddenly lodged in her throat, so big she could barely manage a swallow. What Shayna feared wasn't hypothetical. It wasn't irrational. And it wasn't going to be any part of her fresh start.

She gently pressed her hand against Billy's chest as she pushed out from underneath of him. Shivering from a sudden rush of nervous adrenaline, she scrambled off the bed, her gaze scanning the floor.

"Where's my shirt..." And then she remembered. It was downstairs where Billy dropped it. She picked up his instead.

He moved to sit on the mattress's edge, seemingly perfectly comfortable with the fact that he was still naked—a sight that, in her rising panic, she couldn't fully appreciate.

"What are you doing?" he asked.

"I'm tired." She punched her arms through the sleeves and yanked on his tee. It was miles too big and that was good—she felt way too exposed with so much skin showing. Heat filled her face as she grabbed up her jeans and undies.

"You're running."

A tendril of anger flickered inside her. "Wow. Okay," she said. Even though he was right.

She forced herself to face him again before she left, and tension absolutely ricocheted between them and within her.

He nailed her with a fierce stare, one she wished she was seeing through her viewfinder. Could she capture the disappointed glint in his dark eyes? "Why..." His lips pressed into a tight line like he'd reconsidered his question, but then he shook his head and started again, his voice gentler. "Why won't you talk to me?"

Because I might vomit. "I just can't." She searched those eyes and willed him to understand. "I'm sorry."

He frowned. "Me, too." Was there a coldness to his words or was she imagining it?

Shayna didn't know. If there was, it was just one more burden she'd have to carry—and another of her own making.

Just like losing Dylan.

A long moment of tortured silence followed. She didn't know what else to say, and Billy certainly wasn't making any effort to make this easier for her. Not that he owed her anything. Which just left her with turning away and walking out of his room.

Her mind momentarily debated collecting her clothing from downstairs, but she couldn't take the chance that he'd follow her down and question her again.

Unlike Billy and her brother, Shayna wasn't brave. Which was a really freaking sucky thing to realize about yourself.

Instead, she went straight for the bathroom to get ready for bed, and then she dashed for her room and closed herself in.

And when she couldn't fall asleep, she pulled out her laptop and started searching for an apartment of her own.

SHAYNA WAS the first one to emerge from her room on Sunday morning, proving that she was far braver than Billy.

A little after nine, he heard the shower in the hall bath come on, and a short while after that, her footsteps moved past his room and descended the stairs.

He'd been awake for two hours mindlessly scrolling through the *happy happy, joy joy* of other people's perfect online lives when he finally threw off the covers and made for the bathroom, his back on fucking fire from the way he'd tossed and turned all night.

But that was what being a total asshole did to his sleep, apparently. He never should've—

Staring at himself in the bathroom mirror, he chuffed out a laugh of disgust. At himself. Because the list of things *he never should've* was about a mile and a fuck long.

He never should've touched Shayna again.

He never should've given in to the desire he'd had for her pretty much since the minute she'd dropped that fucking towel. And it wasn't just that he'd seen her naked. He wasn't a complete animal, after all. It was that in the wake of that moment she'd been brave and funny and self-deprecating and easy going and it had obviously really fucking *charmed* him. Like a goddamn spell.

He never should've gotten her naked again because what little willpower he possessed where this woman was concerned had no chance whatsoever when confronted with the bare curves and hidden secrets of her gorgeous body.

He never should've put his mouth on her, because now she was even deeper inside him than she'd already been, and all he had to do was lick his lips and the memory of her sweetness was right there again, filling his senses and heating his blood and making him *want*.

But, having crossed all those lines, he never should've

spoiled the amazing feeling of holding her sated body against his —for once—sated body by expecting her to get even more intimate. As someone who'd more than a few times used sex as an escape, he knew as well as anyone that fucking was not always the most intimate thing that could happen between two people.

Shayna Curtis had a secret. One that scared her. Bad.

He hadn't needed any special instincts or skills to see her near-panic as she'd high-tailed it off his bed and out of his room last night. And seeing that fear both tore him up inside for her and made him want to smash his head into a goddamn wall. Because in his selfish need to find someone who might understand the poisonous guilt he carried inside him, he'd pushed her away.

Billy of all people should've known better. He braced his hands against the counter and hung his head.

As if she hadn't bared enough of herself already.

Not just in getting naked and sharing her body with him. Not just in letting him find his pleasure in her mouth. But also in admitting before the first piece of clothing had even hit the floor that she'd always had a crush on him. So she'd already laid some not insignificant emotion on the table.

Yet he'd pushed for more.

He wondered what awesome curse words she'd come up with for him overnight. Whatever they were, he deserved them.

Fuck, how was he going to make this right?

Another thought followed close behind. One that either made him an even bigger asshole or, just maybe, one that had him finally on the path to doing the right thing.

Maybe he shouldn't make it right. Maybe he should let her stay mad at him. Keep her distance. Until it was time for her to move on.

Something panged inside his chest hard enough that it caught his breath. Because if her living here had highlighted how fucking starved for company and companionship he'd been, what the hell was her leaving again going to throw some much unwanted light upon?

With that thought, Billy hit the shower and wondered how else he might yet fuck things up with his best friend's sister.

Fifteen minutes later, he was dressed and coming downstairs with nearly the same mix of determination and trepidation with which he might've approached the hideout of a suspected terrorist. He wasn't even at the bottom of the steps when he saw Shayna heading for the back door, a big camera bag on her shoulder.

"Hey," he said, rounding the plate-glass bannister. "Where you heading?"

She paused at the door and peered over her shoulder at him. And, *fuck*, the wariness there cut him deep. *You put that there, Parrish.*

"Oh, hey. Uh, work, actually. My editor called and asked me to fill in for someone who was supposed to cover a community event over in Southwest today."

Standing there at the door, she looked not a little badass in a pair of jeans, black T-shirt, with a pair of black sunglasses on her head and the camera bag on her shoulder. And fucking hot, too. Which was exactly the kind of thing he shouldn't be noticing but couldn't help noticing.

"Sorry you got called in on a Sunday." It was the least thing he should be apologizing for.

She shook her head. "I'm pretty psyched about it."

He crossed to the kitchen counter, but no closer. Both because he didn't trust himself and because she was throwing off that wariness like a fucking wall. "Well, go knock 'em dead then."

"Yeah." She nodded. "Okay. Well. See ya." She gave him another long look.

"See ya, Shay," he said, looking right back.

Whole conversations passed between them. He just didn't know what any of them meant.

Then she was gone. And it took everything he had inside him not to go after her. Because he had the shittiest, most foreboding feeling that she was never coming back. Which was bullshit, of course. And just a reflection of how bad he'd screwed up.

Not to mention a total gut check that he shouldn't let it happen again.

CHAPTER TWELVE

Was it bad luck to look for shelter on a website that otherwise featured offers of stained sofas and people seeking other people via dick pics and screeds in all-caps? Shayna really hoped not as she stood in front of the three-story brownstone which had a basement sublet that she'd found on that site.

After she'd gotten home yesterday from covering the unveiling of a new heritage walking trail in Southwest DC, she'd picked up where she'd left off the night before—looking at apartment listings and making some appointments to begin seeing them.

It was not going to be easy.

There were so many ways that housing could go wrong: crazed roommates with weird habits, unseen bugs, evil landlords, a family of rats taking up residence in your walls, or a whole host of weird noises, smells, or other quirks of an apartment you'd only learn about once you lived there.

All of which were among the reasons why she'd ruled out finding an apartment from a distance before she ever got to DC.

And if all of that weren't enough, there was the intense competition for the best places. Shayna had already had one appointment cancel on her for a $950 studio near Gallaudet University in Upper Northeast—rented by someone else before she'd even seen it. And it had literally been the only available apartment under a thousand dollars per month located in the parts of the city where she most wanted to live.

If she absolutely had to, she could maybe go as high as $1,250 a month, but beyond that and she'd be in a position of deciding between repaying her student loans and eating.

Which brought her to the basement in the brownstone. She knocked on the front door, and a middle-aged woman almost immediately answered, a man hovering right behind her.

"Hi, I'm Shayna Curtis. I'm here about the sublet?"

"Hi, I'm Brenda, and this is my husband, Robert. Come on in," the woman said. "Of course, the apartment has its own entrance, too. So, you wouldn't come in this way typically."

Shayna nodded and tried to peer around their part of the house just to get a feel for them. It was old in that quaint sort of way, but clean and nicely decorated. It gave her hope.

In the kitchen, Brenda unlocked a door, revealing a set of steps down.

There was no lock on the inside. That was the first thing Shayna noticed. So they could lock her out of the upstairs, but she couldn't do the same.

Still, she determined to keep an open mind. They hovered as they hit the basement, pointing things out and watching her as she looked around the one-bedroom apartment. It was a cave with a low ceiling, small windows, white-cinder-block walls, and a beige carpet that had seen better days, but it was fairly spacious and the bathroom included a combined washer/dryer unit.

"Rent includes utilities except for phone and cable," Brenda said. "We just ask that if you have to hold parties here, they end by eleven o'clock. It's an old house and sound can travel." Robert was still standing there, having not yet said a word. Which was a little weird. But, whatever.

Shayna nodded. "And it's $1,050?"

Brenda arched an imperious eyebrow. "Yes. Is that going to be a problem?"

Annnd now the apartment was decorated in attitude.

Whoa, bitchtits. That's what Shayna thought. But what she said was, "No, not at all." Because she could make this place work despite its cave-like qualities. "I have a few other appointments set up, but I should know within the next few days."

The woman sighed audibly. "Very well. But know *we* have other appointments, too."

"Of course," Shayna said, itching to get out of there. She made for the door to what would be her private entrance, and the landlords followed. "Thank you for your time. Your apartment definitely has a lot of what I'm looking for."

"Good luck," the woman said, opening the door for her. Was she imagining it or was the man pleading with his eyes? The dynamic between them was kinda creepy.

"Thanks." Shayna jogged up the steps, feeling like she could finally breathe again. She made for the metro station for another appointment, unsure what to think about the place she'd just seen.

"Miss? Hey, miss?" came a voice from behind her.

She turned to find a woman about her age jogging toward her. Covered in colorful tattoos and a face full of piercings. "Yes?" Shayna asked, wary.

The woman caught her breath and began gesturing. "I know you don't know me, but I saw you come out of the basement apartment at 519." Shayna nodded though she had no idea what to expect next. "The couple who owns that place fights all the time. Like knock-down, drag-out fights. Everyone on the block can hear them. People call the cops on them but nothing ever seems to happen. I just thought you should know."

Shayna's jaw about hit the street. *It's an old house and sound can travel...* "Holy crap, thank you for telling me. I was tempted by that place."

"No worries," the woman said, already retreating. "Sorry to be the bearer of bad news."

"I really appreciate it," she called back, putting her hand to her forehead. Well *that* was a freaking near miss.

Which put her on edge as she knocked on door number two across town, a sublet of a one-bedroom plus den apartment. The woman had said she could have the bedroom, so at least Shayna would have a door.

This time when she knocked, a girl in pigtails and pajamas answered. A girl who was at least college-aged based on the conversation they'd had in advance, but who appeared much younger. "Hey, you Shayna?" she said by way of greeting.

"Yeah? Corinne?"

The woman yawned and nodded as she waved her in, and Shayna could immediately smell the cat. "So, this is the place," Corinne mumbled as she shuffled her fuzzy slippers against the badly scuffed wood floors.

They passed the galley-style kitchen first, which was a little messy but not terrible, before arriving into the living room with attached den.

And *Jeebus fannyflaps Christmas*. The living room was a seven-layer dip of actual carpet, cat hair, discarded clothing, gum and PopTart wrappers, magazines, and hairbands. The coffee table bore the load of more than a few dishes growing their own ecosystems.

"This is the shared space and my room's beyond the curtain," Corrine said, still mumble-showing her the apartment despite Shayna's growing freak-out. "Your room is there." She pointed to a mostly closed door near the den.

Shayna was afraid to look. Like, legit had no idea what to expect.

She pushed the door open and was hit by a wall of acrid cat urine odor. Because the litterbox sat against one wall. Otherwise, it was empty. Unless you counted the tiny ants parading across the windowsill and the bug carcasses in the grimy ceiling light fixture. Stomach dropping, Shayna peered out the window and wasn't at all surprised to find a view of an alley.

"I appreciate your time, Corinne. But I think I have too much stuff to fit here. I'm a photographer so—"

"Yeah, okay. Whatever. Can you see yourself out?" she said, collapsing into the futon couch.

"Uh, sure."

Out on the street again, Shayna didn't know whether to laugh or cry. She almost wished someone had been with her so that she could've gotten a reality check about whether all that craziness had actually happened.

Thank God she hadn't tried to rent a place sight unseen before she'd arrived in DC, because if she'd have been locked into either of the two places she'd visited tonight, it would've been terrible.

She arrived home at nearly eight o'clock still feeling a little shell-shocked. Billy stood at the stove sautéing vegetables in a big wok.

"Hey," she said, too fuzzy-headed to remember that things were weird between them. From the way she'd broken her word to talk to him and run out of his room in the middle of a near panic-attack. After they'd given each other oral sex.

Amazing oral sex. Like, *mind-blowing* oral sex.

And then her past had caught up with her and ruined everything. Like it always did. On a sigh, she dropped into a chair at the breakfast bar. "That smells good," she said, realizing she hadn't eaten. Although dish ecosystems didn't necessarily inspire an appetite.

Billy was studying her, a wariness in his eyes that she couldn't quite read. "Want some? I made plenty. It's just chicken and vegetables in soy sauce. And I steamed some rice."

"Sounds amazing," she said, heavily dropping her purse onto the chair beside her. Scrolling through her phone, she saw that a few other potential roommates and landlords had responded to her inquiries and wanted to set up meetings.

"You okay?" Billy asked after a long moment.

"Um, yeah. I, uh..." She put down her phone. No way could she respond to anyone in her current frame of mind. "I went to see a couple of apartments and they were legitimately terrible."

The pan knocked loudly against the stove like Billy had nearly dropped it. "Sorry," he said, intently stirring the veggies. "Apartment hunting already? No, uh, no rush, you know."

"I appreciate that," she said, her belly doing a little flip. Because she wasn't sure if she believed him after their fight—or whatever it had been—on Saturday night. Or maybe he did mean it because Saturday just hadn't been that big of a deal to him? Shayna really didn't know. "But it's obviously going to take a while, so I figured I shouldn't wait until the very last second."

Billy nodded as he turned off the burner and set the pan aside. He scooped out a portion of rice for each of them and topped it with the stir fry. "Did you go alone, Shay?" he asked as he settled a plate in front of her.

She moved her purse from the other chair to make room for him and dropped it to the floor. "Yeah. I mean, I was meeting with women so it seemed okay."

He sat and dug into his first bite. "I know it's none of my business, but I think you should take someone with you."

"Really?" No doubt, it would be more fun to do with someone, but it wasn't like she couldn't handle herself.

He threw her a look that was almost hilariously identical to one Ryan might've given her. Typical overprotective Rangers.

She shrugged as she savored how perfectly he'd sautéed the vegetables. Sexy *and* a good cook. It was a killer combination. To say nothing of the fact that he was, without question, also a trained killer. Maybe that shouldn't be hot, but it was in a heroic soldier kinda way.

She glanced at him and caught him licking sauce off his lip, which reminded her of what else he was good at doing...

Because, *dear God*, that man's mouth was *lethal*.

He frowned at the way she was looking at him, and she ducked her chin. "Well, no worries, I'm being careful. I even have pepper spray in my purse—a gift from Ryan."

"Which is great if you have time to fish it out from the bottom of your bag or unless someone jumps you from behind," he said, eyebrow arched.

She made a face at him. "Well, thanks, numbnuts, I wasn't worried about that *before*."

"Sorry, I'm not trying to freak you out, but I'm kinda wired to think through and prepare for the worst-case scenario."

She softened at that because of course he was. "You don't have to be sorry. And it would be fun to have a wingman to look with. But I don't really know that many people here yet. And I hate to feel like I'm impos—"

"Seriously?"

His tone made her look at him again, and his expression called all kinds of bullshit on her. "What's that for?"

His eyebrow arched higher. "I told you I'd help you with whatever you needed."

Her belly went on a loop-the-loop. "You're doing enough."

"Shayna."

"What? I wasn't going to bother you after..." She couldn't figure out the best way to finish the thought, so she let her words trail off. She didn't need to spell it out for him to know what she was talking about.

"Fuck." He dropped his fork noisily against his plate. Shayna's heart tripped into a sprint. "This was why I shouldn't have started something with you. Because I was an asshole and now you're too uncomfortable with me to ask for what you need. And my helping you getting settled in here was the whole point of this arrangement." He put a hand on her arm. "I'm sorry, Shayna. I know you're pissed and you have every right to be, but—"

"Wait. What?" She blinked at him as she struggled to take in everything he'd said and figure out her reaction to all of it. "That's not...I'm not mad at you. I thought you were mad at me. And that you had every right to be."

His whole handsome face slid into a frown. "Why the hell would I be mad at you?"

"You're not?"

"No. Jesus. I was a pushy, invasive asshole."

Relief flooded through Shayna so hard and so fast that she grasped the edge of the counter. "I thought you were disappointed in me for going back on my word and running away."

Billy shook his head. "I shouldn't have said that. It wasn't fair. And it wasn't the right time to bring any of that up."

"Oh," she said, a burning sensation suddenly tingling against the backs of her eyes. He *wasn't* mad at her. Wow. Okay. But why was it impacting her this way?

She glanced down at her plate again, blinking fast to try to stem the tears before they started. And then the answer smacked her in the face—this emotional letdown was because of how scared she'd been to lose Billy from her life *altogether*. Because she'd already had quite enough loss in her life as it was.

"Hey. I'm really fucking sorry, Shay."

"Me, too," she managed.

He pulled away, picked up his fork again, and took a big bite. "So, consider me your wingman whenever you need."

The sweetness of the offer was *not* helping get rid of the sting in her eyes. Or the ballooning warmth in her chest.

"My wingman and my muscle?" She gave him a hesitant smile, part of her not quite believing that they were okay and therefore not quite sure he'd appreciate the humor.

He frowned for a moment and then his whole expression morphed into amusement as he remembered that earlier exchange.

He smirked at her. "You better fucking believe it."

OVER THE PAST TEN DAYS, Billy had accompanied Shayna to see three apartments. One with a roommate and two studio apartments without.

And Billy was fucking horrified at the idea of Shayna living in any place remotely similar to what he'd so far seen.

There'd been the studio above the fish store that fucking smelled like death in the heat of the afternoon. There'd been the very clean but twelve-by-twelve windowless box of a studio.

Which just, no. Fuck, no.

And there'd been the sublet with the horror show bathroom, in which the toilet was covered in pubes and the shower surround was outlined in furry mold. Billy had nearly wanted to puke.

No, no, and no.

And that was to say nothing of what she called the 'cave basement' and 'seven-layer-dip' apartments she'd seen without him.

So far, Shayna was oh for five.

He felt bad for her because she was clearly frustrated and nervous about finding something. But there was also a part of him that fucking prayed every new place would be a nightmare before they walked through the door.

Because something was happening inside him—the more time he spent with her, the less he wanted her to go.

It wasn't just the apartment hunting, it was that they'd go to dinner after, and Billy would get to try to cheer her up. They ate good food and had interesting conversations and he got to go to bed at night knowing he'd made Shayna Curtis smile. Which was maybe a stupid fucking thing to feel so satisfied about, but he couldn't deny that it hit him that way—like he was doing something important, something *meaningful*.

She'd also come to WFC with him again—in large part because she'd wanted to have the chance to see his friends at least once more, and last Saturday was the last day of her week-long visitors' pass. But it made him wonder if she maybe saw herself moving on from not just his house, but his life—and hell if that didn't poke at some uncomfortable shit within his chest that he was avoiding examining too closely.

And when they weren't out visiting potential apartments, they were at home on the couch or at the breakfast bar looking at listings together, because the dearth of decent housing options that she could afford was making him fucking crazy.

In all that time spent together, they *talked*. They talked about everything.

It was only a slight exaggeration to think that he'd had more deep, consequential conversations with Shayna during the weeks since she'd moved in than with any other single person since he'd discharged from the military.

So much of his life operated at the surface these days.

He was coasting through a job he was good at but didn't

love. He had friends, but not as many close friends as he'd once had. And outside of WFC, there was nothing in his life about which he felt passionate anymore. Once, that'd been the military and the mission and the Ranger creed. Now, he wasn't sure he gave "one-hundred-percent and then some" to anything like a Ranger pledged himself to do.

Amid all that superficial bullshit, his time and conversations with Shayna stood out as different. Deeper. Important.

Even though the one conversation Billy was dying to have with her they still hadn't had. About her secret. He'd learned his lesson there.

If and when Shayna was ready to talk to him about the burden she bore, she'd let him know. Maybe she wouldn't ever be ready, but he was familiar enough with burdens to know that he couldn't force her to share it. As much as he wanted to know, he had to be okay with that.

Which brought them to apartment number four, for him. A fourth-floor walk-up near Catholic University, which he liked because it wasn't too far from his house. It was a two-bedroom place and a sublet, and the potential roommate was a thirty-year-old woman who worked as an administrative assistant. Shayna had threatened to smother him with a pillow if he ran a background check.

He'd run one anyway, she just didn't know it.

"Maybe sixth time's a charm," she said hopefully.

"Well, to find out what's behind door number six, you gotta knock," he said.

She did. A woman opened the door wearing a smile. "You must be Shayna. Come in. I'm Clara."

"Hi, Clara. Thank you. This is my friend, Billy. He's along for the apartment-hunting ride with me." They all shook and made the necessary pleasant noises, and then he and Shay followed Clara from the little hallway into the living room.

Billy nearly swallowed his fucking teeth.

Clowns. There were fucking clowns *everywhere*.

Porcelain figurines and stuffed dolls and framed paintings. Like, not a few clowns. Not a squad's worth or a platoon's worth or even a whole goddamn *company* of clowns. Easily a whole fucking *battalion* of clowns inhabited just this one room.

"Oh, wow," Shayna was saying. "How fun is this? How long have you been collecting them?"

Billy blinked at her. Was she serious?

Shay went up to examine a two-foot-tall doll in a stand that had an absolutely grotesque face, its features like wax that had melted. No. No way she thought this was okay. There was a hundred-and-twenty-six-thousand-per-cent chance these fuckers came alive at night and would kill Shayna in her sleep.

And then Ryan would kill Billy. And just fucking no.

"Oh, for years," Clara said, smiling at Shayna's interest. Clown lady crossed the room to a glass cabinet and opened the door. Shay followed at her invitation to see what the woman wanted to show her and threw Billy a glance as she did so.

One that clearly read *help me God!*

Billy just managed to bite back a laugh that he had to cover with a feigned cough.

Finally, Clara led them further into the apartment. Except for the clown infestation, he had to admit this was the nicest of the places they'd seen. The kitchen was decent sized and spotless, which he appreciated. Same with the bathroom.

"This one's my room," Clara said, inviting them to look in... to see more fucking clowns. How could anyone in their right mind sleep with all those clown eyes boring down on them? "And this one would be yours." She pushed open the door.

"Hey, this is a nice size," Shayna said, flipping on the lights and walking into the long rectangular space.

Billy's gut dropped because he wasn't imagining the cautious hope in Shay's voice.

"What's this?" Shayna asked, pointing to a square card table in the far corner. It was the only thing in the room.

Billy walked over to find it covered with beads, candles, incense, and doll-shaped things made of dried husks. No clowns, though. Still, WTF. He reached out a hand to examine a jar filled with strange-looking—

"Don't touch that! Don't ever touch anything on this table. Ever!" Clara yelled, rushing over and worrying over the table like he'd broken an irreplaceable antique.

Billy looked at Shayna's wide eyes and was about two seconds from fucking exfiltrating her right out of this place.

Clara placed a hand to her chest. "I'm sorry. It's just that, this would be your room, Shayna. But a male spirit lives over here."

She gestured to the table, and Billy's gaze followed to look at the empty air over the table with a refrain of *are you fucking shitting me* running through his head.

Clown lady continued, "He's pretty friendly overall. He just occasionally makes things hover or move or fall. But if anything on this table gets touched, well, it's just better not to touch anything on here. *Ever.*" She gave Billy a pointed stare, unblinking for so long that her eyes had to have air-dried.

"O-oh okay. Well, it's such a big room, I'm sure I can share my space," Shayna said, her tone no longer cautiously hopeful. Nope, now it was just south of hysterical. Thank fuck.

Clara smiled. "Oh, good. Well, if you want the room just say the words and it's yours. I think we'd get on well."

"I, um, I have a few more appointments in the next couple days but I am interested and I will be ready to make a decision without too much more delay." She delivered the words in the same rehearsed way she'd said them all the other times her answer was in the negative, so Billy hoped that was the case again here.

They'd only made it to the second-floor landing when Billy grabbed Shay's arm.

She wouldn't meet his eyes. Her head was shaking and her shoulders were shaking and she grabbed his arm right back and hauled him down the steps.

"Not yet. Not yet," she gasped, sputtering with humor she could barely restrain.

Billy grinned. "Fucking clowns," he whispered back. "Like, a whole *fucking army* of clowns."

She held out her hand as if to tell him to stop, and finally they spilled out onto the front sidewalk laughing and crying and gasping for breath.

"The ghost...the ghost table. You should've seen your face when she yelled at you." Shayna clutched her stomach and fell against his arm. Tears streamed down her face, which was red from how hard she was laughing.

She was so fucking pretty. Happy and funny and full of life.

"I know. 'Bout had a goddamn heart attack," he rasped. "But Shay there were *bones* in that jar, I swear to Christ."

She burst into laughter again, so hard that she was leaning nearly all her weight against him, her face buried against his chest. And it felt so damn good.

"Those clowns come to life at night," she managed. "You know they do..."

"Right? I thought that same thing," he choked out, his cheeks hurting from how big and hard he was laughing.

When was the last time *that'd* happened? Fuck. He'd still been in the military. Without question. Not one thing since the ambush had made him laugh like this.

Until Shayna.

"If a clown shows up in our house we'll know it followed us

home from here and I will *die*," she said, chortling and gasping for breath.

"A clown shows up in our fucking house and I'm burning that sonofabitch down."

Our. They'd both said our.

Shayna nodded and wiped at her eyes. "Ooh, lordy. God, I need a burger," she said. "Tell me you're hungry."

"Hell, yes. Food is immediately necessary," he said, his brain still spinning on the *ours*.

"Yes. Yes, it is." They started down the street away from the House of the Clown Army. For fuck's sake.

And, Jesus this all felt good, even as it highlighted that he had this kind of easy, fun rapport with so few other people in his life anymore. Mo and Noah and Sean—they were becoming his new brotherhood.

And Shayna...what was Shayna to him?

Beyond being his best friend's sister, Billy didn't know.

All he knew was that he was feeling torn in two when it came to this woman—torn between letting her go before he crossed anymore lines, and staking a claim and letting the chips fall where they may.

CHAPTER THIRTEEN

It turned out, the choice wasn't going to be his.

"Billy?" Shayna said after they'd finished their burgers and fries and sat contemplating splitting dessert.

"Yeah?" He looked up from the mile-long menu. "You know what you want?"

She dropped her menu to the table and looked at him with a too-serious-to-be-about-ice-cream expression on her face. "Yes. Um, yeah, I think I've figured out something that I want."

He frowned. "This isn't about dessert, is it?"

"No. It's about you. Or us. Or, I don't know, about the fact that we were together and then never really had any conversation about whether that meant anything," she said in a rush.

Wait. She thought there was a chance that hadn't meant anything to him? He'd told her how crazy she made him...

Oooh, fucking hell, had she thought he'd only meant physically? "Shayna—"

"Please." She held up a hand. "Can I just get it out while I'm momentarily brave enough to talk about this?"

He had no idea where she was going, but his intuition was

skating ice down his spine in a feeling of deep, crawling foreboding. "Say it. Whatever it is."

"So, I've been thinking... You've become a really good friend to me these past few weeks—"

Oh, fuck.

"—and even though there's obviously, um, really crazy chemistry between us, I'd like us to be friends. I mean, *just* friends."

Oh, fuuuck. Billy's gut was making a slow slide to the floor.

"I don't have that many here, and no one else who knows Ryan or my life before DC. I don't want to lose that or mess it up. I hated when I thought you were mad at me. Of course, if you thought we were only friends anyway, I probably sound like an idiot right now. But I still wanted to officially let you know what I was thinking. In case there was any question. Or anything." She clenched her eyes shut. "And now I'm going to stop talking forever."

He couldn't even chuckle at her self-deprecating humor. Because she'd just put him in the friend zone. And, in the process, made the debate that had been raging inside him completely meaningless.

Even worse, *her decision* suddenly made one side of that debate a whole lot more compelling. More than that, *obvious.* Like there'd never really been any choice at all and he'd just been too moronic or cowardly to see it.

Wasn't that always the fucking way? It took losing the choice about whether to turn right or left to highlight which path you'd really wanted to go down all along.

Now, a giant neon sign flashed in his brain over *claim Shayna once and for fucking all and figure out the rest as you go.*

Except she'd just pulled the plug.

And sonofabitch, it *was* better this way, wasn't it?

Better for her in so many ways, not the least of which was all the bullshit he clearly hadn't resolved from what'd happened to him in Iraq. Better for his relationship with Ryan. Better for them—him and Shayna—because he'd hated thinking Shayna was mad at him, too. He didn't want to fuck up what he'd found with her either.

"Friends, huh?" he managed as his brain spun and his heart fought the idea.

She gave a nervous shrug. "Yeah."

He inhaled a deep breath, manned up, and did the right thing—finally. "I'm honored to be your friend, Shayna. Of course. But for the record, our night together absofuckinglutely meant something to me."

He was willing to let her go if he had to, but he wasn't willing to let her think he hadn't cherished the hell out of being with her.

Her gaze whipped up and he saw the confusion there. And maybe a little disbelief, too.

Which were two more reasons why respecting her wishes and quashing his belatedly apparent ones was the right thing to do. He'd screwed up that night with her enough that he'd left her doubting. If that wasn't all his failings and insecurities in a nutshell, he didn't know what was.

"But friends is great. So, *friend*, what are we having for dessert?"

When they got home that night, Billy was grateful to find a whole pile of messages in his inbox from new clients confirming that they were hiring him.

The new caseload was going to require all his time, in part because he'd agreed to two short-term surveillance cases—another infidelity case and a workers' comp case to investigate the validity of the injury. And in the vein of *when it rains, it pours*, he had an offer from a law firm to do surveillance in another case where he'd be gathering evidence for an upcoming trial. Add to that four new background checks he still had to do and Billy was going to be a busy fucking boy.

He didn't think he'd ever juggled so many cases at one time.

God bless referrals from former clients and the network of veterans who had each other's backs in the civilian world just like they'd done on the battlefield. And since new jobs tended to come in fits and starts, he was hesitant to turn any of them down.

But it meant that he wasn't going to be able to spend as much time helping Shayna.

That cut both ways. Good, because it would help ensure the platonic distance between them—and he might need that help given his newfound insight into his own misfit emotions. But bad, too, because he thought it was much safer for her to be doing this with someone at her side.

Billy broke the news to her the next morning. "Hey, Shay," he said, hitting the first floor wearing sleep pants and a T-shirt.

"You're up early." God, her smile was pretty.

And he was a fucking idiot. It was maybe the hundredth time he'd thought that since their talk the night before.

On a sigh, he slid into a chair at the breakfast bar. "Wanted to let you know that I picked up a bunch of new cases, two of which are surveillance. It's going to cut into my schedule for the next stretch of days. Not sure how long just yet."

"Oh, okay." She poured herself some coffee. "Want some?"

"No, thanks," he said, earning a pair of raised eyebrows from her. "Gonna try to grab a few more hours sleep before I head out since I'll be pulling nights for a while again."

"More sleep is good. Your last surveillance case kinda trashed you. I'm a little worried about how you're going to juggle two." She sipped at her coffee, then added more milk.

"I'm not sure either yet, which is why my wingman availability's up in the air." Wingman. He didn't want to be her wingman. Or, at least, not *only*. Goddamnit, Parrish.

"I'll see if Havana can come with me. Right now I just have one tonight and another tomorrow night on my calendar."

"That's good. I really don't love the idea of you going into strange apartments by yourself."

Shayna smirked. "I suppose that makes sense. I mean, you never know when someone might pull a gun on you and scare you so bad that you drop your towel."

He lovingly gave her the finger. "*That* is the perfect example of why you shouldn't go off somewhere on your own, woman."

"Yeah, but you turned out to be completely normal," she said with a laugh.

"If I'm normal then your fucking meter needs recalibrated." Billy grinned despite himself. "Okay, just wanted to touch base with you before my schedule goes haywire. Sorry I'm not available like I told you I would be."

"I understand you have a life that, you know, doesn't revolve around me twenty-four/seven. The nerve!" She winked at him.

Fucking *winked* at him. After making a joke about the extent to which their lives revolved around each other.

She could've just punched a hole through his sternum and squeezed his heart and it would've been less uncomfortable then the irony-laden taunt. "What can I say?" he managed. "Shoot me texts and keep me posted though, okay?"

"You got it," she said.

"Have a good day at work." Billy slid off his stool and made for bed for just a few more hours. "And let me know what your friend says about going with you."

"Ten-four, good buddy."

He smirked over his shoulder. "Now who's the fucknugget?"

"Touché." Her laughter lit up the room and the inside of his chest. Just like it always did. But that was something else he'd now be keeping to himself.

SHAYNA WENT to find Havana when she got to work on Thursday morning. She was bummed that Billy wouldn't be able to go apartment hunting with her, because they always had so much fun together. On the other hand, maybe it was good to get a break from him, because she wanted him so damn bad that she could barely stand it.

Which made it especially impressive that she'd managed to deliver her let's-be-friends speech.

His friendship and companionship had really come to mean a lot to her over the past few weeks, and she didn't want to risk losing it. The certainty of that friendship was more important than the long-shot of a relationship with him, especially when nothing more had happened between them, he'd never said anything about being with her, and it had sucked so bad thinking that he'd been mad at her when he wasn't. Shayna had therefore decided to make the call and put the whole were-they-or-weren't-they question to rest once and for all.

And Billy had readily agreed.

Which made her even more glad that she'd done it, even though her head clearly had very little control over her heart. Or her traitorous body, for that matter...

On a sigh, she rounded the corner into Havana's cubicle and found it empty. A lady at the next desk popped up and said, "She's in a design meeting."

"Oh, okay. Thanks." Frowning, Shayna hustled back to her own desk. She'd handed in an assignment the afternoon before and expected to get something new first thing today. Sure enough, she had an email from her editorial team sitting in her inbox, so her butt had no more than hit the cushion of her chair before she was right back up again to meet Joe and Rose in the conference room with one of the reporters who Shayna didn't yet know very well.

"Hi," she said, coming into the room. "Hope I didn't hold everyone up."

"No, we all just got here," her news editor, Joe, said. "Shayna, do you know Andy Katz yet?"

"No. Hi, Andy." She extended her hand and they shook.

"Hey, Shayna. Looking forward to working with you."

They all took their seats, and her belly did a little flip in anticipation of learning about the new assignment.

"Andy," Joe began, "why don't you share the feature idea you pitched?"

The man nodded. Probably in his forties with round wire-framed glasses and salt-and-pepper hair, he had a kind face and a passionate energy about him. "It's on the Big Brothers Big Sisters program, which pairs volunteers with area school-aged kids to provide additional mentoring, support, and opportunities for new experiences."

Shayna smiled. This was going to be fun.

"I want to profile some of the matched bigs and littles. Talk about how the program is changing kids' lives. Interview parents about the ways that the program supports them and their families. Track down alumni of the program to do where-are-they-now follow-ups and gather their reflections about how being a little impacted their lives. All leading up to a gala fundraiser they have in a few weeks," Andy said, his enthusiasm absolutely infectious.

Her picture editor, Rose, sat forward. "Shayna, everyone here has seen the photos you took for the heritage trail unveiling event and we thought you'd make a good fit for this assignment."

Shay gave herself an inner fist pump, because her morning was totally looking up.

Andy nodded. "In fact, you've already met one of the big-little pairs I want to feature. Josiah Johnson and his sixth-grader little, Barry Huss."

"Of course." From the heritage trail event. They'd been at the front of the crowd when the mayor did the ribbon-cutting, and she'd captured a shot of them in profile looking on as the mayor grasped the ribbon.

Conversation with them had followed afterward, because it turned out that Barry was really interested in cameras and photography. So he'd been completely excited to let her get another shot of him, this time with his little black hand pointing up at one of the heritage trail signs that had a picture of the former slave and civil rights activist Frederick Douglass on it.

The latter photograph was her first that had appeared in the printed *Gazette*, the cut-out of which was now framed and sitting on her desk. "What a small world."

"It is. And you made a good impression," Andy said. "Some of these families are going to be shy about talking, and Josiah thought you were great with his little." Inside, Shayna was squeeing so hard.

Rose slid her a sheet of paper. "This is a preliminary list of names, contact information, and events to cover. The program is going to be emailing everyone on the list that you two might be in contact for the story, so that should lay some groundwork." Shayna scanned it over, nearly chomping at the bit to get started, even as the length of the list meant she was going to be running her ass off for the next few weeks. Which, bring it on!

"I'll email you more names as they emerge," Andy said. "The first thing to note is the back-to-school Little Celebration at the Northeast Recreation Center on Sunday. Is that going to be doable for you?"

She nodded and made a mental note to move an appointment for an apartment she was scheduled to see on Sunday afternoon. "Yes, no problem. I live not too far from there and I'm available all day."

"Good," Andy said. "It's like a festival with food and games and a moon bounce and a DJ, so it'll be a good opportunity to meet some of the families in a laid-back environment."

A *lot* about journalism rested on relationship-building, and this event was going to be a perfect first step for gaining the trust of everyone involved. "This all sounds great. I'm really excited to get to work on this."

She spent the morning making calls and sending emails, and only when her stomach growled around twelve thirty did she realize she hadn't asked Havana if she was up for a probably crazy house-hunting adventure. Shayna found her in the lounge, eating lunch and reading a book. Leah and Malik were there, too.

"Hi, everyone," she said as she threw leftover stir fry into the microwave. They all made small-talk while she waited for her bowl to spin round and round, and then she joined Havana at her table.

"Hey, girl. How's apartment hunting going?" Havana turned her book face down, revealing an intriguing black-and-white cover of a beautiful woman in profile wearing a glittering crown.

"What is *that*?" Shayna asked, spinning the book so that she could read the title. *The Controversial Princess*.

"It's a romance about the daughter of the king of England who has a torrid affair with a hot American actor. It entirely fictionalizes the royal family and it's rocking my world."

"Ooh, I might need to borrow that when you're done," Shayna said, waggling her brows.

"Why not read a book about the actual royal family?" Malik asked, grinning as he came over to take a look.

Havana smirked up at him. "Because I've read every freaking thing that exists about the real royal family and I can't get enough. I need more royals. *All* the royals. Damn Harry and Meghan ruined me. I'm obsessed."

Shayna laughed. "It is pretty cool that we have an American princess now."

"Mm-hmm. And I don't even care if Brits wanna say that she can't be Princess Meghan. She's Princess Meghan to me." Havana threw everyone a look that brooked no arguments.

Malik held up his hands in surrender. "You recall that we purposely threw off the monarchy, right?"

Havana was not amused. "Yes, which is why we can now admire it from afar." They all laughed. "So now, back to your apartment-hunting..."

Shayna sighed. "I actually wanted to talk to you about that. I have appointments tonight at six thirty and tomorrow at seven to see some new places. Any chance you can come with me? My roommate's busy, and I'd go myself, but it's more fun with someone. And also it gives me witnesses for the craycray that's out there because you wouldn't believe the half of what I've seen the past few weeks."

Havana's whole face slid into an expression of regret. "Damn, I'm sorry, Shay. I can't. My mom and I are heading out of town tonight for my cousin's wedding on Saturday."

Oh, shoot. Shayna had totally forgotten. "That's right. I knew that. Don't worry about it." She really could go herself. It wasn't that big of a deal, even though she knew Billy wasn't going to be thrilled.

"I'm free," Malik said, shrugging. "I mean, if you want some company."

"Really?" Shay grinned up at him, feeling like she was

slowly building a community—and a life—here. Just like she'd wanted. "I warn you, it's a battlefield out there."

He smirked. "I grew up in NYC. DC is a baby city by comparison."

"Okay, then, you're on."

That afternoon, she texted Billy: *I found a friend from work who can go with me tonight. Just FYI!*

She wasn't sure why she left off that it was a male friend, but given Billy's over-protectiveness, maybe it was for the best.

Barely a minute had passed before he replied: *Good. And good luck. –Wingman*

She stared at that word. It was a cute and funny way to sign off. But it also made her wish that Billy Parrish could be so much more than that to her.

CHAPTER FOURTEEN

"Who calls a studio a two-bedroom apartment?" Malik asked after they left her Thursday night appointment.

Shayna rolled her eyes and shook her head. "Now I know why the listing said two *hyphen* bed *hyphen* room apartment. I thought the second hyphen was a typo." Instead it turned out that someone was really subletting a studio—one room with two beds—and asking $900 a month to do it.

"Damn, I'm sorry, Shayna." They paused out in front of the apartment building that was *not* to be her new home.

"Don't be. Something will come along. At some point. I hope." She chuckled and mentally scratched possibility number seven off the list. "You wanna grab something to eat? My treat."

It was the least she could do, even though the comparison to the routine that she and Billy had created made her miss him something fierce. Which was probably stupid since it'd only been a day since they'd last gone out together.

God, she had it bad, didn't she?

"I'm game to do that tomorrow, but tonight I have to finish a piece so I can have it on my editor's desk before morning," he said, his bright hazel eyes filled with regret.

"Oh, good luck with that, then. And tomorrow sounds great. Thanks again, Malik. I appreciated the company."

He smiled. "I told you I'd be happy to explore the city with you."

Shayna laughed. "Bet you weren't expecting to start with the seediest parts."

They said good-bye at the metro, each of them needing a different line. Forty-five minutes later, Shayna was walking up Farragut carrying a bag of Indian take-out. She found Reuben sitting on his front porch with Ziggy. "Hi, guys," she called out.

"Oh, Shayna. How are you this fine night?" Reuben asked. Zig got up, chased his tail, and barked all at the same time.

She laughed. "I'm okay. I've been trying to find a new apartment but it's surprisingly not that easy."

Reuben waved her in. "Come on and join us if you have a minute."

"I do," she said, greeted by a very happy Ziggy the moment she stepped through the gate. "Hi, Zig," she said, bending down to give him a pet as best she could with the take-out in her arm. As she approached the porch, Reuben went to stand. "Don't get up," she said. "I'm happy with the stoop where I can pet Ziggy."

Smiling and nodding, Reuben settled himself in again. "So what's going on with finding an apartment?"

She put her takeout behind her where Ziggy wouldn't knock it over and gave Reuben the run down. "I've looked at seven places so far, and every place has either had strange personalities or poor conditions. And several more have cancelled before I had a chance to see them because someone else rented them first. Those were probably the good ones." Ziggy pushed his head under Shayna's hand, making her laugh.

"You can't stay with that young man of yours?" Reuben asked.

And there went the laughter. Oh, man, the way he'd

phrased that question did things to her heart. Because Billy wasn't hers. Not by a long shot.

"Billy's happy to let me stay there until I find a place, so he's not rushing me out or anything. But it was always a temporary arrangement—one my brother made for me."

"I see," Reuben said. "Shame, though, 'cause it seems like you two get on real good."

They did. They really did. She took Ziggy's block head into her hands and scratched behind both ears. But it wasn't like Billy wanted a roommate. He hadn't had one before she came. And he'd only taken her in because Ryan had called in a favor.

"Well, I have another place to look at tomorrow night and one more this weekend." Which reminded her that she needed to reschedule Sunday. "So keep your fingers crossed for me."

He nodded. "I'll say a prayer and we'll see if we can't get the big man upstairs to help you out."

She smiled. "Thanks. Hey, have you eaten dinner? I got Indian take-out and have way more than I could possibly eat myself." Given how much she'd been eating out lately with all the evening appointments, she probably shouldn't have splurged when she was coming home anyway, but she'd been tired and craving comfort food after another strike-out.

"No, I haven't. But you should save it for Billy."

"I don't know when or even if he'll be home tonight. He's working some extra shifts for the next few days. I'd love to share it with you."

"Well, okay then. Do you want to eat inside or have me grab some plates and we'll eat picnic style out here?"

Fifteen minutes later, they were settled around Reuben's dining room table using his wife's nice china. He said it was a plenty special occasion for it, which totally charmed Shayna.

His place was tidy and chock-a-block with mementos from a long and eventful life—framed photographs, trophies, kids' art projects, and more. But it also had a quality of stillness in the air that spoke to the likelihood that little had changed inside these walls in many years.

They ate and talked about everything and joked about Ziggy until the sun had gone down and Reuben's daughter had called for her nightly check-in. And Shayna thoroughly enjoyed herself—making her realize that she was going to miss Reuben and Ziggy when she moved.

The thought sent an unexpected shock of sadness through her.

In just a few weeks, she'd come to adore seeing these two each morning as she left for work and many evenings when she came home. Sometimes she took walks with Reuben and Ziggy around the neighborhood, and on a few occasions she'd dropped in just to say hello. They'd become part of her routine, part of her circle, part of the community she was trying to build here.

She'd have to come back over here and visit them. Of course, she would. Then why was she so sad?

That feeling still had its tendrils in her the next evening when she and Malik approached apartment number eight, which was a studio on the fourth floor of a brownstone in Adams Morgan. At $1,200, it was at the top of her price range, but it would be an awesome neighborhood to live in.

A realtor met them at the front door and gave her a big smile. "Hi Shayna, I'm Mark Wilson."

"Hi Mark. Thanks for meeting me tonight. This is my friend, Malik Morrison."

The men shook, and then the realtor guided them up the four flights of stairs. "There is an elevator, but it's currently out of service," Mark said.

She wondered how often that happened. By the time they made it upstairs, Shayna's shirt was sticking to her. The hallways weren't air conditioned and it was stifling on the upper-most floor, where they found two doors.

"This is it right here. 4A." Mark fished through his keys and finally opened the door. "There isn't central air, obviously, but you could buy a window unit."

The room wasn't huge but the place had a lot of character. Despite being a studio, it was L-shaped, so it would give her bed a bit of separation from the rest of the living area. There was a built-in bookcase between the windows, crystal knobs on all the doors, and a really pretty cut-glass light fixture hanging from the ceiling.

"And this is the kitchen," Mark said, flipping on the light switch.

Shayna saw Malik's eyes go wide as he peered in, and she nearly chuckled. It was very likely that the kitchen was in a space that had once been a closet, because that was how wide and deep it was. Which explained why neither the sink, the oven, nor the fridge were the full, normal size.

"It's really cute," she said. Even with its faults, it was the best place she'd seen. She wasn't sure if that was saying much. She peeked into the bathroom next.

"Shayna," Malik whispered. "I don't think I could fit on that toilet without my knees hitting the glass."

She winced. "I see that." The toilet was super close to the shower enclosure.

"I have to test this out," Malik said, amusement plain in his tone. He sat. And promptly cracked both knee caps on the shower door. "Ow. Damn."

Shay couldn't help but laugh. "You knew that was going to happen!"

"I know, but still," he said, standing and rubbing his knees.

They returned to the main room when Shayna suddenly heard footsteps out in the hallway. A door opened and closed.

She remembered the lady from the cave basement saying how sound traveled in old houses, and it was obviously true here, too. Still, that wasn't so bad.

She peered around the space. "So, I'd put my bed there," she said, looking at the nook created by the shorter side of the L. "And I could maybe do a loveseat-sized sofa and a small two-seater table. I'm not sure about my desk, though. Or where I'd store my camera equipment." To say nothing of her hope to set up a darkroom space. "But I could probably figure something out—"

She'd barely pronounced the 'T' in 'out' when it started. A headboard banging against a wall and guttural moans.

Shayna froze. Someone was having sex. From right next door, it sounded like. She looked to Malik and found him wide-eyed and slack-jawed. But it was the realtor who most caught her attention. His face was beet red.

"Is this a regular feature of this apartment, do you know?" she managed.

Mark um'ed and shuffled and wiped at his brow before finally saying, "So, your neighbor is a very nice lady named Lacie, who, um, runs a business out of her, uh, room."

"A business. What kind of a—" Which was when Shayna got it. "She's a *prostitute*?"

"For real?" Malik asked, coming to stand at her side as she faced off with the realtor. She appreciated the support, too. Because this was...not gonna work.

"Uh, well, yes," Mark finally said.

Her shoulders fell as she looked around at the quaint space. Her imaginary furniture layout poofed before her mind's eye.

"Come on, Shayna," Malik said. "You can't put up with all that racket at all hours. And you have no idea what kind of people her johns are."

She nodded. It was a good point and possibly the first time

she was glad that Billy *wasn't* with her. She could only imagine what his reaction would've been.

Outside, she stared up at the place and shook her head. "Too bad I didn't pitch my apartment-hunting journey as a story. I wonder if anyone would even believe it."

Malik gave her a sympathetic look. "You deserve a really nice dinner somewhere. Do you like Italian?"

"I love Italian," she said, grateful for the distraction from her housing woes.

Thirty minutes later, they were seated at a table in a below-street-level Italian restaurant in Georgetown, famed for its celebrity sightings, over-the-top Victorian décor, giant portion sizes, and—Shayna stared at the massive devil and skeleton dog hanging from the ceiling just to her right—all-out holiday decorations. Despite the fact that it was only late September, the place was *full-on* Halloween. Everywhere she looked.

It was fun and ridiculous, and it gave the space a shadowy, candlelit atmosphere that was also kinda romantic. Which of course made her wonder if Billy had ever been there. Because Shayna was a glutton for punishment. Obviously.

"I wonder when their Christmas decorations go up?" she mused, peering around.

Malik chuckled as he opened his book-like menu. "Probably the minute these come down."

She grinned as she flipped through the huge array of choices. Everything looked amazing. After they placed their orders, Shayna asked, "How'd your story go last night?"

"Got it done," Malik said. "And my editor only had a few changes so I'm feeling pretty good about it."

"Oh, good for you. What was it about?"

They talked shop until their dinners arrived. Her eyes went wide as she took in the absolute mound of gnocchi della mamma on her plate. "We could've shared this."

"Or fed a small village," Malik said, digging into his tortelloni stuffed with braised beef brisket in a sauce of pine nuts, mushrooms, butter, and cream.

"I'm a big fan of leftovers, though." Shayna moaned around a bite.

"You'll definitely get a couple meals out of this then. See? I knew this place would lift your spirits."

"It really has. Thank you." Shay grabbed a piece of Italian bread and dipped it in the amazing meat sauce. "Speaking of spirits…"

The comical look on Malik's face made her laugh.

"That reminds me of one of the apartments I saw earlier in the week. In fact—" She peered around at the gabillion ornate Halloween decorations filling every available space, many of them big standing witch, vampire, or mummy figures, among others. "—this whole place reminds me of that apartment."

"I think I'm scared," Malik deadpanned.

"But which would've scared you *more*? The table full of voodoo-looking items in what would've been *my* bedroom because my would-be roommate believed a mostly friendly male spirit inhabited the room? Or the approximately ten thousand clown figurines and decorations that filled the living room, some of which were disturbing enough to have fit in here as Halloween decorations?"

"Where are you *finding* these places?" he asked.

"I don't know," she said with a chuckle. "On roommate-finder websites and Craigslist and one realty site that specializes in rentals and sublets." She shrugged. "So? Ghosts or clowns?"

"Uh-uh," he said around a bite and shaking his head. "Both are a nope for me. Just no. No. No. Nope. No way." He nailed her with a stare.

"Yeah, that was pretty much Billy's reaction, too."

"So, Billy's the current roommate, right?" he asked.

"Yeah. Well, it was never the plan for me to be his room-mate. He served in the Army Rangers with my brother, who asked him if he'd put me up for a few weeks until I found a place of my own. I'm crashing in his office."

"Oh," Malik said, shaking his head. "And you can't stay there, then?"

Okay, universe, you can stop having people ask me that any time now! Kthxbai.

Shayna shook her head. "Not forever, no." In addition to the other reasons she'd laid out for why her arrangement at Billy's was temporary came the realization that, despite knowing how challenging of a time she was having, he'd never offered for her to stay.

Which was the first time that she'd ever had *that* thought. And it was really freaking depressing.

No, he hadn't offered. Which, fine, was his right. Didn't make it suck any less, though. Crap, how had it taken her so long to realize that?

"Well, this might be crazy, Shayna, but I have an extra room in my rowhouse. It's three bedrooms, one of which I use as an office. But the third room's just sitting empty. It's only me. And you'd be more than welcome for however long you'd like to stay. Being roommates could be fun."

She blinked. "What?"

Malik grinned. "I don't think I have too many strange quirks, except maybe that I'm a rabid Giants fan. And I pick the green M&Ms out of the bag first. And every once in a while, my family might invade. There are a lot of them."

She blinked again. Malik...was offering. "Malik, that's amazingly generous of you but I can't invade your home."

He shrugged. "Why not? It's a nice, safe place and we could work out rent and all that. We already know each other and know we'd get along."

She shook her head, completely overwhelmed by how nice this offer was. "I don't think I could afford my fair share of a three-bedroom rowhouse." And it wouldn't truly feel like she was on her feet if she was still accepting hand-outs from a friend, would it?

"Shayna, not to be gauche, but I made a lot of money on Wall Street. I don't need a roommate or to share expenses. So, we can figure out what would be doable and fair."

Dropping her fork to her plate, she sat there, kinda gobsmacked. Could she really do this? Was it possible that she'd just found her new roommate? Would it be weird to live with a colleague? Her head was spinning a little at the unexpected turn of events and all the questions that came with it.

"Oh, I guess I should tell you I'm gay, in case that matters. Not that there's a boyfriend in the picture, but, you know, hopefully someday there will be." He winked at her.

Shayna burst into tears.

"Oh, hell," he said, reaching across the table to hand her a clean napkin. "I've had girls be disappointed before when I had to tell them I wasn't interested, but this is new."

She laughed through her tears. "No, no. Of course, I don't mind that you're gay. I'm crying because I didn't realize how heavily this situation had been weighing on my shoulders until you just lifted it off for a moment. I...I don't even know what to say." She wiped her face.

"You don't have to say anything right now. I'll show you my place. We can negotiate rent. And you can think about it. I know you have some other places you were scheduled to see, right?"

She nodded.

"Well, if you like one of those, great. If not, you know where to find me." He grinned. "Okay?"

"Okay," she said. "Are you sure you don't want to change your mind after this?" She waved the tear-soaked napkin.

Malik laughed. "Nah. It's not every day I get to be someone's white knight. I'm kinda digging it."

That made her laugh, too. "Thank you."

He shook his head. "Don't worry about it. Now, do you want to split a dessert or are we each getting one of our own?"

"Um, I say we both get one so that we can have some of each."

"You see, that's a very good point." He tapped at his temple and then pointed at her. "We're going to make a good team, I can tell."

"Should we go look at the desserts?" she asked, remembering the massive glass case they'd passed when they'd come in.

"Hell, yes." Malik got her chair for her as she rose.

And then they picked out the decadent chocolate truffle cake and the cookies and cream mousse cake. Malik had debated the cheesecake, and she was really glad he hadn't gotten it. She'd had enough reminders of Billy as it was.

Which made her wonder when she'd have the chance to tell him about her potential new situation. Or what he'd think about her living with another man.

CHAPTER FIFTEEN

"You ready to tell me what's going on with you?" Noah asked Billy as they hit the locker room after WFC on Saturday afternoon.

"I'll second that," Mo said, revealing just how shitty his performance had been out there today. Had everyone noticed? For fuck's sake.

Billy probably shouldn't have taken the time away from his cases to come to the club. But forty-eight hours of being alone doing surveillance had left him nothing to do but sit and spin on his fucking mistakes. Naturally, he felt like a powder keg about to explode.

He'd needed the release. Even though he didn't have the focus or discipline of mind right now to achieve it.

And it'd shown. Obviously. Sonofabitch.

Hands on his hips, Billy dropped his eyes away from Noah's and Mo's too-perceptive gazes, hung his head, and swallowed back a growl of frustration. "I fucked something up."

"What kinda something?" Mo asked.

Billy glared. He didn't want to talk about Shayna. Or how

his failure to make a decision, to admit his own fucking feelings, even to himself, and to ensure she knew where she stood with him had lost him a chance at something—*someone*—he really wanted. Her.

But apparently, his silence was its own kind of answer, because Mo said, "With Shayna?"

He did growl then. Turning away from his friends, he raked his fingers through his hair and scrubbed his hands over his unshaven face.

Noah cleared his throat. "Do you remember that day we were in the ring and you'd tapped out but I didn't hear you?"

Hands locked atop his head, Billy nodded. He knew what was coming next before Noah even said it.

"I just kept on pounding on you a good thirty seconds after you were out. And after that, you said to me something like, 'I see where you are. I know it because I was there.' And you told me that I'd better get a handle on it before it consumed me."

"Yeah." Billy leaned back against a locker on a resigned sigh. Advice that was a helluva lot easier to give than to take.

The younger man came closer. "Well, I'm saying it right back to you now. I see where you are, Billy. And I know what it is because I was just fucking there. And you gotta get a handle on it before it consumes you. I can see by the look in your eyes that it's damn close already."

How had the tables done this one-eighty in just a few months' time? Because Billy couldn't deny that they had.

Nor that Shayna was at the heart of it all. In ways both good and bad.

In daring to hope that she could be his, in finally letting himself want her, he'd crashed against the rocks of his survivors' guilt and his fear that Ryan wouldn't find him worthy because Billy didn't fucking find himself worthy.

Shayna Curtis had made Billy want more from his life. She'd thrown light on all the dark, twisted places inside of him from which he'd been hiding. And now he was a goddamn wreck and a pressure cooker of rage and guilt and shame besides.

"He's not wrong, is he," Mo said, opening his locker. It came out as a statement, not a question.

"No," Billy bit out.

"She got under your skin—"

"Goddamnit, I don't wanna talk about Shayna," Billy said, cutting Noah off.

"Too bad," the Marine said, risking Billy's ire by coming closer. All that separated them was the bench between the rows of lockers. "Because it was falling in love with Kristina that did the same damn thing to me."

"I'm not fucking in lo—" His voice cracked on the lie.

Jesus Christ, it *was* a lie.

Billy braced his hands on his knees and heaved a breath.

Because he was in love with Shayna Curtis. The girl—*no*, the *woman*—who was supposed to have been off limits had stolen his fucking heart.

A big, meaty hand grasped his shoulder. "You gotta talk to someone, Billy. And you gotta talk to her."

He forced himself into an upright position and met Mo's dark stare. He didn't know what to say. Not really. Not yet. So he just nodded.

"Or you could come take an art therapy class with us," Noah said, a bit of humor playing around his mouth.

"Fuck that," Billy managed, earning a few chuckles from the other men.

"Don't knock it 'til you try it, Parrish," Mo said, folding his big arms.

Noah clapped Mo on the shoulder. "You know the big guy here's taken so many art therapy courses that he's on a first-name basis with all the instructors and helps out like a damn teaching assistant."

Mo's laugh was a deep rumble. "That shit chills me out. And you do *not* want to meet me unchilled. That's all I'm saying."

Billy managed a smirk. He couldn't imagine Moses losing his cool like he was currently doing, nor did he wish the way he was feeling on anybody else anyway. Because this out-of-control shit sucked ass.

"Text her and tell her to come to dinner with us." Noah gave him a no-nonsense look.

Mo nodded. "Longer you put it off, the more you're going to build it up in your mind as something big and insurmountable."

"All right," Billy said, even though a part of him remained hesitant. He didn't want her to see him when he was mid-losing-his-shit, but just talking to the guys had made him feel a *little* better. Though his problems were clearly too big and fundamental to be fixed by a single conversation no matter how helpful it'd been.

He saw that now. Still, maybe hanging with Shayna in a big group of friendlies was the perfect way to ease into the conversation he needed to have.

Once and for fucking all.

So he sent the text and invited her out.

And then he pecked out an email to Ryan:

Hey Ryan – Need to talk to you ASAP. Let me know when you can Skype? Nothing's wrong, so don't worry.

Now Billy just had to figure out what to say to both of the Curtises that would give him a chance in hell of earning him a chance at what he really wanted.

A woman. A relationship. A life that was bigger than himself.

———

SHAYNA WAS a bundle of nerves by the time she arrived at the barbecue joint where she was meeting Billy and his WFC friends. She'd been excited and really pleased that Billy thought to invite her, not to mention glad for him that he'd taken a break from working. And she was happy to get to see his friends again because she really liked them.

But she was also nervous because, without question, her apartment search was going to come up. And she'd have to tell Billy that she was leaning towards taking Malik up on his offer.

His house had been, of course, fantastic. Not fancy. But a quintessential DC row house, spacious and well-appointed with lots of natural light in a quiet neighborhood up Wisconsin Avenue. The room that would be hers was bigger than some of the apartments she'd seen, and the basement had a roughly finished bathroom that would make a perfect darkroom.

No moldy showers, ghosts, or clowns in sight.

She found Billy's party at the back of the restaurant. They all had drinks but still had menus, so she wasn't too late. "Hey, everyone."

Mo, Noah, and Tara got up to say hello to her, and being embraced by all of them like they were old friends was really freaking nice. Just like she'd done with her parents, Shayna had isolated herself a lot these past two years.

At first, it'd been because she was hurting and, with both a broken arm and ankle, it'd been difficult getting around. And then it'd been because, if her own family and closest friend blamed her for Dylan's death, what would mere acquaintances who knew about the accident think of Shayna?

So once she was able, she threw herself into work with a frenzy, which was what led her to realizing that the museum wasn't where she wanted to be. Once she got the newspaper internship, she'd had to take on a second job that actually paid, and that'd left her even less time for other people.

So having friends again...well, it'd been a long time for her. And it felt damn good.

Billy was standing at his seat when she finally went to sit down next to him, and he pulled the chair out for her and gave her a smile, sending her heart into a tumble and rushing heat over her body. From the way she wanted him. Lusted after him. Loved him.

Because she did. Finally knowing that she had somewhere else to go had meant coming to terms with leaving Billy's—and leaving Billy himself—and that was the very moment her heart had made it clear just how hard she'd fallen.

The sadness she'd been feeling the last few days hadn't just been about the stress of the search or missing Reuben and Ziggy. It had been about missing *Billy*.

It'd *always* been about Billy. For her.

He leaned in close. "I need to talk to you after dinner. Would that be okay?"

"Uh, sure. Of course. Is everything all right?"

An array of expressions crossed his face before he finally settled on a little frown and gave a shrug. "Yeah. I mean..." He shook his head. "Yeah, everything's fine."

Prickles skittered across her scalp. "How are you surviving all the surveillance work?" she asked him, wondering if that was what accounted for how run down he seemed in just a few days' time.

"It's fine," he said. "I'm going to be able to wrap one of the cases up pretty quickly, so that'll help."

"Oh, good."

The waitress appeared and asked them if they were ready to order.

Everyone turned to her. "Go ahead," Shayna said, flipping open her menu. "Just do me last." Her belly was a bundle of nerves, so she struggled to figure out what she could put into it. She finally decided on the barbecued chicken and baked potato. When the waitress departed again, she asked, "Where are Dani and Sean tonight?"

"Working," they almost all said in unison, which resulted in a round of laughter.

"They're both kinda workaholics," Tara said. "But I guess that comes with those particular professional territories." She sipped at her soda. "Oh, hey. I've been meaning to say congratulations to you. I saw your name on a photo credit in the paper."

Shayna smiled. "Why, thank you. That was pretty cool, wasn't it?"

"Is that right?" Mo said, grinning at her. "I want to see it."

"I might be able to find it online," Shayna said, fishing her phone out of her purse.

"I got it," Billy said. His web browser was open to the page.

Shayna did a double take. Her gaze lifted from his phone, which he passed around the table, to him. "You have my picture on your phone?"

Was she imagining the pink in his cheeks or was that just color casting off the stained-glass light fixtures? "I set a Google alert for your name so it would catch your credit lines and I wouldn't miss any of your photos."

Her jaw was on the floor. She knew it was. But she couldn't pick it up.

He didn't want to miss any of her pictures? That reached into her chest and squeezed something awful. Because it was so bittersweet. An amazingly thoughtful gesture from a man she wanted but couldn't have.

Billy gave a little shrug, like maybe he was embarrassed. "Plus I wanted to be able to send the links to Ryan. Figured he'd want to see them."

For a second, the reality check of him doing this for Ryan's benefit threatened to crash her back down to earth. But somehow she stopped that kneejerk reaction, because her gut was insisting that the look in those dark eyes wasn't about Ryan.

Not about Ryan, at all.

Then what *was* it about? Shayna didn't know, and Mo's voice interrupted her ability to think on it just then.

"This is a powerful shot, Shayna. This little boy looking up to Frederick Douglass like that. It's really good," Mo said.

She beamed. "Wow, thanks Mo. That means a lot to me. Oh, and guess what else?"

"What?" Billy and Mo both asked.

"This picture landed me an assignment working on a feature on Big Brothers Big Sisters of DC. The reporter is going to be interviewing bigs and littles, the littles' parents, and alumni of the program to show how powerful its impact is. I'll need to take shots of everyone involved and at a couple of different events. It's my biggest assignment so far."

Big enough that her photo editor had decided that they'd run a photo slideshow with the story online to make use of more of the pictures than could be published in the print edition. A whole slideshow of *her* photographs!

"I think that deserves a toast," Mo said. "Because that sounds awesome." Everyone raised their glasses and toasted her with a round of sodas and beers.

Shayna laughed. "You guys sure know how to make a girl feel good."

Their food arrived, and everyone dug in. Her stomach gave a flutter because anticipating the apartment-hunting question was making her a little crazy.

And then it came.

"So, Shayna," Noah said from the other side of her room-mate, "Billy says you've been looking for an apartment. Find a place yet?"

The chicken and potatoes went on a loop-the-loop in her stomach. She set down her fork and took a deep breath. "Yeah. Um. It's been kind of a nightmare, actually, but I think I've found a place."

Billy's gaze whipped to her and his expression was like she'd just kicked his puppy. Hollow and gutted.

Why was he looking at her like that?

She swallowed hard and let the rest of her news fly. "I have a colleague with a really nice three-bedroom row house in Glover Park. He went with me to see a few of the apartments and after walking a few miles in my apartment-hunting night-mare with me, he proposed that I could rent a room from him. His house is really nice. Much better than anything I've looked at so far."

Now Billy's jaw was ticking and his shoulders had gone tense. When he looked at her, his eyes were black fire. "So you've decided this?"

"Uh, pretty much," she said, surprised at how upset he seemed. Which confused and annoyed her, because it wasn't like her apartment hunting should be a surprise to him. And he hadn't offered, had he? "I have one more showing scheduled, but I might cancel it."

"Glover Park is a great neighborhood," Tara said, seemingly unaware of the weirdness between Shay and Billy. "A ton of great restaurants and, depending on where you are, you might be able to hear the Naval Observatory playing the sound of colors synchronized to the nation's master clock."

Shayna tore her gaze away from Billy's over-the-top inten-sity. "Colors?"

"Sorry," Tara said. "The music that accompanies the raising and lowering of the flag."

"Oh! That would be fun to get to hear," she said with a laugh.

"When are you moving?" Tara asked.

"Um, I'm not sure yet. I have to shoot an event tomorrow at the Northeast Rec Center and I don't know how long that'll be. So, probably next weekend." It wasn't like she had a lot of stuff, but the event started at noon, which was smack in the middle of the day.

"If you need any help, Shayna, just say the word," Mo offered.

Was she imagining a strange tone to his voice? "Thanks. I will."

It got oddly quiet around the table.

Shayna picked up her fork again and took a bite. But she could hardly taste anything around the weird feeling in her belly.

"How was fight club today?" she asked, trying to kickstart the conversation again.

Billy suddenly rose and dropped his napkin atop his half-eaten meal. "Sorry," he said. "Just realized how late it is. I gotta get back to one of my cases or the night will be a wash."

Shayna's heart tripped into an aching sprint. What about the talk he'd wanted to have?

Mo and Noah traded a look before they rose to shake Billy's hand.

"Why don't you stay a little longer?" Mo asked, eyebrow raised.

"Gotta pay the bills," Billy said, his tone flat and tight.

"Remember what we talked about," Noah said in a low voice.

What was going on? She felt like there was a whole conversation happening but she couldn't understand the words.

Finally, Billy looked to her. "You okay getting home?"

"Uh, yeah, I Ubered, but what about—"

"Another time maybe. It wasn't anything big," he said, and then he was gone.

Shayna felt like they'd just had a fight. Except they hadn't. Was he really that upset about her moving out? Or was he just pissed off at her for considering a male roommate? Because she couldn't see any other reason for all the intense weirdness that'd just transpired.

"Wow," she said. "I'm sorry. I think my news killed dinner."

"You don't have nothing to apologize for, Shayna," Mo said.

She appreciated that he said it, but she couldn't help but feel like she'd done something wrong. And that started to piss her off. So much so that she was glad when dinner was over so she could be by herself and avoid taking her temper out on anyone else.

She was so filled with restless anger that she spent the night packing. Bags. Boxes. Whatever she could jam her stuff into, she did.

By two o'clock, she was nearly done and completely spent.

Especially when she tried to add writing an email to Ryan on top of it all. She drafted and deleted it at least a half dozen times because it kept ending in a way that essentially said *I fell in love with your stupid friend who doesn't feel anything in return! Thanks for nothing, thundercunt!*

Yeah, that wasn't happening. Even though she knew he'd give *thundercunt* a solid A.

Finally, she just wrote:

Hey Ry—I just wanted you to know that I found a new place. I'm going to be subletting from a colleague at work who has a really nice three-bedroom rowhouse in NW DC (address below). His name is Malik Morrison and he's a new reporter at the Gazette, *too. I'm pretty psyched about it. Everything else is good. Take care of yourself!*

   Love, Shayna

It was mostly true. Which was the best she could do just then.

CHAPTER SIXTEEN

BILLY DROVE around the city for more than an hour. Just drove. To nowhere and everywhere.

It was a perfect fucking reflection of the chaos whirling in his head.

Shayna was leaving and it was his own goddamned fault. And on top of it all, she was moving in with another man. That didn't necessarily mean anything, of course, and maybe it shouldn't have crawled underneath Billy's skin. But it did. Bad. Because it made him feel replaced and replaceable.

And really fucking jealous.

On top of his terrible session at WFC and his realization that he probably needed to talk to his shrink again, it all combined to brew a toxic cocktail that had turned his blood into a raging fire. He'd suddenly been overwhelmed with a feeling like he was going to explode. And rather than chancing spewing any of that at Shayna or his friends, he'd bounced on dinner like a sonofabitch. He was well aware that nothing about his departure had been inconspicuous or natural, but he couldn't help it.

Because Shayna was *his*.

Except, because he was a total fuckhead, she wasn't. And,

really, he hadn't even fought for her, had he? He'd taken too long to get his damn head together and been too late. So every bit of the shit sandwich that was his life right now was on him.

And hell if the guilt over surviving when others hadn't wasn't beating his ass a little harder as a result.

Which was maybe why Billy ended up in front of an old warehouse in Upper Northeast. One he hadn't been to in a long string of months. One he'd convinced himself he wouldn't need to come to again.

Warrior Fight Club hadn't taken the edge off the way he'd needed it to. And the idea of turning to one of his former lays to try to find some release was a total non-starter now that his heart had set its sights on Shayna.

All of which left him one option—the underground fight club ring another Army buddy had first invited him to more than a year ago.

The guy had come out for WFC but been frustrated that it *hadn't* been more about fighting. A few weeks later, he'd found what he'd dubbed "the real thing" and sent Billy the information in case he was interested, too.

Billy's curiosity had been piqued.

Especially once he found that getting pounded on helped to quiet the accusing voices in his own head. Not that he couldn't give as good as he got. But here, the guys didn't fight by the rules of any particular style of martial arts or and they didn't fight fair. And back then his recovery hadn't been quite far enough along to give him the physical edge that he'd since gained. Thanks to Warrior Fight Club, which had provided enough release and solace for him that he'd stopped coming here.

Until tonight.

Billy pushed out of the car. He needed the fucking voices to shut the hell up. He went to the door around the corner in the shadows and knocked.

A metal plate slid to the side, revealing a pair of dark eyes that immediately went wide in recognition. The door swung open and a giant mountain of a man filled the breach.

"Billy Parrish, what the fuck are you doing here?" Abe said. Billy only knew him by his first name. They clasped hands.

"Same thing everyone does here," Billy said. "I'm here to fight."

"Well, come on in then."

Billy nodded and went in the direction of the voices, not that he needed that clue since he'd been there before. At the back of the warehouse, he founded a set of stairs down and followed them to a basement level. Twenty men stood around, some already shirtless and shoeless. Others were heading in that direction.

His friend wasn't there, though. Billy was glad.

And didn't that tell him a whole helluva lot about what he thought down deep about being here. He didn't want anyone from his real life to know. Because talk about fucking reckless. He knew it was. But he also knew it'd been effective before at releasing the pressure valve in his head.

Right now, the benefit outweighed the risks.

Billy kicked off his boots and stripped off his T-shirt. Earlier, he'd worn his compression vest under his tee at WFC to protect a back already achy from all the hours of sitting. But that wasn't allowed here. He felt the eyes on his ruined skin before he saw them. And he met the gazes of every goddamn man.

Go ahead and underestimate me, assholes.

He grinned and a lucky-if-he-was-eighteen-year-old nearly scampered away.

By the time Billy was called out to fight, four pairs had already gone at it and he was nearly itching to get this over with.

And then he was in the ring with a twenty-something guy

with a lot of ink and even more attitude. Sneering, the man came at him.

His defensive instincts kicked in and Billy dodged and caught the man with a hard back elbow strike into his kidney. His opponent careened into the circle of onlookers around them, who helpfully shoved him back into the center.

Billy could've probably taken the motherfucker out with a few well-placed jabs to his vulnerable rib cage, but winning wasn't what he was here for. He let the guy get squared off again. He even let the guy gain a little confidence by not dodging some easily avoidable hits.

But in the end, the asshole was all powerless, unfocused bluster, and it was pissing Billy off because it wasn't giving him what he needed.

So he finished him with a combination of hooks and upper-cuts until the guy was laid out on the floor and yelling, "Stop!"

Which brought Billy another opponent.

A much more promising one. A little taller and bulkier than Billy, and with an air about him that was entirely unrushed and relaxed. The guy wasn't arrogant and didn't gloat, both of which were often hallmarks of someone whose confidence was backed up by actual skill.

Billy smiled.

The match began. They circled each other for a few seconds, and then it was on. The guy knew how to mix up the kinds and pacing of his strikes so that Billy couldn't predict him, and he was good at defending his own vulnerabilities. He obviously had some training.

Which explained how his opponent landed an absolutely brain-rattling hook to Billy's face.

Jesus fucking relief.

The feeling that erupted throughout Billy was almost euphoric.

It made him smile even more. He recovered himself and was right back in it. He landed a few fucking satisfying hits himself, making the guy bleed from the corner of his mouth. And leaving Billy feeling more alive than he had anywhere else for a long time.

Except for when Shayna had been in his bed and at his side.

The thought was a total fucking distraction, of course, giving the guy an in to deliver a brutal hammer strike to Billy's bad shoulder that just barely missed his face. And even though it hurt like hell, Billy relished it.

Because those voices? They weren't saying one goddamned thing.

So he didn't stop the fight. He didn't give up despite the fact that he was bleeding from a cheekbone and his shoulder. No. *This guy* knew how to fight. They were well matched and gave each other real competition.

Exactly what Billy needed. Which was why he went right back in for more.

———

SHAYNA SHOULD'VE BEEN MORE excited this morning.

This Big Brothers Big Sisters assignment was a fantastic opportunity for her career. And while she was excited, she was also exhausted, strung out from how poorly she'd slept, and increasingly pissed off at Billy for making her feel this way.

Maybe food would help.

She was downstairs toasting a bagel and spreading peanut butter on apple slices when the front door sprung open.

Shayna nearly jumped out of her skin. "Holy crap, you scared me," she said, surprised to see him home.

Billy closed the door with a strength that could only be

described as slamming it. "Sorry," he mumbled, chin and eyes down. He staggered towards her.

"Dude, are you drunk at ten o'clock in the morning?"

"No," he said, making for the fridge. He reached in and grabbed the half-gallon carton of milk. And then he tilted back his head and chugged it.

Which was when she saw all the cuts and dried blood.

"Jesus, Billy! You're hurt. What happened?" Her pulse exploded into a sprint as she tried to catalog his injuries.

There were cuts on his cheekbone, the bridge of his nose, and the corner of his mouth. A bruise was blooming at the corner of one eye. And a bloodstain on his shoulder in the same spot where she'd patched him up before seemed to indicate that his scars had opened up again.

He shook his head and gave her more of that weirdly flat and overly mellow tone. "Not hurt. Actually feel pretty decent. For once."

She gawked at him. "What does that mean? Did you get in a fight? Or a car accident? Or...just tell me what the hell happened to you."

He ignored her. "You moving out today?"

Shayna frowned—both at the non sequitur and because they'd discussed this the night before. Did he not remember her telling Tara? Or, oh God, did he *want* her out today? "What? No. I have to cover an event at the Northeast Rec Center. Don't you remember?"

He chugged another long drink of milk. "Oh, that's right."

"Billy, you're really worrying me right now."

"You don't have to worry about me, Shayna." He gave her a look that was...so sad it made her chest hurt.

"Of course, I have to worry about you. You're my friend." The word was so wholly inadequate as to be ridiculous. But it was the best word she had. The parameter they'd both agreed to.

"Right. Well, *friend*, I appreciate it, but I'm good." He dropped the milk back into the fridge.

"You're bleeding. And your shoulder's open again." A knot of emotion lodged in her throat. She was truly worried about him. And she wasn't sure he should be alone. But she also couldn't be the one to stay with him. Not that she was sure he'd want her to if she could, given his strange mood.

Billy just shrugged. "Gonna go get some sleep."

She frowned again. This was just all so unlike him. "You don't have to work?"

"I will later," he said in that same monotone.

"What about the conversation you said you wanted to have with me?"

He paused at the bottom of the staircase. "Just, uh, just forget I said anything about that." He disappeared up the steps.

She stood there staring and wondering what the hell had just happened. Glancing down at the counter she saw her now-cold bagel and the apple she'd been peanut-buttering. She ate a few slices of the latter, but her stomach was so in knots that she couldn't finish.

On a deep breath, she went upstairs. And found Billy leaning against the doorjamb to her room.

"Why don't you let me clean up some of those cuts?" she said. "At least the one on your shoulder. If your shirt sticks to it—"

"You're packed," he said. Had he even heard her? Or was he purposely ignoring her?

She rubbed at her forehead, where a headache was spreading like spilled ink. "Yeah, I just figured I'd get a head start—"

"Maybe you should go today then."

Shayna's heart stopped. For a moment, she would've sworn it did. And then it restarted in a booming beat that made her tremble. "You want me to go?"

Still peering into her room—and not even deigning to face her—he shrugged with one big shoulder, as if it didn't matter to him either way.

It would've hurt less if he'd stabbed her with the butter knife she'd been using.

"Wow. I feel bad for whatever happened to you, Billy, but that doesn't mean I'm okay with you being an asshole." She crossed her arms and bore a death glare into the back of his head.

He finally turned to look at her. "I kinda specialize in asshole, Shayna, so all the more reason for you to go."

She flinched. That was how hard the words hit her. And they cut her even deeper.

"Fine. I'll ask Mo to meet me here after my event." Her eyes had the weirdest stinging sensation. Like she needed to cry but couldn't. Like he'd stunned her so badly that her body wasn't functioning right.

Something flashed behind Billy's dark eyes. For just a moment, she would've sworn it had. But then it was gone again. And there was just the two of them facing off in the hallway. The same place their story had started a month before

Except all the hopefulness she'd felt then was gone. And all she had in its place was a broken heart. One she'd thought couldn't have shattered any more than it already had two years before.

Clearly, she'd been wrong.

Without saying another word, she marched past him to where her camera bags sat laid out on the foot of her bed.

No, *his* bed. Get it right, Shayna.

She did a quick double check of her equipment, making

sure she had a decent variety of lenses, sufficient batteries, her notebook, and her Nikon D850 in case she wanted to grab some video, too.

Shayna was good to go. In every way.

Billy was still standing near the doorway when she turned around. An ache bloomed harder in the center of her chest—hard enough it nearly stole her breath. So she forced her gaze away and left.

She had a job to do today and she wasn't letting anyone get in her way.

KIDS MADE it really hard to stay in a bad mood or wallow in sadness.

Which made Shayna feel even more grateful to be working on this assignment. She and Andy had been at the Littles Celebration for about two hours, and she'd met about half the people on her preliminary contact list and gotten dozens of shots. Everyone was friendly and helpful and only too happy to talk about their experiences with the organization. Plus, it was a gorgeous day, so they'd decided to host the whole thing outside on the rec center's grounds.

Everything was going great. Shayna had even been able to set aside some of her worry about Billy when she'd mentioned to Mo by text that she thought something was wrong with him. Mo said he'd go over to their house before she got home to check on Billy and then he'd be there to help her move when she was ready.

That was all as good as it could be. Which really wasn't saying much.

She was setting up to take some video when Barry came up and peered into her bags.

"Whatcha doing?" he asked.

She pulled out the D850. "This is my favorite camera, and it takes both photographs and pretty amazing video. I thought I'd shoot some of the latter and put together a little movie for the Big Brothers website or Facebook page."

"Oh." He watched her like a hawk. Shayna smiled. She easily remembered how fascinated she'd been by cameras at a pretty young age, too. "Are cameras expensive?"

"There's a pretty big range, actually. You can get a high-quality compact with 25x zoom for about two hundred dollars. Or you can spend a couple thousand dollars or more on a DSLR, which is just a digital single-lens camera as opposed to one with film, that has all the bells and whistles."

"Huh," Barry said. "I hope I can have a camera someday."

"You will. Know how I know?" she asked him as she zipped her cases closed again.

"How?"

"Because you already know this is something that interests you. And I believe you can do anything you put your mind to."

He grinned, and that smile did a ton to make her feel better. Kids had a way of putting your problems into perspective, that was for sure.

After that, Shayna had an assistant for the next thirty minutes while she grabbed video of kids jumping in the moon bounce and playing games, of families gathered around tables heaped with food, of toddlers dancing without a care in the world in front of the DJ's table, and of the event signs rustling in the breeze. She'd get it all edited into a forty-five-second spot in between other things at work this week.

When she was done, she found Andy with his notebook closed and recorder turned off just sitting and enjoying the event. "Ready?" he asked.

"I got everything I need," she said. "And had a lot of fun besides."

They said their good-byes and walked out to their cars together.

"I'm down the block there," Shayna said, pointing past a line of utility repair trucks that had taken up a lot of the street when she'd looked for parking earlier.

"Here, give me one of your bags and I'll walk you down. I wanted to touch base with you on a few scheduling things."

"Sure, no problem," Shayna said. "But you don't have to carry anything. How did you feel today went?" They started down the block, then crossed after the last of the utility trucks.

"Better than I expected. Everyone was very open. It was clear that Big Brothers Big Sisters did a great job laying the groundwork and explaining why the article would be important to the program. This feature is almost going to write itself." He smiled.

"Bet it's nice when that happens."

"*So* nice."

They reached her car, and Shayna popped her trunk. "Did you have some interviews you wanted me to accompany you on?"

Andy nodded. "Three so far confirmed for next week, but I expect two others, too."

"Okay. Let me just put my bags in here..." She lowered everything off her shoulders and retrieved her phone from her back pocket. "And I'll pull up my calendar on my..." She frowned. "Do you feel that?"

Andy barely had a chance to react to her question.

The world exploded around them.

A deafening boom was accompanied by everything moving, and then a wall of heat and just sheer force slammed into Shayna and threw her back and to the ground.

She blinked and groaned as debris rained down around her, some of it on fire. Her ears rang and her head spun and her arms and face burned in a million tiny places.

What just happened?

Her back and head protested as she forced herself into a sitting position on the street, the world still a tilt-a-whirl.

Time slowed to a crawl and Shayna couldn't believe what she saw.

A wall of flames towered over the garden-style apartments that sat back about a hundred feet from the street. One whole part of the building had collapsed. People were running and screaming. A few people peered out of second- and third-floor windows and waved for help.

Dear God.

She tried to shake away the fog clouding her head and glanced down to see that her clothes were covered in tiny pieces of glass and wood and metal...and that a two-inch piece of metal had lodged in her right forearm. Dozens of other tiny cuts explained why her skin burned so bad. But otherwise she was fine.

But what about...

On a whimper of realization, she cried, "Andy? Andy, are you okay?"

Shayna forced herself to her feet and found him flattened against the side of her car. The force of his impact had been hard enough to cause a dent above the rear tire.

She went to her knees beside him. "Jesus, Andy, talk to me."

"Are the kids okay?" he rasped.

Her throat went tight. "I...I don't know. I think they should be. They were far enough away."

He nodded on a groan and dragged his phone out of his pocket. "I'll call 9-1-1." He grasped her wrist. "And you...you need to do your job." His eyebrows rose meaningfully, asking her if she understood as he pressed the phone to his ear and started speaking to the dispatcher.

The words hit her almost as hard as the blast wave.

Holy shit, he wanted her to photograph this.

Shayna rose so fast that it made her dizzy, but she braced on the still-open trunk of her car until she could reach her bags. Her mind was racing but she knew what she needed to do.

She fished a tripod out of one bag along with a charging cell and her phone...where was her phone? She finally found it ten feet away where it'd apparently been blown out of her hand. The screen was cracked, but otherwise it worked.

She pressed a number in her contacts and put the phone to her ear. "Rose, it's Shayna. Andy and I just witnessed an explosion in an apartment complex across from the Northeast Rec Center. Can you get me access to the *Gazette* Facebook page? I can stream the scene live."

"Give me two minutes. Are you guys okay?"

"Okay enough. Hurry, Rose." They hung up.

Shayna placed the tripod next to Andy, who was trying to get up off the ground. "Are you sure you should do that?" she asked as she adjusted the stand's height, secured her phone to the clip, and plugged in the battery.

"I'm good. You good?" he asked, not sounding very good at all. Then again, Shayna had a piece of metal sticking out of her arm that she weirdly couldn't feel. So maybe it was like that for him, too? She nodded. "You're gonna stream this. That's smart. What can I do?"

"Rose is going to call back with the login to the *Gazette's* Facebook page. Do a live video. And keep an eye on the charging cell. There are three more just like it in my bags. Don't let it run out of battery."

"Got it," he said.

Shayna went for her D850 next. It could fire thirty frames

per second and had enough resolution to capture an incredible degree of detail. She put the strap around her neck and started shooting.

The flames. The debris. The running people. The gaping hole where a building once stood that she could just make out through the roiling black smoke and fire.

"I'm going closer," she said. Sirens wailed in the distance, thank God.

"Wait," Andy said as her ring tone sounded. It was Rose with the login information. "This is going to get picked up everywhere. Let's do this like a TV intro." Shayna immediately moved behind the camera and logged in as Andy moved in front of it. "Just tell me when you're ready, Shay."

"Move that way a little," Shayna said, setting it up for the best shot. Andy grimaced as he moved, but neither of them were about *themselves* right now. "Stop."

"Okay, go ahead," Andy said. His shirt was torn, there was a crack in one of the lenses of his glasses, and he had the same scattering of cuts and nicks over his forearms and face as she had.

She typed in a short descriptive line for the post, and then the live video counted down 3-2-1 and she gave him a thumb's up.

"This is Andy Katz of the *Washington Gazette* reporting live from the scene of an apparent explosion at the Northern Arms Garden Apartments in Northeast DC. My photographer, Shayna Curtis, and I were here on another assignment when the blast occurred. As you can hear in the background, police, fire, and EMS are on their way but haven't yet arrived."

Ten people tuned in to watch. Then a hundred. Within sixty seconds, there were nearly a thousand people watching and reacting to the live video.

"It's not clear whether or how many residents might've been

inside the building or what caused the fire, but as you can see, inhabitants are streaming out of neighboring buildings."

She gave him another thumb's up. He had it from here. Rounding the far side of her car so she could stay out of the video's frame, she put the viewfinder to her face. Her heart was racing and she couldn't stop sweating and blood kept dripping into her eye, but she couldn't worry about any of that just then.

Crouching out in the field in front of the building, she took wide-frame shots of the blaze and then of the towering column of smoke and flames. She moved closer, and the whole world narrowed down to what she saw through her viewfinder.

People huddled together in raw shock. Gas company employees running from the buildings. One of their utility helmets in the grass. Three people clustered in a window immediately adjacent to the flames.

Jesus, when were the fire companies going to get here?

She'd no more thought that then the first of the emergency vehicles swung onto the block.

In a burst, she captured shots of the first responders unloading and setting up the scene. Firemen unrolling the hose, opening the hydrant, donning their gear. The EMTs laying out a triage area and reaching out to the first of the injured. The police setting up a perimeter.

Which meant she needed to get these close-ups while she could because she knew she was going to get pulled back any second now.

"Help us!" a lady screamed from her window.

Shay went as close as she dared, close enough that the heat hurt her face and hands. "Hold on," she yelled. "The firemen are here. I'll point them right to you."

Shayna let the camera go slack on the neck strap and waved her arms as a line of firemen started across the short field. A group came right for her. "There are three people in that window," she told an older man with a weathered face. "But there were also two in that window just a minute or two ago and I haven't seen anyone come out." She pointed to where she meant.

He nodded. "We're on it. Thanks. You should get back now. This scene's not stable." He jogged away.

And Shayna continued taking pictures. Because telling our most human stories through images was her job, her passion, and the way she made a difference in the world.

CHAPTER SEVENTEEN

THE KNOCKING WOULD NOT FUCKING stop.

After at least ten minutes of it, Billy hauled his ass out of bed and down the stairs, fully prepared to murder whoever was on the other side of that door.

"What?" he growled as he opened it.

"Took ya long enough," Mo said, giving Billy's face and bare chest, both covered in bruises, a once-over before inviting himself inside. "You look good."

"Fuck." Billy buttoned the fly to his jeans. He'd been too strung out to take them off when he'd fallen into bed.

"Yeah, that about sums it up, I'd say. What the hell did you do to yourself?"

"Nothing. Listen, Mo, I was kinda in the middle of something—"

"Sure you were," he said, making himself good and comfortable on the couch. He even propped up his feet on the table and crossed his ankles. The fucker. "Just to move this along, know that I'm not leaving. Because after I figure out what's going on with you, I'm hanging around to help Shayna whom it seems is in a big rush to leave your house all of a sudden. Have any idea why that might be?"

"She found a new place. You heard her," Billy said, dropping heavily onto the couch himself.

"You let her news fuck you up even more, didn't you?" Mo arched an eyebrow. "She said she found a roommate and you heard that you were too late. And then you learned that it was a guy and what you heard was that she wanted someone else. How am I doing?"

Billy let his head fall back against the cushion. "You're really fucking irritating, Griffin."

Mo's low chuckle rumbled through the room. "Translation: I'm batting a thousand. Good to know." When he spoke again, his voice had lost that humor. "She was upset after you left. I get why you got out of there. But what I don't get is whatever happened between you since then. And whose fist you ran into. Repeatedly."

"Do you know a vet named Gordon Rizzo?"

"Aw, you gotta be shitting me," Mo exclaimed. "You went to that underground fight club again?"

Billy's head whipped up. "Again?"

"You think that didn't make its way back to me, son? I've been in this city a lot longer than you."

"Well. Shit."

"Uh huh." Mo shook his head. "Don't even think of pulling shit like that again. Somebody liable to shank you as well as punch you in there. Gimme your word."

"I needed the release, Mo."

"*Gimme your word.*"

Billy heaved a deep breath and all of a sudden he felt every one of his bruises. "Fine. You have it."

"Now, tell me what you did to chase Shayna away."

Fuck. Mo wasn't giving him an inch, was he? Not that he really deserved it.

Boom!

Billy and Mo both flinched as a thunderous noise pierced the afternoon quiet. Whatever it was made the glasses rattle against each other inside his kitchen cabinets.

"What the hell was that?" Billy asked, foreboding crawling down his spine and his heart galloping as his brain threatened to pull Billy back into his past.

Into the ambush. Another explosion. The pain of fire all across his skin.

"Something big," Mo said, frowning. He pulled out his phone and started typing. "Texting Riddick. Even when that boy isn't on shift he's got that incident scanner going."

It only took a minute or two before Sean responded. "He says, *'Probable natural gas explosion at an apartment complex.'*"

"Shit," Billy said, blowing out a shaky breath. "That sounded close."

Mo eyeballed him in a way that made it clear he understood what was happening to Billy. "You could've planned something a little less elaborate to divert me from this conversation, you know."

Billy actually managed a chuckle. He scrubbed at his face and heaved a deep breath.

Mo's phone buzzed another incoming message, and a big frown settled across the man's face as he read it. "Billy, I think you need to go grab your laptop."

He rose. "Why?"

"Just go get it."

Ice skittered down his spine, and Billy made quick work of grabbing the laptop off his bedroom chair. He settled next to Mo on the couch when he returned. "What am I looking for?"

"Go to the *Gazette's* page on Facebook."

Oh, fucking hell. How was the *Gazette* a part of this? Billy did what Mo said. "What? What am I looking for?" he asked again. And then he saw it. A live video of a massive fire.

He shuddered. He fucking hated fire.

A disheveled man with multiple lacerations and a pair of broken glasses narrated the scene. "If you're just tuning in, this is *Washington Gazette* reporter Andy Katz reporting from the scene of an apparent explosion and three-alarm fire at the Northern Arms Garden Apartments. My photographer, Shayna Curtis, and I were at the scene covering an unrelated story when we witnessed the explosion at approximately eight minutes after three o'clock..."

"Oh, fuck. Shayna. Oh, fuck." His heart in his throat, Billy switched over to his text app and fired off a message. His hands were shaking, making it hard to hit the right keys. Then another. Then another. They all showed as *Delivered* but not *Read*.

Shayna are you ok?

Just saw the news. Let me know you're okay.

I'm sorry, please call or text me. Worried.

"I'll call her," Mo said, but a moment later he shook his head. "Straight to voicemail."

Billy slammed his laptop closed. "She's there. She's there, goddamnit. And she might be hurt. Did you see her colleague?" One heartbeat passed, and then another. Jesus, how was it possible that she'd been at the scene of an explosion? Nausea rolled through his gut. "I'm going over there."

He took the steps two at a time. Shirt. Shoes. Keys. Phone. Then he was back downstairs.

Mo stood in the middle of his living room. "It's going to be a mob scene, Billy."

He met the other man's dark gaze. "She thinks I want her to move out, Mo. She's probably rattled and possibly hurt, and she think's I want her gone."

"Then it's going to be a mob scene plus two," his friend said. Just like that.

It took forever and a fucking day to get anywhere close to the scene of the incident, at least that was how it felt. And then Mo and Billy were forced to park and hoof it the last four blocks. Of course, there were barriers everywhere once they arrived, and a crowd ten deep of looky-loos wanting to watch as the disaster unfolded.

And, of course, there was the fucking fire, which made Billy's skin absolutely crawl with the desire to flee. Which, hell no. Not without Shayna.

"We'll find her," Mo said. "The angle of that Facebook feed was from over there."

Billy followed Mo's hand signal and nodded, and they made their way around the crowd, close to where the majority of the emergency vehicles had parked.

"That's Riddick's company," Mo said, pointing at one of the trucks. They made for it, and Mo flagged someone down. "Can you tell Sean Riddick that Mo's here and needs to talk to him when he has a sec?"

"Sure, man," the guy said with a wave.

"Look," Billy exclaimed, his heart suddenly in his throat. "That's Shayna's car and her colleague." And, Christ, she'd been parked so close.

"Billy." Mo grabbed his arm and hauled him a few steps to the right such that they could see around the back of one of the hose trucks. On the grass just beyond, black tarps were laid out on which sat dozens of patients. EMTs moved among them administering first aid.

And that was when Billy saw her.

She was at the edge of the group—just out of frame, as it were—taking pictures. He remembered imagining Shayna as a war correspondent, and it was exactly what she looked like as she moved around a disaster scene littered with debris, discarded bandage wrappers, and empty water bottles.

"Oh, Jesus," he managed, his hand grabbing at his heart. He called her name.

But of course she couldn't hear him over the rumble of the fire engines and the still crackling flames and the spraying of the hoses, not to mention the voices of onlookers, the crying of children, and the occasional voice through a bullhorn.

And then Sean Riddick came around the back of the firetruck, his face sweaty and grimy and his turnout gear smelling like smoke. He took one look at Billy and said, "Shayna's here. She's injured but she won't let them take her to the hospital. Then again, she was the first one on the scene and almost all the initial images and the live stream video are hers. I get why she doesn't want to walk away."

Billy's stomach dropped and his heart squeezed and his chest swelled with pride. "How badly injured?"

Sean looked to the right and left and then lifted the yellow tape. "Come on back," he said. Billy and Mo followed him through the gear and people and around the triage area. "She's got an impaled object wound in her arm. They wrapped and cushioned it, but they don't want to take it out because they don't know how deep it is. And she's got a head lac that needs stitches. Everything else is superficial, though there's a lot of it. She was standing right where they set up their camera."

Right. So, ground-fucking-zero. Billy was shaking—for her and for the memory of what'd happened to him.

"Somehow, though, she still looks better than you." Sean smirked, and Billy didn't even mind the jab since the guy had brought him to Shayna. "Catch ya after."

"I owe you, Sean."

He shook his head. "No you don't. Just take care of her."

Billy stood about twenty feet away from where Shayna was

crouched taking pictures. So in her element. So fucking beautiful even though he could see the head wound and the bandage on her arm from here.

Suddenly, she looked right at him, then she did an almost comical double take.

Billy couldn't stand the distance between them for one more second. Not the physical distance that kept her from his arms. Nor the emotional distance that prevented her from knowing exactly how he felt.

WHY WAS BILLY HERE?

Shayna rose as he started toward her and met him half way at the corner of the triage area.

At first she was wary, given how they'd left things earlier. But he looked so different to her. His eyes were bright and sharp and his expression was all masculine determination. He hadn't done much to clean up the cuts on his face but even they appeared less severe when the rest of his demeanor was so vital.

He came right up to her, his eyes absolutely burning. "Are you okay?"

She nodded. "I'll be fine. Just a few cuts and bumps."

"And a foreign object in your arm?" he asked, in a tone so full of concern.

She looked down at her bandaged right forearm. It was starting to throb, but still it seemed a minor thing compared to what the people who lived here were going through. Last she'd heard, there were thirty-four injuries and four missing people. "Well, yeah."

He peered around at the chaos. "I know you're working. And I know it's important. And I know this story is going to be huge for you and I'm so fucking proud. I'll wait for you here until you're ready to go, and then I'll come to the hospital with you."

Every bit of what he'd just said hit her right in the chest. The respect. The acknowledgement. The pride. "Billy, you don't have to do that. Really."

"Yes, I do. Because I fucking love you."

Shayna's equilibrium completely checked out.

It'd happened once or twice before since the blast had knocked her off her feet, but usually just when she got up too fast. Not when she was standing perfectly still. "What?" she managed.

He gently took her into his arms. "I love you. And I don't want you to move out. I was a complete asshole because I thought I was too late and I was kicking myself for denying what I felt when I've known for a while that I felt it. I'm so damn sorry for all of it, too."

Wait. Was Billy Parrish telling her he loved her when she'd thought he didn't want her around at all?

Cautiously, she placed the hand of her good arm on his hip and peered into his eyes. "Billy, I hit my head on the street when the building exploded. I've got a kinda big knot and maybe a wee concussion, so I'm going to need you to repeat what you just said so I can be sure I heard what I think I heard."

He smiled. "If you think you heard me tell you that I love you, then you heard right."

Just beyond Billy's arm, Mo was smiling and nodding. "You heard him, Shayna."

She blinked, stunned and completely overwhelmed.

"Am I too late, Shay? Have I ruined everything by taking the long fucking route to get here? Because if you really want to be just friends, I'll do that for you, too. Anything for you." Billy gently tucked a curl behind her ear.

Finally, Shayna let herself believe. "You really love me?"

He nodded, and the look on his handsome face was so fucking earnest. Even with the cuts and bruises and three-day growth of scruff he was the sexiest man she'd ever seen. "I really do." And damn if him saying that didn't make him ever hotter.

Shayna swallowed around the knot of emotion suddenly in her throat. "God, Billy, I love you, too. I love you so much that it's been hard to breathe for holding it in."

"Aw, Jesus," he said, pulling her closer, which didn't quite work because her camera still hung on her neck between them.

They both laughed as she tried to hang it over her shoulder instead, but he had to help her because of her injury. And then she was in his arms and his mouth was claiming hers and she held and kissed and claimed him right back.

"You're shaking," she said when they pulled back from the kiss.

Billy leaned his forehead on hers. "I, uh, I really hate fire." His gaze flicked nervously towards the blaze.

Shayna held him tighter even though it made her arm ache more. "Yet you still came here for me."

He nodded. "It feels like I've wanted you to be mine for so long, Shayna. I had to make sure you were okay."

She could hardly believe what was happening, but it was everything she'd been wanting, too, so she wasn't going to waste a minute questioning it. "Well I am yours, Billy. And you're mine, too."

"Better fucking believe it." He gave her another quick kiss. "Okay, baby. Go kick some more ass and come back to me when you're done. I'll be right here waiting for however long it takes."

CHAPTER EIGHTEEN

THEY GOT HOME at five in the morning.

Then slept like the dead in Billy's bed 'til two in the afternoon.

And then they'd taken turns washing the past few days off one another's skin in the shower. Not really talking. Not trying to arouse. Just wanting to take care. Because they were both physically beat up and emotionally drained and needed the TLC. From one another.

Something about the past twenty-four hours had forged them so that Shayna felt closer to Billy than she'd ever felt to anyone in her life.

Maybe it was having shared their feelings and realizing she wasn't the only one in over her head. Or maybe it was how he'd supported her work, waiting at the scene for five hours. Or maybe it had been how he'd ridden in the ambulance with her and held her hand, staying by her side as much as he could as she got stitched up. Or how he'd held her all morning long as they'd slept—how they'd held each other.

Or maybe it was how Billy had admitted his fears about losing her and his fear of fire.

Whatever explained it, Shayna was considering—*really* considering for the first time—telling Billy the thing that *she* most feared him finding out. Because she wanted what they had to be *real*, and real meant that he needed to know her. All of her. Even the ugly parts. And that she had to be brave enough to trust him to...she didn't know. Forgive or accept her, maybe?

So as they stood in the bathroom in nothing more than towels, Shayna took a deep breath and let the truth fly, "It's my fault that Dylan died." The words made her pulse pound like a bass drum, but there was also a kind of freedom for having voiced them.

"What? No. No, baby, it's not." Billy cupped her face in his hands.

"It is," she said, meeting his gaze. A shiver shuddered through her. "I was seeing this guy who Dylan had insisted was bad news. We'd only gone out a few times, and I liked the guy. Dylan and I actually fought over him. But I just wouldn't listen."

"Oh, Shay, no."

"Please, let me get this out." When he nodded, she continued, the words coming faster now like they were a poison she needed to purge. "The night of the accident, the guy had...um..."

This was the part that no one in the whole world knew.

"He'd tried to force himself on me. And then he'd tried to keep me from leaving his house, but I managed to get out a back door before he could stop me. I zigzagged through people's yards on foot in case he was following me. And when I finally felt like I was safe, I called Dylan and asked him to pick me up, knowing he'd been right all along. Even though he didn't gloat about it. Not once."

"Jesus," Billy said, a storm rolling in across his expression, making him look fierce. Lethal. "I'm so sorry, Shayna. But none of that makes the drunk driver who hit you your fault."

She gave a fast nod and could no longer hold back her tears. "Don't you see? If I'd listened to Dylan in the first place, none of that would've ever happened. He wouldn't have been in his car picking me up. The drunk driver never would've been anywhere near us. And Dylan would've gotten married like he was supposed to. And my parents would have all of their children, and probably some grandkids, too. And Ryan would have his little brother. But because of what I did, all of that was lost. And you... you were right. I did run away. From my whole family. Because I know they blame me and it was easier to be alone than to see it."

She couldn't believe she was saying this, but she also couldn't deny how much she needed to give voice to it.

After so long of holding in the guilt and the shame and the overwhelming sorrow.

"Aw, Shayna, you're not to blame. I promise. Dylan died because someone decided to drink and get behind the wheel of a car. End of story. And I can tell you for a fact that Ryan doesn't blame you, either."

She gasped. "How do you know?"

"Because he said as much to me when it happened. He was never anything but relieved that you'd survived. He loves you." Billy kissed her tears away. "And I love you. In case you think this changes a single thing, know that it just makes me love you more."

"Why?" she asked, her belly a nervous mess even as his support and acceptance built her up. Still, how could he love her *more* when her role in this made her feel so damn *unlovable*.

"Because I know what it's like to hate yourself for surviving when people you care about died. I carry that same pain. Maybe...fuck, this sounds stupid..."

She grasped his hips, needing to touch him, to feel him. "What? Tell me."

He twisted his lips. "It's just that, maybe our souls recognized that we carried that same pain. Maybe that's why we were so drawn together," he said.

Those were some of the sweetest words she'd ever heard, even though she ached to hear that he understood her so well *because* he carried the same guilt. "I love the idea of that, and if it's true, maybe we can help heal each other."

"Maybe we can, baby." His kiss was all sweet, caring compassion.

But Shayna suddenly wanted more. "I want to be yours, Billy."

The little bit of smugness in his smile was so damn sexy. "Oh, you're mine, all right."

She grasped his wrists where he still held her face. "I want to be yours in every way. Make love to me, Billy?"

He didn't make her ask twice.

"I want to worship you," he said, guiding her to the bedroom and laying her out. He settled in alongside her and kissed her deeply, his hand exploring her body as his tongue tasted her mouth. He cupped and massaged her breasts, and then his fingers tormented her nipples with little squeezes and twists that had her moaning into his mouth. "I fucking love the sounds you make," he rasped around the edge of a kiss.

"You make me crazy," she whispered.

Billy grinned. "That's my line."

Her fingers cupped the side of his face, soft and sweet. "It was a good one."

Nodding, he trailed kisses down her jaw to her throat to her clavicle, and then lower, until he sucked her nipples into his mouth and flicked them with his tongue. Shayna's hands went to his hair, holding him to her as he licked and sucked at one breast and then the other.

Then he went lower until he got good and settled between her thighs, his big shoulders spreading her wider. It was one of her favorite sights in the world.

Billy, between her legs, looking like a starving man.

"God, Shay, you don't know how many times I've thought about getting my mouth on you again."

"I do," she said, "because I've thought about it, too. Do it, Billy. Taste me."

Holding eye contact, he licked firm and slow right over her clit. On a gasp, her hips came off the bed. Billy slid his arms under her thighs and gripped her tight, holding her right where he wanted her.

And then he was *merciless*.

He alternated between long, hard licks from her opening to her clit to fast flicks that made her hold her breath. His stubble burned so good against her thighs and where his mouth met her skin.

"Give me your orgasm and I'll give you my cock." He arched a challenging brow.

That was *not* going to be a problem.

"So close." Biting on her lip, she watched him worship her, which was exactly what it felt like, just like he'd said.

Peering up at her, he sucked her clit into his mouth and penetrated her with two thick fingers. He flicked at her with his tongue and curled his fingers inside her in a way that drove her wild. Shayna cried out and grasped at the sheets and thrust as hard as she could against his mouth. And then she was coming and rasping his name over and over.

"Holy shit." Her heart was a jackrabbit in her chest.

"Fuck, that sounded good," he said, his face so freaking

gorgeous and his expression not a little smug. But Shayna hardly cared when his lips glistened with her orgasm.

"It was *so* good, Billy," she said. "Can I have you now? Please?"

Kneeling between her thighs, he took the long length of his hard cock in hand and stroked. "You want this?" He looked down to where his hand worked over his erection.

"So much," Shayna said, aching for them to come together in every way they could.

"You can have me every way you want me." He reached into the nightstand drawer and retrieved a condom, and then his big hand rolled it on, and it was a decadent sight that she couldn't help but watch. "You keep looking at me like that, Shayna, and this isn't going to last very long."

She grinned. "Well I can guarantee you this isn't going to be the last time."

He chuckled, and the sound was pure masculine satisfaction. "You better fucking believe that, baby. It's not even going to be the last time *today*."

Shay laughed until he came down on her with all his weight. Then all she could do was moan at the goodness of the sensation.

Looking into her eyes, Billy drove his cock inside her, once, twice, three times, until he filled her to the hilt.

"Oh, God, you feel amazing," she rasped, wrapping her legs around his hips as warmth flooded her chest. She wasn't alone anymore, and Billy was right here with her. Loving her.

He pushed up on an elbow and met her gaze as he withdrew and thrust, withdrew and thrust. The position held a firm fiction against her clit and gave her a big shove toward the edge.

"You're mine, Shayna," he said, thrusting hard, burying himself deep.

"Say it again," she gasped, wanting and needing to be claimed.

"You're fucking mine." Billy clutched at her shoulder, his body driving hers up the bed.

"Again," she whined, her back arching as sensation pooled between her legs.

He buried his face against her ear. "Mine, baby, all mine. Now come on my cock. Come on my cock and say my name."

Her orgasm was like a flash flood barreling down on her out of nowhere. "I'm gonna come. I'm gonna come. Billy."

His thrusts hit her harder, faster, until he was grinding against her and she was coming and writhing and digging her nails into his ass—just like he'd said.

"Fuck, Shayna, it's too good, baby. You're too good."

"Never too good for you, Billy. Give all of yourself to me."

He unleashed himself then, bracing on both arms and letting his hips swing until his orgasm had him shouting and clutching to her shoulders and hunching himself around her in the tightest, sweetest, most intimate embrace.

"I love you, Shayna. And I'm so fucking glad you're mine."

"Love you, too," she said, hardly believing the way everything had turned out.

And feeling, at long last, like she deserved this new life—this new love—that she'd finally found.

THAT NIGHT they lay in Billy's bed again. Truth be told, they'd only gotten out of it to shower and eat. It'd been his very best day since the ambush had changed his life, and now Shayna was changing it again, for the better.

"In case it needs to be said, this is your room now, too," he said, holding her from behind and tucking her in tight all along his body.

She chuckled. "Is that so?"

He nodded, his face against her soft curls, his nose breathing in her sweet scent. "Either that or expect me to sleep in whichever room you decide is yours. Because this whole fucking house is yours now, too."

Shayna shifted so that she could look up at him. "I want to be right here with you. That's enough for me."

He kissed her. "Good answer."

All day, he'd been thinking about how brave she'd been in telling him about what'd happened to her and Dylan. He hated that she took on the responsibility for someone else's actions, but he entirely understood *why* she'd done it since he'd walked a million miles in those same shoes. He hurt for her that she'd cut herself off when she most needed people to lean on, though he got that shit, too. And he *loathed* knowing that some lowlife scumbag had put his hands on her without her consent.

Billy half hoped he learned who that motherfucker was some day. And that he found him alone in a dark alley.

Sonofabitch.

Billy wanted to be as brave as Shayna had been. It felt like the only way he'd know for sure that he deserved her.

"What's wrong?" she asked.

Ever his perceptive woman, wasn't she? But she'd given him the perfect opening.

Billy took a deep breath and a leap of faith. "Right now? Not a damn thing." He kissed her again. "But I need you to know something. Not long after I first got home, back when I was still deep into recovery, I overdosed on pain meds." Her eyes went wide, and Billy pushed on. "I can't tell you what I was thinking. I honestly don't remember anything except just needing the pain to stop."

"Oh, Billy." Shay's hands went into his hair. "I can't imagine what that must've been like for you."

Careful of her bandaged injury, he brought her hand to his mouth so he could kiss it, and then he laced their fingers together. "The other night, I went to a fight club. A, uh, a real underground one. Like you pictured. I promise I won't ever go again."

"Why did you go?" Her voice was little more than a whisper.

"There was so much pressure inside me." He brought their clasped hands to his chest. "Here." Then to his temple. "And here. It made me realize that I still have shit to work out and that I need to start talking to someone again."

Shayna nodded. "I know that can't be easy. But you can talk to me any time, if it helps. Or just let me hold you. Or, you know, *anything else* that might help you feel better." Heat slid into those pretty blue eyes.

And just like that, Billy was hard against her ass.

"Anything, huh?" He kissed her and rocked his hips against her.

"Mmhmm," she said, smiling into his kiss.

"Grab a condom, Shayna. I need in you." He watched as she did, and then as she tore the wrapper. "Touch yourself," he said as he took the condom. And Jesus if she wasn't something to see. Her right hand slid down her stomach until his fingers circled her clit.

Her lips pushed into a pout. "Hurts my arm too much."

"Aw, baby." He nuzzled her cheek. "Don't you worry about it. I'll get you off. Want my hand or my mouth?"

Shay's cheeks went the prettiest shade of pink, and it made him chuckle. "I want us to lay just like this," she said. "So, hand?"

He gave his fingers a good lick, loving how her eyes tracked the movement. Just...loving her. So damn much. And then he was touching her, teasing her, circling her clit and eating up every little moan she made.

"Spread your legs, Shayna." When she did, he slid his hand lower until he could penetrate her with one finger, then two. "So wet for me. Gonna feel so good."

Lust-drunk eyes peered up at him. "Fuck me while you rub me," she breathed.

"Damn, genius really does come out of your mouth," he said, adjusting their position until he was lined up just right.

Her chuckle turned into a moan as he filled her in one long, slow, wet stroke.

"There it is. Fuck, there is it." He gripped her hips and closed his eyes against the goodness of this feeling.

Not just the sex, though that was fantastic. The feeling of belonging to someone—and something—bigger than himself. It'd been so damn long.

And then Billy started to move, decadently lazy ins and outs meant to drive them both crazy. His fingers returned to her clit, and he kissed her ear. "Love you so fucking much, Shay."

"Oh, God, Billy. I feel so full this way."

Jesus, this woman's mouth. He kissed her shoulder and fucked her good and deep. "That's it. You just concentrate on how it feels." He moved his fingers faster, harder, zeroing in on her clit and offering her no mercy.

Finally, her hips jerked. "Billy. *Billy*..." Her orgasm wracked through her, squeezing his dick so good that his own orgasm was suddenly urgent as fuck.

"Roll onto your stomach, baby," he rasped, following her as she moved. Until he was covering her head to toe. Every soft thing about her cradling every hard thing about him. Body and soul.

"Love you under me. Taking me. Taking me so damn good."

His hips moved faster, the sound of their meeting skin and harsh breaths in the air.

"This feels insane," she whimpered.

He nodded. "So fucking tight."

"Yes," she moaned. "Yes."

"Aw, you gonna come again for me, Shayna?"

"I don't...I don't know..."

He laid all his weight atop her and angled his hips so he could drive into her just right. "I do. Come again. Come again and I'll give you mine."

His hips flew. His hands clutched. His breath sawed in and out of him as he took what was his. What he felt like had *always* been meant to be his. Like Shayna had been made for him. And he'd been made for her.

"Fuck, Shayna, it's too good, baby," he said, his orgasm careening through him. And then he was shouting and coming and holding onto her so tight.

"Don't stop," she cried. "I'm so close."

Billy gave her what she asked for, and then she did the same, coming on his cock until he was gritting his teeth from the fucking torturous pleasure of it.

He collapsed on top of her, but she wasn't complaining. "Your arm okay, baby?" he asked.

"I have an arm?" she said, amusement plain in her breathy tone. "Oh, yeah. It's mighty fine."

Billy smacked the luscious curve of her ass. "Oh, yes it is."

Shayna grinned and peered back at him, one eyebrow arched. "Hmm, that felt good, too."

His head thunked against her shoulder. "You kill me dead, Shayna. Absofuckinglutely dead." She laughed and he smacked that ass again, earning himself a squirm and a moan. "And I love it."

Which was how they ended up having sex again. And again. Like it was the air they needed to breathe.

And given how long they'd both denied themselves meaningful relationships with other people, maybe it was that fundamental, that essential, to them both.

"I'M GOING TO THROW UP," Billy said. Because that was what happened when you faced your fears.

And, in this case, it was his fear that Ryan Curtis was *not* going to approve of them. But Billy had to face that fear head-on, because he was willing to fight for Shayna. He'd made the mistake of not doing so once, but never again.

Shayna chuckled as she fiddled with her laptop and set it up in front of them on the coffee table. "That would be gross so please don't."

Billy tackled her to the couch, and her laughter lit him up inside. He let himself go lax on top of her. "I feel a lot better now."

Still laughing, she shoved out from underneath of him, and he let her go so that she didn't hurt her arm. "If you're nervous about what Ryan is going to say, him seeing you laying on top of me isn't going to help."

"Fuck, that's true," he said, sitting upright. He grabbed his crotch. "Okay, I found my balls again, let's do this."

Shay gave him a look. "Your balls are just fine, Billy. I should know since I was licking them less than an hour ago."

"Christ, baby," he said.

And of course that was the very moment that the Skype call came through.

Shayna answered, and then Ryan's face filled the screen. It was about ten at night there, and Ryan looked fucking beat.

Beard on his face. Dark circles under his eyes. Sunburn on his cheeks. In other words, totally par for the course of being deployed in Iraq. "Hi, Ry!" she said.

"Oh, look, it's a twofer!" he said, making her laugh.

"Hey, man, how's it hanging?" Billy asked.

"High and to the right, just like always." Ryan grinned.

"Oh my God, that's TMI, knobhead!" Shayna said.

Suddenly, her brother leaned closer to his screen, his eyes narrowing. "Is our connection shitty or...are the two of you all beat up?"

Shayna took over answering, and Ryan's face was almost comical as she detailed the explosion and the fire and how her pictures had appeared on front pages of the *Gazette* and every other localish paper, not to mention online everywhere. There were even pictures circulating of Shayna herself, a couple of which were really fucking hard to look at, because she'd gotten so damn close to the flames. But there were others that made him even prouder, if that were possible, of her holding a baby, handing out water bottles, and directing firemen to an apartment where she'd seen survivors.

Shayna was a hero. She was certainly his.

Which suddenly made what he had to do a fuck of a lot less scary.

"So, Jesus, what's new with you, Billy?" Ryan asked. "I hope it's not that interesting."

Billy blinked. Then let the words fly. "I'm in love with your sister and we're together now." Shit, he hadn't exactly meant to just blurt it out like that.

Ryan's face froze. And then his brow cranked down. And then his mouth dropped open and he tilted his head.

Shayna busted out into laughter. "I think you shock-and-awed him, baby."

Heat crawled into Billy's cheeks. "Uh, I guess so."

And then Ryan grinned. Fucking *grinned*.

"Good," he said. "I'm surprised, but that's good. Nothing makes me happier than the idea of my two favorite people caring for each other."

Now Billy was probably the one with the struck-stupid look on his face. It was just that easy?

Ryan leaned close to the screen again. "But if you hurt her, Parrish, I'll kill you slowly and I'll like it."

"Ryan!" Shayna said.

But Billy just guffawed, and damn it was good to feel this much joy. "If I hurt her, I'll deserve it." Which wasn't going to happen. Not ever again.

And just like that, they had Ryan's blessing and a whole new life together. And happiness unlike any Billy ever knew he could have.

Worth Fighting For

Getting in deep has never felt this good...

Commercial diving instructor Tara Hunter nearly lost everything in an accident that resulted in her medical discharge from the navy. With the help of the Warrior Fight Club, she's fought to overcome her fears and get back in the water where she's always felt most at home. At work, she's tough, serious, and doesn't tolerate distractions. Which is why finding her gorgeous one-night stand on her new dive team is such a problem.

Former navy deep-sea diver Jesse Anderson just can't seem to stop making mistakes—the latest being the hot-as-hell night he'd spent with his new partner. This job is his second chance, and Jesse knows he shouldn't mix business with pleasure. But spending every day with Tara's smart mouth and sexy curves makes her so damn hard to resist.

Joining a wounded warrior MMA training program seems like the perfect way to blow off steam—until Jesse finds that Tara belongs, too. Now they're getting in deep and taking each other down day and night, and even though it breaks all the rules, their inescapable attraction might just be the only thing truly worth fighting for.

Fighting the Fire - September 2019

The more they fight, the more desire consumes them...

There's only one thing firefighter Sean Riddick doesn't like about Warrior Fight Club, and that's Daniela England, the sexiest, snarkiest, most irritating woman he's ever known. But MMA training keeps the Navy vet grounded, so Sean's not about to give it up, no matter how many times he goes toe to toe with Dani—or how bad he wants to take her to the mats.

A former Army nurse and the widow of a fallen soldier, Dani is done with the military *and* with military men. Fight club is the only thing that eases her nightmares, which means she *has* to put up with Riddick. He might be sex on a stick, but he's infuriating and everything she's vowed to avoid.

But when a crisis throws Sean and Dani together, all that fight bursts into a night of red-hot passion. Now they're addicted to the heat and must decide if the one person they've most resisted might be exactly what they've both been looking for.

And don't miss the sexy and emotional first book in the Warrior Fight Club series:

Fighting for Everything

Loving her is the biggest fight of his life...

Home from the Marines, Noah Cortez has a secret he doesn't want his oldest friend, Kristina Moore, to know. It kills him to push her away, especially when he's noticing just how sexy and confident she's become in his absence. But, angry and full of fight, he's not the same man anymore either. Which is why Warrior Fight Club sounds so good.

Kristina loves teaching, but she wants more out of life. She wants Noah—the boy she's crushed on and waited for. Except Noah is all man now—in ways both oh so good and troubling, too. Still, she wants who he's become—every war-hardened inch. And when they finally stop fighting their attraction, it's everything Kristina never dared hope for.

But Noah is secretly spiraling, and when he lashes out, it threatens what he and Kristina have found. The brotherhood of the fight club helps him confront his demons, but only Noah can convince the woman he loves that he's finally ready to fight for everything.

WORTH FIGHTING FOR

CHAPTER ONE

Nothing chased away nightmares and anxiety like nachos. At least, that was what Tara Hunter hoped.

"Anything else?" Matt asked from behind the bar at Murphy's, her favorite place in the neighborhood.

"A rum and Coke," Tara said, taking off her coat and unwinding the scarf from her neck. She settled both on the stool next to her. It was eleven o'clock on a Sunday night, and the bar was as quiet as she hoped it would be.

Having placed the order, though, she was back to having nothing to distract her from the way her heart wouldn't settle and her breathing couldn't quiet calm. She knew *exactly* why her central nervous system was freaking out—because tomorrow was her first day on a new diving team, and that meant getting back in the water again. But knowing didn't mean she could always control it. Having insight into all the ways her brain was messed up only got her so far.

So Tara took a deep breath and counted backward from five.

Five things she could see. Her reflection in the mirror that was the centerpiece of the big, carved bar. Her long wavy hair pretty much looked like she'd rolled out of bed, because she had. Without any makeup, her face appeared pale in the dim light of the bar.

What else?

The rows of bottles glinting gold and white in the spotlights all along the bar. A couple tucked into the last booth, sitting on the same side and totally wrapped up in each other. Outside the front window, unusual late-winter flurries blew on the night wind.

Tara took a deep breath.

Four things she could hear. The alternative rock song playing on the juke box. Ice clinking in a glass. She peered around, her gaze following the sounds of the other diners. A man sitting in the closest booth was talking on his phone, *loudly*, one of those people who talked louder on cell phones as if he thought he needed to force his voice down the line. At the other end of the bar from where she sat, a customer thanked the bartender as he slid off his stool.

That time, her breath came deeper, slower, calmer.

Keep going.

Three things she could feel. Her nipples against her sweater, because her anxiety attack hadn't been able to abide taking the time to put on a bra before she'd bugged out of her place and gone for a walk in the late-February air.

Matt delivered her drink, and Tara took a long pull from it, mentally adding the fizz of the soda as the next thing she could feel. The smooth, cool glass in her hands—that was the third.

The muscles of her shoulders began to relax. It was working. Keep going.

Two things she could smell. The warm spice of the rum in her drink. The almost stale, malty tang of beer which seemed to be common to every establishment that served it.

Her heartrate was normal again.

Finish it. She took another drink of her rum and coke.

One thing she could taste. She'd already used the rum, so she crushed an ice cube between her teeth and concentrated on the clean, cold taste of the frozen pieces quickly melting in her mouth.

She heaved a deep breath, and the ease of doing so proved for the millionth time that immersing herself in her environment had the power to calm.

The bell over the front door jingled and a gust of unusually bitter wind followed, enough to make Tara hug herself as she glanced over her shoulder to see who else was coming to Murphy's so late.

She almost choked on the ice cube in her mouth.

Because the man sliding onto a stool about five down from hers was freaking *gorgeous*. Tall. Broad shoulders with a trim waist, the quintessential swimmer's build she knew so well after a lifetime of being around swimmers and a career in diving. His black hair was cut short, and his face in profile was a study in hard angles—the square jaw, the high cheekbones, the furrowed brow. She hadn't seen him in Murphy's before. No way she would've forgotten—or missed—him.

Dark eyes slashed toward her.

When her heart kicked up in her chest this time, it had nothing to do with the nightmares she knew so well. And despite getting caught checking him out, Tara managed a smile. "Hey."

As he shrugged out of his coat, his gaze ran over her face, making her remember she hadn't done a *thing* to herself before walking out her door, and he nodded once. "Hey."

The bartender greeted New Guy and slid a coaster and a menu in front of him. "What'll you have?"

"Whiskey, neat, for now," the man said as he flipped open the menu.

Matt made the drink, then disappeared through the swinging doors into the kitchen. A minute later, he returned carrying a massive oval platter piled high with tortilla chips and toppings. He settled the plate in front of her.

"Holy shit, I forgot how big these were," she said with an incredulous laugh.

Matt grinned. "Maybe I'll steal one then."

"Steal two, Matt, seriously," she said, unrolling the napkin from around her silverware.

Her apartment was just down the block, and since she'd frequented Murphy's so much over the past year, she was on a first-name basis with most of the staff. He gave her a wink as he moved down to New Guy. "Care for anything else?"

The guy's gaze swung to Tara. "Are those as good as they look?" He had a slight drawl when he spoke, and Tara couldn't quite place it. It wasn't pronounced enough to be from someplace like Texas.

She smiled as she pulled a chip from the pile, the melted cheese stretching before it broke. "They're freaking awesome. There's just a metric crap ton of them."

He chuffed out a laugh. "So I see." He peered at the menu again, giving her a chance to appreciate the bulk of his biceps under a dark gray Henley. Because wow. "What else would you recommend that's not that big?"

Tara mmmed around the first chip. The crunch of it combined with the gooeyness of the cheese and sour cream and the tanginess of the pico and chili. Oh yeah, getting out of her apartment was exactly what she'd needed.

Matt tapped at the plastic-covered menu in front of the guy. "Wings are good. Pretzel sticks and cheese dip are real good. The loaded potato skins and onion rings are also great, though they're pretty big, too."

New Guy glanced at her nachos again.

"You could share mine. I'll never eat all these." Tara wasn't sure what possessed her to make the offer, except that there was no way she was going to finish them on her own.

The guy's eyebrow went up, and she couldn't tell if he was dubious or intrigued.

She shrugged as she ate a second chip. "Up to you, but if you don't decide soon I'll have eaten all the best ones."

Amusement played around his mouth. "There are best ones?"

"Of course there are best ones," she said, sucking sour cream off her finger.

The guy looked between her and Matt as if he was waiting for the punchline, and then his gaze latched onto hers. "What other appetizers do you like here?"

"Onion rings or wings, hands down."

Matt chuckled. "She's a regular."

"No kidding," New Guy said. "Let's go with the wings." The words were barely out of his mouth when he picked up his things and slid down to the bar stool right beside her. "You sure about this?" His shoulders were broad enough that they nearly touched. And he was even better looking up close. Laugh lines crinkled the corners of his eyes. Two character-adding scars jagged on his forehead. A hint of black ink curled up the side of his neck.

"I offered, didn't I?" She smirked.

He smirked back but held out a hand. "I'm Jesse. What's your name?"

The move seemed a little old-fashioned, but she found it charming nonetheless. She returned the shake, thinking that his name fit the accent. "Tara."

"Tara," he repeated, as if trying out her name to see how it felt on his tongue. She liked the way it sounded in his deep voice. Jesse grabbed a laden chip. "What makes a chip better or worse, Tara?" he asked as he took a bite.

"Well, obviously, the more toppings it has, the better it is. And the less toppings, the worse. And the crunchier chips are better than the ones that get soft under the cheese."

He hummed around a bite. "You have clearly put a lot of thought into this."

"Clearly. Or maybe I just know what I like," she said, instantly hearing the innuendo in the words. And his double-take revealed that he heard it, too. And *Holy Hot New Guy* why hadn't she brushed her hair or at least put on some tinted lip balm before coming out tonight?

"Good to know," he said with a chuckle. For a moment, they ate in silence, an odd intimacy between them from sharing the same plate of food. And then Jesse said, "So what's a girl like you doing at a place like this at midnight all by yourself?"

Tara laughed. Then realized that he hadn't been trying to make a joke. "Oh. *Oh.* You're serious." She laughed again. "Uh, what's a guy like you doing at a place like this at midnight all by yourself?"

His expression immediately read chagrinned. "Fair point. And I didn't mean for that to come out as quite that big of an idiot."

"That's good or you'd be relegated to only the soggy chips."

"That's hardcore." He grinned at her. And, *man*, that grin. It managed to be both sexy and reserved, like he couldn't quite give in fully to the humor. And *that* impression was intriguing. Because she knew what it felt like to experience life as if through a filter. You on one side. The rest of the world on the other. And you could never quite get to where everyone else was. Maybe it was like that for everyone who'd died and come back to life.

Except, nope. She was cutting off *that* line of thinking right now. Or else she'd end up needing to count backward from five again.

He took a chip absolutely straining under a load of cheesy, gooey goodness, and Tara arched a skeptical brow that pulled a deep belly laugh from him. She loved the sound of that, too, which made the sarcastic retort she'd been thinking up get stuck in her throat.

Jesse shrugged with one big shoulder. "All I meant was what are the odds that I'd come in here and meet someone like you?"

Tara froze with a chip halfway between the plate and her mouth, and her heart kicked up in her chest. Was he teasing her now? Or flirting with her? Or both? "Someone like me?"

The smile he gave her was genuine. "Yeah, a pretty woman willing to share her nachos with a stranger."

Her mouth dropped open. Did he just call her pretty? "I don't even have any make-up on," she blurted.

His gaze ran over her face. "I didn't notice that."

Heat absolutely bloomed over her cheeks, and not a little licked down her spine, too. "Uh." She swallowed. "I couldn't sleep."

Now his glance was more appraising. "Me neither. Sometimes it helps me to walk when I can't sleep, which is what led me here."

"Me, too," Tara said, wondering what in the world was happening. Because it was *not* every day that she met a freaking gorgeous guy who not only complimented her but with whom she had things in common. "Of all the gin joints in all the towns in all the world, he walks into mine." She blinked, more heat filling her face as she realized she'd actually voiced the line that'd popped into her head. No one ever accused her of being smooth.

His grin was crooked. "I doubt they have 'As Time Goes By' on the jukebox."

Casablanca was her favorite movie. Beautifully, devastatingly romantic. "You know Casablanca?"

"Of course. One of the best movies of all time."

"Right? Wow. I think this is the beginning of a beautiful friendship." She raised her glass, more than a little embarrassed by her own cheesiness but having fun nonetheless.

Dark eyes intense, he clinked his tumbler against hers. They drank, eyes connected over the rims of their glasses. Butterflies whirled in Tara's belly, making her feel like she'd just crested the highest hill on a roller coaster.

Matt arrived with Jesse's wings. "Can I get y'all anything else?"

"Need a refill?" Jesse asked, nodding at her nearly empty glass.

"Yeah, sure," she said, even though a second was going to make her alarm going off painful come morning. Still, the sweet, fuzzy heat spreading through her blood felt good. And whether that was from the alcohol or her unexpected dinner companion, Tara wanted more of it.

Nodding, Jesse pushed the plate of wings between them. "Dig in."

Grinning, she grabbed a wing. "I love meals made out of just appetizers. You get a little bit of everything."

"So you like appetizers, late-night walks, *Casablanca*, and Murphy's, where you're a regular," Jesse said, sliding the plate of wings closer to her. "What else?"

She chuckled. "I don't know. I'm not that interesting."

He arched a brow, and it communicated disagreement so loud that she had to resist squirming on her stool.

"Um, I like swimming. And fighting." His expression went incredulous, and it made her grin and shake her head. "Not like, beating-people-up fighting. I belong to a MMA training club." She didn't offer more about it, because she really didn't want to get into the fact that Warrior Fight Club was for wounded warriors. Because too often she'd met guys who backed off when they found out she was a veteran. Worse, he might ask how she'd been wounded—something he'd be able to see for himself if he got a look at the other side or base of her throat. She was too much enjoying being fun, flirty Tara. For tonight, she didn't want to be almost-died Tara.

Jesse scratched his jaw. "How you think that makes you not interesting, I have no idea."

She nodded to Matt when he brought her fresh drink, then took a long sip. The rum was sweet and smooth on her tongue. "How about you? Tell me some random things you like."

He shrugged and his eyes narrowed as he thought about it. "The Pacific Ocean. The way the mountains come right up to the beach in California."

"Is that where you're from?"

He gave a head shake as he ate another nacho. "I've lived there on and off over the past decade, but I'm originally from Cunningham Falls, Montana."

That explained the accent, and it gave her pictures of him on horseback, a cowboy hat on his head. And she did not mind those images one bit. "I've never been."

His gaze went distant. "I haven't been back in a long time."

"Still have family there?" she asked, immediately regretting the question when his jaw went tight, making her feel like she'd veered into territory he didn't want to cover.

"Yeah."

The shortness of his answer made it clear she'd read him right, so Tara changed the topic. "What brought you to DC?"

"A new job." He pulled a couple wings onto his plate, then stared for a long moment at their reflection in the bar's mirror. "How 'bout you? DC home for you?"

The water was always where she'd most felt at home. Right

up until a broken cable had sliced through the ocean and nearly garroted her. Other than that, she wasn't sure. Her dad had been in the navy, so they'd moved around a lot when she'd been a kid, and then her own naval career had meant more of the same. "It has been for the past year. Before that, a little bit of everywhere."

Jesse slanted her a grin. "Citizen of the world, then?"

Omigod, she was never going to survive this sexy man quoting Casablanca to her. Never. A ripple of delighted excitement ran through her belly. "Yeah. Exactly."

He gave her a crooked grin and winked. *Freaking winked!* If Tara hadn't been sitting on that bar stool, her panties might've dropped to her ankles.

"I hear that," he said as he raised his glass to her. "To putting down new roots."

"Um, I'll drink to that," she managed as they clinked. "So what else do you like?"

"Let's see," he continued. "I like anything to do with the water. Swimming, boating, surfing, scuba." So she'd been right about that swimmer's physique then. "I used to do a lot of skiing, too. There was great skiing near where I grew up." Something dark and distant passed over his expression. For just a moment, she was sure of it. But then it was gone as fast as it'd appeared. "Haven't done much of it in years now, though."

She wasn't touching the Montana topic again, so she took a drink of her rum and Coke and just enjoyed the unexpected companionship. On the juke box, the song changed, and Tara grinned. "Oh, my God. I danced to this at prom," she said as an old Journey power ballad played.

He smirked at her. "What was the guy's name?"

Tara snorted. "Curtis Miles. We were just friends. Or so I thought, until he started crooning 'When You Love a Woman' in my ear as we danced. Except he changed the *you* to *I*. It was super awkward."

Jesse chuckled. "Poor guy."

"Don't feel bad for him. He ended up hooking up with one of my friends later that night."

"Damn. Sorry."

Tara shook her head. "No need. I didn't mind and the two of them have been married for twelve years and have three kids. They were clearly meant to be."

"You believe in that?" He signaled to Matt for a refill of whiskey.

"What?"

Jesse slanted her a look. "Meant to be."

Twisting her lips, Tara shrugged. "It sure seems to be true for some people." She thought of her coupled WFC friends. Noah and Kristina had been best friends since childhood and were now together. That sure seemed meant to be. And Billy and Shayna had also known one another since she was a teenager and had been roommates before dating, so that seemed like it might've been meant to be, too.

Jesse's expression grew thoughtful as he reached for his fresh drink. "Maybe for some people it is."

A weighted silence settled between them. It wasn't uncomfortable, exactly, but the exchange had definitely held up in front of her eyes that there didn't seem to be a *meant to be* for her. Or else she wouldn't be nearly thirty-two with only one long-term relationship under her belt—one that hadn't survived her injuries and medical discharge from the navy.

Tara mentally pushed the thoughts away as she slid the plate of nachos closer to him. "The more important question is, do you like dessert?"

He laughed, and the deep rumble of it made her smile. "I've been known to enjoy dessert now and again."

Was it just her or did that sound like he was talking about something besides a sugary treat at the end of a meal? "Have you now?"

He turned on his stool toward her, and his knee pressed against her thigh. "Just what is it you're tempting me to share with you?"

Heat slinked through her blood, the arousing sensation originating from where they touched. "The monster ice cream sundae," she said, hoping he didn't pick up on the breathiness suddenly coloring her voice.

One side of his mouth quirked up. "Define monster."

"Three scoops of chocolate and vanilla ice cream. Chocolate and caramel sauces. Chocolate chips, whip cream, and a cherry. All on top of a warm chocolate chip cookie. I can never order it by myself because it's too big so you'd be doing me a huge favor."

His arched an eyebrow, his expression seriously sexy. "Is that right?"

"Mmhmm."

A crooked smile broke through his smirk. "Okay, then. Sounds great. Consider me tempted, Tara." The flirtation in his words was mirrored by the amusement playing around his mouth and an intriguing intensity in his eyes.

She turned toward where Matt stood wiping down menus. "Give us the sundae, please?"

"You got it," the bartender said.

Tara looked back to Jesse. "I hope you think it's as great as it sounds."

His gaze ran over her face again, a slow, purposeful perusal that trailed heat low into her belly. "I'm sure it will be. This has already been one of my best meals in a long damn time."

"Murphy's is fantastic, isn't it?"

He nodded. "From what I've tried so far, it seems like it is. But I was talking more about the company than the food."

The directness of his words nearly stole her breath. "Wow. I, uh, I have to agree," she managed, smiling even as her head spun with the chemistry zinging between them. She had no idea where it might lead, but the longer they hung out, the more she hoped this meal wouldn't be the last she saw of this man.

ACKNOWLEDGMENTS

No book is ever the product of the author alone, at least no book of mine. So I have a number of people I want to acknowledge and thank.

First, thank you to author Jessa Slade, who wrote a post about journalists and journalism that was so fantastic that I asked if I could use some of her words for my photojournalist heroine. Jessa was kind enough to agree and thereby helped me bring Shayna's desire to contribute and serve to life.

Second, a thank you to author Jodi Ellen Malpas, whose *The Controversial Princess* rocked *my* world this past summer. I asked her if I could make my royals-obsessed Havana a reader of her book, and Jodi generously agreed to let me mention the title. If you haven't read this book, I highly recommend it (and so does Havana)!

Next, a big thank you to Lea Nolan who was so many times my sounding board as I worked through drafting the story. And an especially *huge* thank you to Christi Barth, who read and commented right behind me as I wrote and made the story a million times better for her insightful feedback and catches of embarrassing two A.M. typos. Lea and Christi are the kinds of friends every writer should be so lucky to have, and I certainly know I am.

A big shout-out, too, to my Heroes and my Reader Girls & Guys and my new K-Team reviewers for supporting me with so much enthusiasm and excitement. You all make it all worthwhile!

Finally, this book wouldn't have been finished without the support and encouragement of my husband and daughters, for which I am so very grateful. Love you guys!

And last, thank you to you, dear reader, for taking my characters into your hearts and letting them tell their stories again and again. ∼LK

ABOUT THE AUTHOR

Laura Kaye is the New York Times and USA Today bestselling author of over forty books in contemporary romance and romantic suspense, including the Hard Ink, Raven Riders, Heroes, and Hearts in Darkness series. Her books have received numerous awards, including the RT Reviewers' Choice Award for Best Romantic Suspense for *Hard As You Can*. Laura grew up amid family lore involving angels, ghosts, and evil-eye curses, cementing her life-long fascination with storytelling and the supernatural. Laura lives in Maryland with her husband and two daughters, and appreciates her view of the Chesapeake Bay every day.

Learn more at LauraKayeAuthor.com

Join Laura's VIP Readers on Facebook for Exclusives & More!

facebook.com/laurakayewrites

twitter.com/laurakayeauthor

instagram.com/laurakayeauthor

bookbub.com/profile/laura-kaye

Manufactured by Amazon.ca
Bolton, ON

13580884R00144